WITHDRAWN

SECRETS NEVER DIE

SECRETS NEVER DIE

VINCENT RALPH

WEDNESDAY BOOKS
NEW YORK

First published in the United States by Wednesday Books, an imprint of St. Martin's Publishing Group

SECRETS NEVER DIE. Copyright © 2023 by Vincent Ralph. All rights reserved. Printed in the United States of America. For information, address St. Martin's Publishing Group, 120 Broadway, New York, NY 10271.

www.wednesdaybooks.com

The Library of Congress Cataloging-in-Publication Data is available upon request.

ISBN 978-1-250-88215-8 (trade paperback)
ISBN 978-1-250-88213-4 (hardcover)
ISBN 978-1-250-88214-1 (ebook)

Our books may be purchased in bulk for promotional, educational, or business use. Please contact your local bookseller or the Macmillan Corporate and Premium Sales Department at 1-800-221-7945, extension 5442, or by email at MacmillanSpecialMarkets@macmillan.com.

First Edition: 2023

10 9 8 7 6 5 4 3 2 1

For Charlie and Lucas

SECRETS NEVER DIE

Trick or Treat

There's too much blood.

It streams down my face and splats on my sneakers, and my heart is pounding in my chest.

I didn't want this. Every Halloween the plan is the same. We go to Dom's House of Horrors party and, while our classmates drink and dance, we sneak into the woods for the ritual. But this year it's ruined before we've even left the house.

A pool of red spreads across the bathroom tiles, staining the baseboard, and my best friend Haran says, "Sorry."

But I'm barely listening. I'm too busy scrubbing my face until it stings.

"You look fine, Sam. Honest."

"I said subtle," I reply. "You made me look like Carrie!"

"Loose lid," Haran says, pointing at the bottle of fake blood leaking over the bath mat.

I stare at my reflection. My costume is soaked pink, like it's been washed in spaghetti sauce, my hair stuck in red clumps, my face rubbed raw.

"You're still going though?" Haran asks, and I nod and say, "Give me your costume."

"What? No."

"This is your fault."

"So go as Overkill," he says. "Go as Disappointment."

I've never hit him but I'm this close to changing that.

Haran grins and says, "Go as Panic . . . or Desperation." He sees my expression and says "Sorry" again, meaning it now.

I don't really want his outfit. It's store-bought whereas I like to make my own.

"Wait," I say. "I have an idea." And two minutes later we're next door, explaining all the blood to Chloe Atwood.

When we were kids, Chloe and I played together while our moms drank tea. We'd race up and down the hill on the corner and she'd beat me every time; then we'd practice kick-ups in the street until sunset. Back then, it didn't matter that she was a year younger. Now, with different friends and different lives, we mostly smile and wave from separate driveways.

At school, she's one of those quiet, studious kids clustered around the tables in the study center. She's smart, which means, fingers crossed, she can help.

"Aren't you a bit old for trick-or-treating?" Chloe asks.

I know I'm blushing when I say, "Do you have anything . . . my size?"

She raises her eyebrows. "This is unexpected. I'm honored. Come in."

In Chloe's room, watching her spread stuff over the bed, I ask where she's going tonight and she says, "Nowhere."

She's dressed all in black, and I assumed it was the start of a costume. Chloe sees my confusion and says, "I had rehearsals after school."

Black leggings and tops are the school dance team's un-official uniform. But it still seems weird, that she isn't getting ready for tonight.

"How come you're staying home?" I ask, and Chloe sighs and says, "My mom hates Halloween, you know that. She makes us sit with the lights off, so people think we're out."

"You want to come with us?" Haran asks, and I give him a look he ignores.

Chloe pulls a face but doesn't answer. She takes the bottle of blood from Haran and busies herself in the corner for a minute. Then she turns back.

"Try this," she says, dumping an armful of clothes into my arms. I change in her bathroom, then stare at the result, wondering if it's enough.

I'm wearing gray shorts, tights covered in tiny skulls, black boots with metal toe caps, and a white T-shirt with SCARED OF LIFE, TIRED OF DEATH written with the last of my fake blood.

It's not what I'd planned, but it's something.

Through the door, Chloe shouts, "Show us," so I open it, and she grins and says, "Perfect."

Haran nods, then turns to Chloe and says, "So, you gonna come?"

She shakes her head and asks who will be there.

"Everyone," I say.

"I don't have a costume."

"It's not compulsory."

"Says the guy who turned up on my doorstep asking for one. And what's *he* dressed as?" she asks, giving Haran a once-over.

Haran spreads his arms, unnaturally long in his outfit, and says, "I'm Slenderman."

"Well, it's fucking creepy."

Haran takes her hand in his spindly fingers, bows, and says, "Chloe . . . would you like to come to a party with us?"

She sighs, stares at the ceiling, then says, "All right. But it better not be lame."

We drive toward the trees, their branches pointing in all directions but leading us to only one.

The woods loom over the far end of town, ominous in the gloom. If you want to leave Hayschurch, drive the other way and hope that, unlike most, nothing brings you back.

We've been here lots of times, but it always feels like we arrive by accident, as if country roads are pieces of string juggled and dropped by the wind.

I know just one person who lives like this, wrapped in skinny lanes and creaking trees.

When my headlights merge with the fog, it reminds me of the horror movies Dad let me watch when I was little, while Mom was out with her friends. I remember that mixture of fear and fascination; of being excited that my father was sharing a moment with me but knowing, deep down, that it was wrong.

"What's this place like?" Chloe asks, and I say, "Imagine a haunted house."

"Okay."

"It's like that. But Dom lives there."

"Dom Simmons?"

"The one and only."

Chloe frowns and says, "I should have stayed at home. That guy is the worst."

"He's okay when you get to know him," I say weakly. Then add, "He's one of my oldest friends." As if that's an explanation.

When we arrive, empty cars line the shoulder that leads to Dom's house and I wish we'd got here sooner.

As if he can read my mind, Haran shrugs and says, "Accidents happen." Then he strides confidently toward the open front door as dance music and screams spill into the night.

I hold back for a moment, the house a gray mass above us, and Chloe sighs.

"Finally, I get to attend one of Dom Simmons's famous Halloween parties," she says. "I can tell the other losers what the fuss is about."

"You're not a loser."

Chloe grins and says, "That depends who you ask."

I poke my head in the living room, nod some hellos, then go to the dining room, where a vast wooden table stretches along the back wall, covered with drinks and snacks and Halloween decorations.

Dom has gone all out this time—the familiar decor of previous years surrounded by even more new purchases. It probably cost the same as most people's yearly food budget, but the Simmons family aren't most people.

"Well?" I ask, ducking under a massive cobweb, and Chloe shrugs and says, "It's not terrible."

"It's the best night of the year!" Haran shouts.

We fight through the crowd to get some drinks, sticky punch in red plastic cups, then head to the kitchen, where someone in a yeti costume is DJ'ing. Their decks cover the center island and I wonder if Dom paid for this as well. We used to spend days arranging playlists for these parties. Now even that's gone to another level.

There are lots of Deadpools and Harley Quinns and a who's-who of movie killers.

Three zombies slither past in a groaning conga line while Pennywise and Scarlet Witch dry-hump against the dishwasher.

"Classy," Chloe says, and I wonder if bringing her was a bad idea.

Tonight—not the party, but the other thing—is special to us. We do something no one else knows about. As much as I like her, Chloe isn't part of that. I hadn't thought that she probably doesn't know anyone else here. What if we can't shake her off?

I stare around, at all the strangers I'm unsure about underneath their masks and their makeup, all the older people and the ones from other schools. I know why they're here, but it still feels disconcerting.

The kids from Hayschurch Academy are the worst. It's not a private school but it acts like it is. The students are all given a smirk on their first day that they wear even on weekends.

"I'm going to find Dom," I say, nudging my way toward the stairs. The first room is locked and I don't try the second. In the third, everyone is watching someone else play the new *Resident Evil*.

The toilet is occupied, at least three voices inside.

I head back downstairs and rejoin Chloe and Haran. In the hall, someone spins me around and, before I can focus, Dom is shouting, "I thought you were going to be ... *whatever* you said."

"The Zeitgeist," I mumble.

"What's this then?" he asks, looking me up and down.

He smiles but I can see he's not happy.

Dom tells everyone what he'll be wearing three months early to avoid clashes. His costume is nothing like mine, but I went off script and he doesn't like that.

Everything he wears is expensive and this is no different. He's a manga character I've already forgotten the name of, but I *do* know he paid hundreds to ship it over from Asia.

"There was an accident," Chloe says. "He got blood on his other costume. Too much blood."

Dom stares at her, then looks at me and says, "No Elisha tonight?"

"She's coming."

"Good." He grins at me. "It would be a shame if one of us was missing."

Dom winks at Haran, then turns to Chloe and says, "Enjoy."

When he's gone, she says, "That guy is a dick," a little too loud for him not to hear. But he doesn't turn around. He just disappears into a crowd that has grown even bigger since we arrived.

"He's not that bad once you get to know him," Haran says. Our standard Dom response. The truth is, he's not that bad to *us.*

Chloe yanks my arm and says, "I'm going to the bathroom." When I turn back, Haran is in the corner on his phone. He's probably chatting to his boyfriend, Brendan, so I leave them to it. They are the poster couple for long-distance. No jealousy, no drama, always together at a party, even when they're one hundred miles apart.

I head to the kitchen, hoping to find a familiar face in the crush. But all I see is a girl wearing a mask with a creepy smile and intense stare. When I look closer, two black contact lenses peek through the fabric. She screeches, "*Hey, you!* I haven't seen you in *ages,*" and I nod, thinking, *I haven't seen you ever.*

"Have you seen Patrick?" she asks.

"I don't know him."

The girl punches my arm and says, "Fun-*eee*! *Everyone* knows Patrick."

"So where is he?"

The girl shrugs and says, "You'll find him. I know you will."

"Okay."

"You'll. Find. Him," she repeats, jabbing my chest. I edge away into the crowd, and when I look back, she's staring after me.

When I find Haran, I ask if he's seen this Patrick guy and he says, "Don't know him. Is he cute?"

"I have no idea."

He puts his hands on my shoulders and says, "I'm genuinely sorry about messing up your costume. You know that, right?"

"This would feel more sincere if you had a face."

He lifts his mask, grins, and says, "Better?"

"Much."

Someone with a white sheet over their head is scrounging through the fridge. On their back it says *Lastminutecostume.com*.

"You okay?" Haran asks. "You seem a little . . . distracted."

"I'm fine," I lie, catching Elisha's eye as she elbows her way across the room.

"It's busy," she says, kissing me and squeezing my hand

because she knows how I'm feeling. She replied to my message about the spilled blood with two words—*It's fine*—but only now can I relax.

She's made her own costume—a crimson-soaked hand bursting from her stomach, its claws sharp and twisted, fake ribs jutting out like broken prison bars.

"Sam is unhappy," Haran says, and Elisha hugs him, then says, "I heard about the accident. But this is . . . interesting."

My girlfriend steps back to get a better look at my outfit, then sees Chloe standing awkwardly in the doorway and waves her over, saying, "I hear you saved the day."

"Desperate times." Chloe smiles then, because Elisha has a way of making everyone feel better.

"How's chemistry?" Elisha asks, and Chloe says, "It's good, actually. Maybe *I* can be Mrs. Ryder's favorite next year."

"I have no doubt."

I've lost count of how many kids Elisha has tutored during high school. Even at her darkest point, she never said no to a teacher. That's why, while Chloe and I mostly share neighborly nods these days, she and my girlfriend have private jokes about science.

There's yelling in the hallway. When I force my way through, I see three trick-or-treaters standing outside, the stars on their costumes glistening in the light of the pumpkins on the porch.

"Fresh meat!" someone yells, and the yeti DJ pulls the smallest kid over his shoulder and runs back into the house.

The girl screams, and the other boy steps forward, then back, then forward again.

"Don't worry," I tell them. "He'll be fine."

When the girl starts to cry, I say, "There's lots of candy in the dining room. Fill your bags with whatever. And take double for your friend."

There are cheers from another room. Then the yeti bounds past, chanting "Trick! Trick! Trick!" while the boy hangs on and shrieks.

Dom crouches next to the girl and says, "You shouldn't knock on strangers' doors. Anyone could answer."

She and the boy run to the end of the path, where their friend is waiting with a look of sheer terror.

"That was fun," the yeti says, high-fiving Dom as he walks past.

"It's nearly time," Dom whispers to me. "Find Haran and Elisha. And get rid of that other girl."

The Dark Place

No one notices when the four of us sneak away.

We go through the gate at the end of Dom's massive garden and step into the woods, the music and laughter softening then silenced the farther we walk into the black.

"How many people are there this year?" Elisha asks, and Dom says, "Enough."

What he means is: It's a lot easier to leave your own party unseen when it's absolutely crammed.

Elisha squeezes my hand and I squeeze back. It's our secret sign that we're safe, because the noises are just animals and the shapes only shadows. At least, that's what I tell myself.

"I can't believe it's been a whole year," Haran says.

Our steps are slow and careful, while his are fast and

thoughtless because he can't wait to get there. A few times we lose him in the darkness, but he never goes far.

Eventually he stops and waits for us, because even Haran is cautious in the woods.

Dom holds his flashlight out straight, never moving from the path, never risking a sideways flash.

Your eyes play tricks in the dark, and it's better to focus on one direction. We come in, we go out, we never deviate.

Someone's footstep cracks louder than the rest, and I shiver. It's only a twig or a pile of dried leaves, I tell myself.

The first year I took part in the ritual, my fear was mixed with uncertainty. I was twelve, and Dom said it would help after what had happened to me. I had no idea how much.

Back then I wanted to hide. I wanted to be alone. Yet Dom's pitch was impossible to ignore. That's when I realized how good he is at getting his way. No matter how many excuses I made, Dom always had an answer.

We walk into a small clearing, the lights from our phones bouncing off the trees and casting long shadows around us. In the far corner is our secret hideaway. Where our secrets are buried.

"We're here," Dom says, pointing his flashlight at a wooden hut with a sheet-metal roof.

The door is ajar and candles flicker through the gap; then a shadow fills the wall and someone inside coughs.

Haran doesn't pause. He runs forward, pushes the door open, and shouts, "Happy Halloween!"

There's a laugh and I feel relieved. Dom's sister, Lauren, is waiting for us, the only one brave enough to come alone.

"Hey," she says. "Welcome back."

Lauren is a year older than Dom and, technically, she's in charge while their parents are away. She's supposed to be protecting their house from bad decisions, but we have more important things to do than party.

She graduated last year, left for a summer internship, then came back empty-handed.

"So," Dom says. "Who wants to go first?"

We call it the Dark Place.

I don't know who built it or when but, for us, it's a sacred spot. And now Haran is alone inside.

The rest of us sit beneath the twisted elms—an arch formed by two bent trees that have wrestled each other toward the ground. We wait here until it's our turn and then we go inside and confess our secrets.

We save up a year's worth of worry and chuck it into the gloom. Then we come out a bit happier, a little lighter.

Dom and Lauren had been doing it for years and then, when I needed it the most, he invited me and Haran to join them.

When they were kids, they buried tiny secrets in the ground, like bad thoughts and stolen sweets. If Lauren told a white lie, or Dom did something naughty, they hurried to the woods and left a confession that let them off the hook. But my first time was different. I told the Dark Place something too big to bury.

The noises of the night are calmer here. Tree branches sway in a suddenly silent breeze, while falling leaves drift toward the ground in slow motion. Elisha's face turns toward mine, and her smile forms in a thousand tiny moments.

Dom and Lauren are talking, but their words float just out of reach.

It's as if the sound has been sucked into the shadows, but that doesn't scare me. It's thrilling, because it means we've arrived.

Elisha rests her head against my chest, while the soft murmur of Dom's and Lauren's voices feels calming and familiar. This is what tonight is really about—not the costumes or the party or the people I barely know. It's about the five of us doing something that makes the rest of the year tolerable. We can say our secrets out loud.

An owl hoots above us, and I wonder how many other creatures are watching from the shadows.

I bury my hands in the pockets of my jacket and try to focus on Elisha's warmth, but I can't stop a shiver running down my spine.

"Okay?" Elisha whispers, and I watch the cloud from her breath slowly fade, then say, "Yes."

That's easier than admitting the truth. I'm scared. I always am.

I can feel the truth inside me, stretching, waking up. I put it in the Dark Place years ago but it's embedded in my soul.

I watch Haran walk back to us. He sits in silence, deep in thought, and I wonder what he said in there. I would never ask . . . and he would never tell. That's our only rule.

"I'll go next," Elisha says.

It's weird to think that a party is happening right now.

I smile at Dom, hoping it hides my anxiety, and he grins back.

Elisha kisses my cheek and walks to the hut. For a second,

I see the light inside; then the door closes and the darkness snaps back.

"You all right?" I ask Haran, and he nods.

"All better now," he says.

Five minutes later, Elisha slips into the space next to me.

She's always a little different after we do this. Her body feels stiff and her eyes are darker.

I kiss her and she whispers, "I'm fine." But she won't look at me.

Lauren is in there a long time. Dom not so much.

These days he's always quick, and sometimes I wonder if he says anything at all. But that's Dom all over. He doesn't waste time with small talk, so I guess this is no different.

"Sam," he says. "You're up."

The Dark Place feels heavier when you're the fifth, weighed down by things I will never know.

The door creaks as I pull it closed. There's a lock on the inside, and I slide it across out of habit.

I sit on the floor, breathing in the familiar mustiness and watching the candles paint strange scampering shapes across the walls. It's warm in here, calm without the wind, welcoming, nothing like it seems from the outside.

If you passed this hut without knowing what it is, you'd call it junk. The woods are full of it—broken bikes, abandoned tree houses, burned-out caravans. But one person's rubbish is someone else's everything.

The metallic smell of the rusting roof creeps into my nostrils.

You have to settle into the gloom like sinking into the softest mattress. Then I focus on the silence until that's all I can hear. No nighttime noises, no animals, just . . . this.

It's what you would hear if, for once, the whole world shut up.

We say out loud what we don't want anyone else to hear.

It feels energizing and brave and scary.

This is where secrets come to die. That's what Dom says.

The first year I did this, he performed like the showman that he is. And yet, behind the bravado was something else—kindness. He knew, long before I did, that it would help.

I smile at the memory; then I speak.

At first, my whispers hang in the air like threads from a severed cobweb. My skin is sticky and my brain feels tight. But soon my heart slows and the words come easy.

I imagine those words drifting toward the candles, catching fire, then turning to smoke.

When I'm done, I wait awhile, enjoying the calm.

That's when something smashes against the side of the hut.

I scramble to my feet. There's another bang, then another, as though someone is punching the wall from the outside.

"What are you doing?" I shout. If this is Dom's idea of a joke, it isn't funny.

There's another bang, so loud it echoes through the hut, and I go to the door, reach for the lock, then stop.

I close my eyes, slow my breathing, and say, "Who is it?"

"Open the door!" Haran yells.

As I do, something else strikes the hut and he screeches.

"What's happening?" I ask, but Haran doesn't answer. Instead, he runs back to the twisted elms, and I follow as specks from the candlelight I was just staring into distort the dark.

"Are you okay?" Elisha asks.

Everyone has their phone out, shining light into the places we never go.

"Yes," I whisper, freezing as I see the fear on their faces. "Who's making all that noise?"

"We don't know," says Lauren, her eyes darting from the woods to me and back again.

The banging has stopped but no one moves. Then a scream rips through the night and I grab Elisha's arm.

"What . . . the actual . . . fuck?" Lauren whispers.

Dom points deeper into the woods and says, "It came from there."

The peace I felt in the Dark Place is gone, replaced by nausea and terror. My ears ring with the scream and then the silence that comes after it.

Haran stares at me and I know what he's thinking. He wants to leave and so do I, but I'm frozen to the spot.

Then Elisha steps forward and Lauren follows.

"What are you doing?" I ask.

"Someone screamed," Elisha says. "They could be in trouble."

"Or *we* could," Dom mumbles.

I follow them. Something moves in the trees above us but I keep my phone pointing forward. Animals chitter nervously in the undergrowth, but Elisha is moving too fast and I can't lose her.

"Lish," I whisper. "Slow down."

I hear Haran and Dom behind us, mumbling to each other. Then we step into another clearing and Elisha shouts, "Hello! Is anyone there?"

"This is it," Haran says. "This is how we die."

He's not smiling, because this isn't a joke. He's the only one not holding their phone.

We wait and listen. Nothing. Eventually Lauren says, "Maybe it was someone at the party."

Haran breathes out and says, "That's probably it. Noise travels around here, right?"

Dom looks at me then away. For half a second, I wonder if this is a practical joke. It's the kind of thing he'd do. But his hands are clenched and his face looks tense in the flashlight beam.

Eventually he says, "We should go back," and we follow him to the hut.

I'm waiting to see the reassuring flicker of the candles, a sign that we're almost safe. But there's no light now. The hut is as dark as everything else.

The wind must have blown them out, I think.

Dom touches the open door and looks inside. For a long moment, he doesn't move.

"What's wrong?" Lauren asks.

Dom looks back at us. Lauren shines a light on her brother's face, and in the moment before he shields his eyes, he looks angry.

"What's that?" Elisha says.

She's pointing her cell at the hut, and something wet is oozing down the outer wall.

I look closer. The ground is covered in broken eggshells, tiny pieces clinging to the mess. But it's not yolk. It looks almost black in the phone's light.

I reach out a finger, touch the wall, then hold it close to my face. The smell is heavy and horrible and I retch.

"Sam . . ." Elisha says. "What is it?"

I jolt back to being in the Dark Place, the sound of something smashing against the hut, the sudden feeling of confusion and terror; then I turn to the others and say, "It's blood."

Home Time

Where have you been?" Chloe asks.

For the briefest moment I want to tell her. I want to say we snuck off to leave our secrets in the woods but someone egged our hiding place and those eggs were filled with blood. But instead, I say, "Nowhere. There's just . . . a lot of people."

Chloe nods and says, "Dom has lots of friends."

She doesn't know the truth—that tonight is a lie that allows us to disappear. Dom knows more people than I do, but that doesn't fully explain the "guest list." He's branched out, giving an open invite to friends-of-friends. Only, this time, someone must have followed us.

I look around at all the strangers hiding in plain sight. It could have been any of them.

There's a crash in the living room and I glance inside.

Someone has pulled the curtains down while jumping through the window.

Dom's parents would be pissed if they knew what sort of party he was having, but it's another secret on a night full of them.

They are staying in some fancy hotel, like they do every Halloween.

I turn to see Lauren pause halfway up the stairs. She glances at the damage, then keeps walking.

She was quiet all the way back from the woods. Haran filled the silence with nonsense, and Dom was mumbling about catching whoever did it. Elisha and I just held hands and squeezed, but for once that didn't make things better.

And now Chloe is looking at me expectantly. I brought her here but I just want to run.

Someone nudges me, and when I turn, a person in a *Scream* mask is standing there, Hannibal Lecter on one side and Chucky on the other.

"You're him, aren't you?"

When I don't reply, Ghostface moves closer and says, "I asked you a question."

His voice is muffled under the mask, and like so many tonight, I don't know him.

"Yes," I say. "I'm him."

"I knew it."

I start walking away but he grabs my arm and says, "You think you're too good to talk to me?"

"No, I just . . ."

"Stop being a prick," Haran says.

He fronts up to all three of them at once, and they look at each other, then walk away.

Most of the time, Haran is just my best friend. But sometimes he's also my bodyguard. That's what happens when you've been friends since birth. You're there for each other, no questions asked.

"What was that?" Elisha asks, and Haran puffs out his chest and says, "Just doing my job."

When he catches my eye, his grin softens into a smile, and I love that he's always got my back.

"I want to go home," Elisha says, and I nod and say, "Me, too."

Chloe doesn't argue. We leave without saying goodbye to Dom and walk silently back to the car. On the way home, she tries to start a few conversations but our silence shuts her down.

The only thing we want to talk about is off-limits—how someone followed us into the woods and threw blood-filled eggshells at a place we thought was our little secret.

Was it kids messing around? Maybe it was the trick-or-treaters we pranked getting revenge. But that scream. It didn't sound like someone was in trouble. It sounded like a warning.

I drop Elisha off first, then drive home, as Haran is staying with me.

"Well," Chloe says. "Thanks for the invite."

Her house is in darkness but her mom is by the window, staring out at us.

"You'd think she'd turn the lights back on now," Chloe says. "All the trick-or-treaters are in bed, Mother."

I look at her pale face in the shadows and don't laugh.

I watch Chloe go inside, the hall light flashing on and her

mom stepping back and closing the curtains. Then I turn to Haran and say, "What the hell happened tonight?"

"I keep thinking about the candles," he says. "They were all lit when we heard the scream. But when we went back to the hut it was pitch black."

"So? It was the wind."

Haran shakes his head. "The door was closed." His eyes meet mine. "I think someone blew them out."

"It's probably nothing," I say, trying to keep my voice steady.

"Yeah," he replies. "Probably."

As we approach my house, I kneel down next to the pumpkins and blow the candles out one by one.

It's supposed to make me feel better but, somehow, it makes things worse.

"Do you really think the scream came from the party?" I ask.

Haran's hands turn to fists as he says, "I hope so."

Neither of us mentions the blood.

Family

"**S**am . . . Sam . . . Sam . . ."

I open my eyes. Molly is standing over me with that look. The one that says playing is far more important than sleeping.

My sister is five and she's the best thing in my world.

When you meet her, she will tell you she was a mistake.

"Mom and Dad didn't want me till I came," she'll say.

She doesn't see that as a bad thing.

Then she'll watch you, and something in her huge blue eyes will make you look away. What she likes best is to watch people think.

No one says it out loud, but we know Molly can read minds. She can't see all your thoughts. Just the ones closest to your eyes.

That's why I can't look at her this morning—because I'm scared that she will see everything that happened last night.

She moves away from my bed, satisfied that I'm awake, then kneels next to Haran and starts whispering his name, too.

He wakes with a shout but she doesn't flinch. She just says, "Hello," and, once he blinks away the confusion, Haran smiles.

"Mom says you're both lazy and you need to get up," Molly says, before marching out the door.

I check my phone, and there are lots of messages on my social accounts. They're all from the same person—a Sasha Craven—and they all say the same thing.

You've probably heard of me so I wanted to say hi.

I check her Instagram, looking for people I recognize. But there are no personal details, we share none of the same friends, and every photo is her on her own, which is clue number one that something's off. Most of her pics look like stock images, and all the backgrounds are unfamiliar.

It's best to ignore messages like that. It could be a bot or it might be someone phishing. Either way, ignore it and they will disappear eventually.

Haran stretches and says, "We should talk about last night."

"Not yet," I say. "Molly's ears are everywhere."

I smile like it's a joke, but I don't want the Dark Place creeping into here. I keep picturing the cracked eggs and the dark blood dripping down the hut. I keep hearing the scream. But in the daylight, in my bedroom, with my stuff all over the floor, they seem a bit less real. Someone pranked us, I think, that's all. Although that means someone from the party knew where we were.

"Come on," I say. "We've been summoned."

Technically, our house is old. The first brick was laid in 1858, but the reality is more complicated than that. Most of the upstairs and the front was rebuilt after a fire tore through it the year I turned thirteen. Now there are two halves of our house, just like there are two halves of my life: a before and an after.

The kitchen is in the before part, untouched by the flames. That's why it's my favorite.

Mom, Dad, and Molly are already at the table when we come down. Breakfast is a big deal in our house, and it's even bigger when we have guests.

"Congratulations, Molly," Dad says. "You've stirred them from their slumber."

She grins and Dad winks at her. It's an unspoken fact that my sister is his favorite.

"Morning, boys," Mom says.

She's looking at me a bit too closely, searching for a hangover.

Eventually, she smiles and says, "Did you have fun?"

"Yes," Haran and I say at exactly the same time. Even though it's just one word, it sounds like the biggest lie we could tell.

"That's good," Mom says. "I know how much you love those parties."

Used to, I think.

"Any trouble?" she asks.

Dad frowns but quickly rearranges his face so he just looks interested. This is for Haran's benefit. Mom and I know the truth.

"No," I say, thinking back to Ghostface. *You're him, aren't you?*

I hate it when people recognize me, and Mom knows that. I catch Molly's eye and quickly look away. She can pick out a lie from a hundred yards. I think she got that from our mother.

"I hope not," Mom says.

This is all passing Haran by. He's too busy stuffing his face—the only thing that can stop my best friend from noticing passive-aggressive table talk and worrying about blood-filled eggs is food.

Sometimes he pauses, mouth half full, to stare at the fruit and cereal and muffins that cover the table like he's at a banquet. I wish I could enjoy it, too, but I'm thinking of something else.

I didn't want to be on TV. That was Dad's idea.

He saw an ad for the auditions, and a few months later I was cast as Isiah in *Future Force*.

From age eight to twelve I was famous. When I was ten, I really came into my own on the show. That's what the critics said. It was the season I started getting more namechecks in reviews, more lines with substance, and, in the final few episodes, more jokes.

What started as a dark sci-fi became a mission-of-the-week dramedy about a family tasked with pushing back the apocalypse one year at a time. It was clever. It had a loyal fan base and a few awards. And the budget was huge.

I was famous. Then, for a while, I was infamous. I was the boy whose career crashed and burned . . . literally.

I didn't want any of it. That was Dad's dream, and when it didn't happen for him, he passed it on to me like a family heirloom.

My father is a photographer who thinks he's one lucky break away from stardom. He's always loved photography, ever since he was a kid, and the attic is stuffed with albums and boxes of his pictures. He wanted to study photography properly but had to make do with online courses. He wants to capture an image critics talk about for centuries. Mostly he takes pictures of food.

Those serving suggestions on the front of packets? That's what Dad does. When he talks about his day job, he says it "pays the bills," which is another way of saying he hates it.

It was a big day in our house when Dad found Instagram. He put all his "free-time" photos online and waited to be discovered.

He's still waiting.

That's why I agreed to *The Sixteenth Minute*—a documentary series about former child stars. By then, I was old enough to say no, but one look at Dad's face and I knew I couldn't. So, I said yes—on one condition.

"I don't want Molly on-screen," I said. "Ever."

That was the bravest I've ever felt, because I'd always done what Dad told me to. I'd always complied, even though that ball of anxiety bobbing in my stomach grew so big that I couldn't tell where it ended and I began. But this time I took a piece of that pain and bargained with it.

For a few horrible weeks, I was interviewed about how it feels to be irrelevant, forgotten, a has-been before your thirteenth birthday. My father came with me to the studio in the city, while Mom stayed home with Molly.

Dad was only happy until he realized I wasn't trying. When I was a kid, I learned my lines, stood where they put me, and mistook my father's happiness for love.

I didn't know what *living vicariously* meant then, but I do now. It's what Dad did every day on set. He never wanted me to be a star for *me*. It was just the closest he could get to the glow.

Sometimes people recognize me. Like Ghostface, last night. That's why Haran was so quick to step in.

He was my friend before, during, and after. He stands up for me when I can't do it myself.

"Sam took Chloe to the party," Molly says, and Mom pulls a face.

"*We* took her," I reply. "And you shouldn't be spying."

"I wasn't spying. I was looking."

Haran laughs, and I catch my parents giving each other funny looks.

Mom blames Dad for all the times I'm recognized in public.

Maybe when I finish school, go to college, get a job—at some point I'll be the me I am now, not the kid I was then.

That's another reason I like our Halloweens so much. In the dark, with only my closest friends for company, I can forget about the outside world. I can't protect myself from the truth . . . or the lies. But during our ritual, once a year, at least I have some control.

Dad puts his hands behind his head and yawns, his burn scars sneaking out of his sleeves. It's enough for the worst of that night to race through my brain like a tornado. Coolly, as I eat my cereal, I put the wall back up. The wall that blocks out what happened. The wall with a thousand weak spots.

Back in my room, Haran's phone vibrates and he mumbles, "Fuck off."

"What is it?"

"Someone's spamming me. Sasha Craven. Do you know her?"

I hold out my phone and say, "Same."

Haran shows me her latest message.

Don't be shy. I just want to be friends.

I've got exactly the same one.

"What are we thinking?" he asks. "Creepy or . . ."

"Definitely creepy."

We think the same thing at the same time. Has Sasha Craven got anything to do with what happened last night? For a moment it looks like Haran wants to say something else. But he just stands awkwardly until I'm the one to speak.

"Hopefully it's nothing to worry about."

"Maybe."

We don't usually talk about the Dark Place when we're not actually there. Even us—best friends since birth—we hide it in our looks and the gaps between our words.

If we said it aloud, nothing bad would happen. That's what we tell ourselves anyway.

Now, after last night, I'm no longer sure.

Nobody's Friend

What are you doing now?
Sundays are the worst!
I'm bored.

The messages carry on all weekend. I ignore them. Sometimes I get random DMs from strangers, and I know how quickly they can turn from nice to nasty. Replies open doors for strangers to walk through ... and I don't trust strangers.

On Monday morning, I meet Elisha outside Slice of Life, our favorite bakery.

Maybe it sounds boring but that's one of the things I love about my girlfriend: our routines. We watch the same shows over and over, racing each other to the punch lines. We start and end every day with the same messages. We love cake.

After everything with *Future Force*—the long hours, the reporters, the speculation around its cancellation—now I appreciate the little things. Except they don't feel little to me. They feel a lot more important than the stuff I once thought was big.

As we walk to school, I want to talk about the woods but Elisha is more interested in Ghostface and his friends.

"That's the problem with a come-one-come-all policy. You get assholes like that. They'd better not be there next year."

Her eyes sharpen. She means it, I know she does. But I can't shake the feeling that Haran messaged her, too.

It wouldn't be the first time. He knows how insecure I am, because Elisha is my first proper girlfriend and she scares me sometimes—what she says or doesn't say, how she says or doesn't say it.

"You think there'll *be* a next year?" I ask. "I can't stop thinking about the eggs. That was premeditated. And the scream? Someone attacked us on purpose."

"It's Halloween, Sam. People try to freak each other out. That's what happens."

I picture Elisha's face straight after the scream. Her eyes were wide and focused. Was she as scared as the rest of us? She was certainly braver—running toward the noise. Sometimes she can be as selfless as Haran. But she usually saves that for her family.

"I think you'd feel differently if you were inside when it happened. It was some serious *Blair Witch* shit."

Haran joins us by the school gates and I can tell he's desperate to talk.

We haven't messaged each other, because the Dark Place isn't something we put in writing.

When Haran's phone beeps, he rolls his eyes. "Another one."

"Another what?" Elisha asks.

"We have a stalker," Haran replies.

Elisha looks at me with different eyes now—intrigued and a tiny bit jealous.

"You don't know someone called Sasha Craven, do you?" Haran asks.

Elisha pulls out her phone and shows us the messages.

"I thought it was just me. I've been getting them all weekend."

"You think she's spamming the whole grade?" I ask.

"If she is, she's got a lot of time on her hands."

We compare messages. Elisha's right because, whoever this Sasha is, she's sending us completely different words now. And yet, they feel strangely similar.

Can we be friends?

I want to be seen.

Please don't ignore me.

"Why is she doing this?" I ask, and Elisha huffs and says, "There's only one way to find out."

She's typing before we can stop her, hitting send on a message that says: *Who are you and why are you messaging my boyfriend?*

The three of us stare at Elisha's phone, waiting for a reply that doesn't come. Then Miss Benning is yelling from the main doors. "Classes started three minutes ago!"

I'm in film studies when my phone vibrates with Sasha's latest message.

She doesn't need to be jealous. It's not you I'm interested in.

Who are you? I type, and the reply is instant.

Someone hid me in the Dark Place.

The First Secret

It's got to be Dom," Haran says when we're in the common room. "He's messing with us."

"Why?" I ask.

"Because he's a tool."

Haran must see my eye-roll, because he huffs and says, "You know he can be horrible."

I do. But something tells me this isn't as simple as that.

I think back to the Dark Place—the sound of smashing that seemed so much louder than eggs, the blood dripping thick and dark toward the ground, the scream. Was it all just Dom fucking around?

"Was he with you?" I ask.

"What?"

"When I was inside . . . was Dom with you?"

"I think so."

"What do you mean, you think so? Either he was or he wasn't."

"I needed a piss," Haran says. "You know I can't go when someone's watching. I went behind a tree, so . . . maybe he had time."

He catches my eye, then stares at the ground.

"I'm sorry," he mutters. "I didn't realize I was meant to stand guard."

"It's all right."

I think back to that night. Dom looked as terrified as the rest of us. And even if Haran wasn't there, there was no way he could have done anything with Lauren and Elisha watching.

When we were younger, he loved making us jump. He'd sneak up on us at school or lurk in an alley if we'd arranged to meet nearby, then cackle when we leaped out of our skin. So, I can see where Haran's coming from.

Haran and Elisha both think Dom is bad news, and they're right. And yet: Dom saw me at my most broken and found a way to help. He took me to the Dark Place. He might blow hot and cold, but we have history.

He was a bully, although never to me. He'd picked on a few wide-eyed kids and made their lives worse for two horrible semesters. He was sly about it, though. Parents think he's the nicest kid in school.

The teachers love him, apart from the ones who think he's too cocky. But even they *like* him. The weird thing is, Dom hasn't always been like this. I remember him on our first day of elementary school. He was just like the rest of us—quiet and scared and a little bit weird.

We're all older now, me, Chloe, Lauren, Haran, and Elisha, yet if you scratch the surface, that frightened five-year-old peeks through each one of us. But not for Dom. You'd need a sledgehammer to find the kid we met on our first day.

Haran types something, then shows me his phone.

Is this Dom screwing around?

"There. Now we'll know."

I feel uneasy. We're giving too much away. Words and names that we can't take back.

The common room door swings open, and Dom marches over and flops down next to us.

"Hey," he says. "I hate dentist appointments."

He takes his phone out, and I glance down to see a message on his screen.

I'm not a lie

But he slides it quickly back into his jacket before I can read the rest.

When we were seven or eight, Dom took us into the woods. I remember that it was getting dark, howls breaking through the trees. He told us a story about these creatures called Snappers.

The Snappers would creep up on you so quietly, then *snap!* If you turned around, they'd drag you into the darkness. The trick was to stand silent and still, no matter how close that sound got.

We had no idea that Dom had persuaded his cousins to hide in the woods that day. When they snapped their branches in the shadows, we didn't stand silent and still. We screamed and bolted back to the house.

That's what I'm thinking right before I turn to him and say, "Do you know a girl called Sasha Craven?"

Dom goes pale, looks everywhere at once, then shakes his head.

"Why are you asking me that?"

"So, you *do* know her?"

He shakes his head again but doesn't speak.

"We've been getting messages. Me, Haran, and Elisha. She knows about . . . what we do on Halloween. I think it's the same person who was in the woods with us."

Dom shakes his head for a third time, as though he doesn't believe what's happening. Then he holds his hand out and mumbles, "Show me."

We pass him our phones and he reads the messages.

"Elisha got these, too?"

I nod.

"Leave it with me," Dom says.

"What does *that* mean?"

"It means I'll deal with it."

"Do you know who's sending them?"

Dom tries to smile but it falls flat.

"Just trust me, okay?"

I check no one's listening, lean in, and say, "If someone knows about the Dark Place, that affects us."

"Don't talk about it here," he whispers. "I said I'll deal with it, so stop worrying."

He stands and walks away before I can work out how to reply. I want to call after him, but Haran touches my arm and says, "Wait."

"He knows something. Did you see his face?"

Haran nods and says, "That's why we're going to follow him."

Spying for Beginners

Dom hurries out the school gate and we follow.

Whoever Sasha Craven is, they can't be dealt with later or with a text. Dom is cutting class, and he never does that.

"I have biology this afternoon," I say.

"Go then," Haran replies. "I'm trailing him."

"In what? It's *my* car."

Haran stops. "Please, Sam?"

His eyes are pleading. A voice in my head says I shouldn't be ditching, that the bell is about to go for next period. But there's another voice—a louder one—telling me to find out what Dom's up to.

"Okay."

We're already at my car and we scramble inside. I can see Dom's is parked a few spaces down, so we wait until he pulls out, then follow.

"Faster," Haran says. "You don't want to lose him."

"I'm not going to lose him. He's literally right there."

There are two cars between us, but I'm still scared of catching Dom's eye in his rearview mirror. If he sees us, he'll know we don't trust him.

"Faster," Haran mumbles, and I breathe out all the words I want to yell at him.

He turned seventeen six months before me but he still hasn't taken his test.

Dom turns right and crawls over the speed bumps into town. Then he pulls into the parking lot and hurries to the library.

My stomach flips because that's where Lauren has worked since she finished school last year. And, before I can process what's happening, she is striding out, Dom following. They stand on the sidewalk, facing each other. Dom is doing the talking, moving his hands. His sister is silent.

"What's going on?" Haran asks. "Do you think Lauren is Sasha?"

She's speaking. No, not speaking—she's shouting.

Then Dom is holding his hands out, trying to calm her.

"We should get closer," Haran says, but I have another idea.

I pull out my phone and start filming them. Passersby are noticing their argument. One woman stops, and Lauren turns, forcing a smile.

The woman walks away slowly, looking back a few times while Dom and Lauren continue talking, more quietly now.

The passenger door opens, and Haran is halfway out when I grab him and say, "What are you doing?"

"Spying. What good is this if we don't know what they're saying?"

"At least we know Lauren's involved. Maybe she'll tell us what's going on. But not if we charge right up to her now."

Haran huffs and closes the door. "Fine. Plan B."

He quickly types another message to Sasha Craven—*We're watching you right now*—hits send, then stares at Lauren and Dom.

"Do you have any binoculars?" he asks.

I pause my recording. "Sure, they're in the glove box."

"Really?"

"No! Why would I have binoculars?"

Haran shrugs and says, "For this exact situation."

I wait until I'm sure he's stopped talking, then click record again.

Lauren has been crying. She wipes her eyes, and Dom tries to hug her but she steps back.

Haran's cell vibrates and we both jump. I look over. Neither Lauren nor Dom are holding their phones. It's not them. I think I knew that all along.

"Is it her?" I ask.

I watch as Haran opens the message. His eyes go wide.

"What is it?" I ask.

"She was there," Haran whispers. "Look. She was there."

He holds out his phone. It's an image. Cracked eggshells and blood, oozing down the outer wall of the Dark Place.

There's a message underneath.

I'm a lot worse than Dom.

Fan Mail

What now?" Haran asks when we're back at school.

I try to think. Dom and Lauren aren't sending the messages, but they know something. Based on this morning in the common room, Dom won't talk. I need to speak to Lauren, and she's more likely to talk to me if Haran isn't there. All he'll do is lob out questions and talk over her answers.

"I need time to think," I say.

"I've seen this film," Haran replies. "It doesn't end well."

"Lucky it's not a film then."

"That's what they all think."

He's talking about the characters we love to shout at on our movie marathons. The ones who don't run, the ones who make jokes when they should be making weapons, the ones who say "I'll be right back."

Haran loves horrors, and between him and my dad they've

made me watch practically everything. To me, they're just stories. To my father, they passed the time until Mom came home. To my best friend, they're something else.

Haran and I go to our separate classes, and I don't wait for him in our usual spot afterward. Instead, I head straight home, and if he's angry at having to get the bus, he doesn't tell me.

Someone was watching us that night. Someone was lurking in the woods, waiting for me to go inside the Dark Place and then playing their own horrible "trick." And it feels like they are still watching.

I've felt the grip of unseen eyes. I know what it's like when people watch you because they think they have a right to.

Most of my fans were just fans . . . but not everyone.

No one is home when I get there. I pull myself into the attic, then push the boxes and old toys aside until I see it. Mom wanted it gone but Dad doesn't do what he's told. He said he'd thrown it out; then he tucked it up here, hidden until the year his bad back meant I was the one who came up for the Christmas decorations.

I guess we all have our secrets.

My father won't let any of my fame go. Even the horrible parts.

I open the box. The notes feel strangely familiar, like a story I read as a kid. They start off nice, then slowly morph into something else—the sentences sharpening, questions becoming demands, compliments replaced by threats.

> *Isiah is the best thing about Future Force. You're my favorite actor.*
>
> *When can we meet? I have so much to tell you.*
>
> *You'll regret not answering me, Sam.*

The last few messages aren't words, just drawings. I didn't see them until I discovered this box, and I'm grateful for that. If I'd seen them when I was eight, I would have been even more scared of the strangers who stood outside our house.

Lots of them were just ordinary people—fans, or superfans. But I knew there was something wrong. Even when everyone had gone home, I knew I was still being watched. I could feel them, the eyes in the shadows.

That's why I did it: the biggest secret I ever told the Dark Place.

Confession

I call Lauren that evening, and she picks up so quickly I'm caught off guard.

"Hi. It's Sam. Um. Dom's friend, you know?"

Lauren laughs and says, "Of course I know who you are, Sam."

"How are you?"

"Fine," Lauren says. But the word stretches too long for it to be true. It sounds more like a question. She's confused about why I'm calling her.

There was a time when this wouldn't have been quite so awkward. Dom painted his big sister out to be a certain way—sometimes annoying, mostly irrelevant—but that wasn't true.

He might not have cared for *her* friends, but Lauren definitely cared for his. When my life changed forever, she gave me her number and said, "If you ever need a chat, call me."

We didn't talk often, but whenever we did, it helped. That's why I feel so guilty phoning her now. I don't want to upset someone who has always done right by me.

I wonder whether she's alone. I picture Dom sitting silently next to her and almost chicken out. But I keep going.

"I've been getting these weird messages," I say. "Haran and Elisha have been getting them, too. From some girl we don't know called Sasha."

Lauren is quiet and eventually I say, "Have you had any? It's just . . . she knows."

An intake of breath like her words are almost ready . . . then nothing.

"Lauren? Are you okay?"

"What did the messages say?"

"They said she's buried in the Dark Place. And there's something else. She was there that night. She has photos."

There's another pause.

"Have you ever told anyone about the Dark Place?" Lauren asks. "Anyone at all?"

"No. Just us five. I swear."

"What about Haran or Elisha?"

Haran wouldn't tell a soul. He loves the ceremony, the tradition, the fact that, one night a year, we do something no one has a clue about. He wants his secrets hidden, just like me.

Elisha came to the ritual late. I had to convince Dom to trust her. I don't think she'd break that trust.

"They wouldn't tell," I say. "I'm sure of it."

Lauren is silent for a long time. Then she lets out a big breath and says, "In that case, we have a problem."

"Why?"

"Sasha is one of my secrets. I put her into the Dark Place."

"So you *do* know her."

"Not exactly," Lauren says. "Sasha doesn't exist."

Questions

I **barely slept last night. What Lauren said went around** and around my head, tying my thoughts into knots.

Sasha is a secret. But she doesn't exist. What does that even mean?

I tried to ask more but Lauren shut me down.

"Everyone needs to hear this together," she said. "Tomorrow."

The messages from Sasha have changed. As I lie on my bed, I get four emojis, twice in a row. A car, a camera, a question mark, and a girl.

I think of the box of old fan mail, now under my bed. I said things in the Dark Place that I've never told anyone. That's why I can't go to Mom, because then she'd know, too, and it would break her.

My relationship with Dad is complicated. There are knots inside knots. There is grief and anger and guilt, and I don't want that with my mother.

There are no knots with her. Our feelings are straight lines, and I will do everything I can to keep them loose and free. I was supposed to leave the Dark Place feeling lighter. I usually feel better afterward.

Sasha stole that from me.

I can feel the storm rising inside me. I close my eyes, searching for that calm—the calm the Dark Place usually provides. There are ways I've found to settle the storms, like playing with my sister or listening to music. But those storms have to be small. Too big and Molly becomes a hindrance, while my favorite songs sound wrong.

The only thing that worked, that *really* worked, was the Dark Place. And now it's drenched in blood.

Thirty minutes later I pull up outside Haran's house and think about sounding my horn or calling him from the car, but that's not what we do.

I get out, I knock, and I talk to his mom and dad for at least five minutes. Because Haran's always late and his parents are always friendly.

"Samuel," Lena says. "It's good to see you."

I smile, because I feel exactly the same. Sometimes I think Haran's mom loves me as much as she loves him. Seeing her gives me the comfort I desperately need right now. If only we were kids again.

Lena must sense that something's not right, because she touches my arm and says, "Is everything okay?"

What would she think if I told her the truth—that for years her son and I have been holding funerals for our secrets and now one of them has come back from the dead?

Lena is holding my gaze, forcing me to look away; then

her husband, Naveen, appears behind her and says, "I see our son's taxi has arrived."

He grins and shakes my hand, which I usually hate but not when Naveen does it.

"How's the family?" he asks, and like always I say, "Fine."

Haran's dad and my dad were once super close. When we were young, Naveen would come over for poker nights and barbecues. It's why Haran and I are such good friends. We grew up together and, like our fathers, were always destined to be. But Dad spends most of his time alone now.

"Haran!" Naveen shouts. "Don't keep Sam waiting."

My best friend bounds down the stairs, kisses his mom on the cheek, and slips past.

As soon as we pull away, I'm spilling everything I know about Sasha.

"What do you mean, she's not real?" Haran asks.

"That's what Lauren told me. She said Sasha doesn't exist."

"Who the hell is messaging us then?"

"I guess we'll find out today. Lauren is meeting us at lunch."

Haran shakes his head. "I don't think we're going to like what we hear, Sam." There's nothing to say to that.

At school, Dom barely looks at us when we catch him in the corridor, just waves and vanishes into the stream of kids heading to class.

"What's up with him?" Elisha asks.

We tell her everything.

"This is . . . a lot," she says when we finish.

"I had five messages from 'Sasha' last night," Haran says. "It's creeping me out."

I take his phone and scroll through.

She made me

She used me
I was nothing
I was everything
I am REAL

I pass the phone to Elisha and she hands it quickly back to Haran.

"Have you had any more messages?" I ask, and she shakes her head. "Nothing at all?"

"Nope."

She looks odd, like she's tensing every muscle in her face. When she sees me staring, she shrugs and says, "What?"

I've always secretly hoped that she'll tell me what she leaves in the Dark Place. But she never does.

Two years ago, when we started going out, she told me, "I don't share personal stuff." That was the first time I heard the sound a full stop can make. But it's not as simple as that. The self-imposed barrier may seem to cover Elisha's entire world, but it is strongest around one horrible memory.

I know her mother up and left when Elisha was thirteen, because the whole school does. In a town like ours, where people usually don't leave, gossip lingers, and the gossip from that time was ferocious. But that's *all* I know about that part of her life—facts, not feelings.

And that's why I never push it, because I'm terrified that one of Elisha's full stops will be the last thing I ever hear her say.

"Isn't it weird that the messages are so different?" I say instead. "Haran's getting these ones but I'm getting emojis. Look."

I hold out my phone and show them. A car, a camera, a question mark, and a girl.

Elisha stares at the symbols, then puffs out her cheeks and says, "This is probably some stupid joke, you realize that?"

Maybe, I think, *maybe not.* Elisha was there in the woods. She chased that scream into the darkness. How can she be so casual now?

"How do you explain this then?" Haran says. He holds out the photo of the Dark Place, the walls sticky with blood, and Elisha shivers.

"It could still be someone messing around," she says unconvincingly.

The truth is we won't know any more until we've spoken to Lauren. But I'm starting to wonder. Maybe we've been making a mistake all these years, hiding our secrets in the Dark Place.

Maybe some secrets should never have been buried.

Answers

At lunchtime I see Lauren standing by the school gates, talking to my old math teacher Mrs. Akinfenwa.

They're laughing like they are old friends. Lauren was one of those students who was popular with kids and teachers alike. Not because she was pretending, like her brother sometimes does. Dom's big sister got the "genuine" gene.

I wonder if I'll ever visit once I've left. I don't think so. I think I'll leave school behind the minute I've graduated.

Stoneleigh Road is the ugly sister to Hayschurch Academy, but I know where I'd rather be. The teachers here genuinely care, probably because you have to be a certain kind of person to work in a school where the computers take half a period to turn on.

Dad went to Stoneleigh and Mom went to the Academy, but she didn't seem disappointed when I chose this place. Our school has memories in every room and on every surface. It has history, like all my favorite places. Plus I wanted to stay with my friends.

It's not just the school that's full of memories. There's the hill Grandpa used to climb even when his limbs seized up, because the view from the top was Granny's favorite. He'd stare into the distance and roll his wedding ring around and around his knuckle, as if he were trying to turn back time. But he was always smiling, so when I go up there now, I smile, too.

There are the rock pools at the beach Haran and I explored as kids, jumping from one tiny world to the next while our parents lounged in the sun. Every visit we'd take one shell each, before tossing the ones from last time back into the sea.

There's the playground I went to every week before I was famous, shrinking as I grew older, then expanding again once Molly took my place on the one swing that flew higher than the rest.

Now Elisha and I hang back, watching Lauren talk to Mrs. Akinfenwa like everything's fine. And I think about Mrs. Akinfenwa, who always seems so composed, and every other staff member and pupil here at Stoneleigh Road.

They all have secrets. Every last one of them. We only know what they want us to. We only see what they show us.

A stranger might watch Lauren right now and think she doesn't have a care in the world. Until she waves goodbye to her old teacher and walks over, her smile shifting, her eyes narrowing, and the truth breaks through.

"Are you ready?" she asks, just as Haran arrives.

"Where's your brother?" Elisha asks.

"He's meeting us there."

We follow her to the rec, and I see Dom sitting in our usual spot. He's watching a couple of people in the skate park, and I remember the summer we thought skateboarding was as easy as standing on some wood.

Dom's dad, Steve, built boards for all three of us and we sanded them down in his workshop, then impatiently waited for the paint then the varnish to dry. Eventually, we ran to the park, ready to show off our skills. The problem was, we didn't *have* any skills. Not that I cared. I was just excited to have something that used to be nothing—this colorful, one-of-a-kind wonder that, a few days earlier, was a plain piece of timber.

I always thought Dom's father was cooler than mine, which is odd because I think Dom thought the same in reverse. He loved my dad's photographs and he was fascinated by the garage we'd converted into a darkroom.

Dom loved watching Dad dip and dry the photographic paper. Loved seeing the picture emerge from nothing. Sometimes Mom would ask why it took so long and Dad would just say, "Respect the process."

That was Dad's catchphrase until his studio was lost in the fire.

I push that thought from my head now as I sit on the bench opposite Dom.

I glance at him. He smiles but it's not real. His lips are trembling.

He's usually the one in control but not today. Today it's Lauren who clears her throat and says, "Okay, let's get this over with."

Elisha sits next to me and squeezes my hand and I squeeze back.

"First off, I made Sasha up," Lauren says. "She doesn't exist."

She looks at Dom, then says, "Well, she *didn't* exist. But I guess she does now. She was . . . a lie I told to make life easier."

Lauren closes her eyes and I think that's it. Then she sighs and says, "I was with someone called Malika. We met during my internship in the city. It was great for a while and then . . . I was going through some stuff. I needed a break. Usually when you end it with someone it's because you don't love them anymore, right? Or because you never did. But I couldn't use that excuse because I still loved Malika. I still *love* Malika.

"I couldn't explain things to them. They would have done everything they could to help me. It *wouldn't* have helped, though. So, I broke their heart. I made them hate me so they'd leave me alone. I made a girl up because it was easier than telling the truth."

I think of how kind Lauren was to me when I needed it the most. How she shifted from being Dom's older sister—a pain in the butt when we were younger, a friendly blur once we hit double figures—to something else; someone important. In recent years she raced from place to place like her life depended on it. But I had never wondered where she was going or who she was seeing.

Now it feels like I should have known—about Malika, about their relationship, about its end.

I see sadness in Lauren's eyes and realize she hasn't been hiding her sorrow. It's always been there. We just weren't looking closely enough.

"So, it's this Malika who's messing with us," Elisha says.

Lauren shakes her head. "Malika has no idea about the Dark Place. They don't know any of you. And if they *did* know the truth, it would be me they're angry with, not you."

"Who is it then?" Haran asks.

"I don't know. All I ever did was name her. Sasha. That's it. When Dom started getting the messages, I didn't connect the two at all. But then I got this."

Lauren holds out her phone and I can see a message from the Sasha Craven profile.

You only thought of me. Someone else brought me to life.

"It was from Sasha. Only now she's got a last name and a face. All her social accounts were set up last week. Everything on the same day."

There's silence. How did we not spot that?

"Whoever planned this knows what Lauren did," says Dom.

If they know Lauren's secret, I wonder, do they know all of ours?

I watch Dom. He looks genuinely puzzled, worried.

I used to know him so well. Haran, Dom, and I were super close. A trio. But, when he hit thirteen, Dom changed. When he blew hot, it was like old times. When he blew cold, Haran and I did our own thing.

We became a two within a three. I never thought Dom noticed or cared much. But maybe he did. Something kept us connected—history, I guess. Whenever it looked like we would drift apart, an invisible string pulled us back.

"And you've never told anyone else about the Dark Place?"

I'm looking at Lauren but I'm talking to everyone.

The slightest pause before she says, "No one."

"Who cares if someone knows about what we do on Halloween?" Elisha says. She looks around at us defiantly. "It's not as if we killed anyone."

Dom stands up so quickly he almost stumbles.

"Look," he says. His hand is shaking and it takes me a few

seconds to focus on the phone; then I see it. It's another photo of the Dark Place. But this one was taken in the daytime.

"They went back," Dom says.

"It was probably just those kids who came to the door," Elisha says. "You tricked them so they got revenge."

I remember the terrible smell of the blood, the feel of it, and I don't think that's something a few trick-or-treating kids would do.

Under the photo, a caption reads: *I'm not the only one who hears their whispers.*

"What do you think it means?" I ask.

Dom wrings his fingers until the blood drains from their tips. "I don't know."

"We saw you both talking at the library," Haran says. "We followed you."

Dom and Lauren stare at him, then at each other. I didn't think we were telling them that. But I guess Haran is going off script.

Lauren gives the tiniest nod and her brother sighs.

"I knew Lauren had made up Sasha," Dom says. "It took me a while to figure it out, but . . . she used to keep me awake for hours, chatting to someone until the sun was almost up. I guess that was Malika."

Lauren gives her brother the smallest smile and nods.

"Then one day she sounds upset, mentions this Sasha girl. Only, there were no more phone calls. Lauren replaced Malika with silence, so I knew something wasn't right. When I got this, I started to wonder."

Dom scrolls through his phone, then shows us the message I saw that day in the common room.

I'm not a lie anymore. I'm ali(v)e now.

They look at each other again and something passes between them. It's a look I know well, because Molly does the same with me. She trusts me implicitly and I think, deep down, Dom and Lauren are the same.

"The fact is," says Haran slowly, "that no one except you two knew about Sasha. And yet she's messaging all of us. This can't just be a prank."

I close my eyes. Then I open them again, stare at each of my friends in turn, and say, "The Dark Place is important to me. It's important to all of us. We don't talk about what we say in there and maybe we never will. We've always tried to protect it. Never questioned what happened in there. But now—we can't ignore what's happening. Someone who doesn't even exist is contacting us from the Dark Place. It might be a hoax, it might be something else, but I think we need to find out what's going on."

No one replies for a long time. Then Dom nods and says, "Agreed."

And so, it's decided. We investigate—even if it means shining a light on the Dark Place.

Second Time Lucky

My anxiety lives mainly in my stomach and my arms. One is heavy and the other is light, my guts twisted and my fingers fidgeting like I need a sugar hit.

When I was younger, I assumed everyone felt like this. I thought the fears that settled in my head like birds of prey were universal. I'd search for it in my friends' smiles because I was sure, no matter how happy they seemed on the surface, that they were fake.

I lied to my parents every time they asked if I'd had a good day on set. I showed Haran and Dom the face they expected to see whenever they called me a "star." I deceived them, so, surely, they must have been deceiving me.

But they never seemed to show it and, gradually, I realized that I was different from most people.

I needed the Dark Place more than anyone. That's where,

ever since I was twelve, I've put all my guilt and anxiety—
letting me be a person who is almost okay.

I'm in my bedroom, steadying my breathing, when I hear
Dad shout. I ignore him. When he shouts again, only Mom
moves.

Then *she's* shouting, too, and I walk to Dad's office. They're
bending over something.

"It's good," Mom says, and Dad says, "*Very* good."

"Who took them, do you think? Sam?"

"What are you talking about?" I ask, and they spin around
in unison.

Dad holds out his phone, and for a moment I wonder if
Sasha has messaged him, too. But he's grinning.

I take the phone. There's a photo on the screen. Not just
any photo.

It's a picture of our cat—Lola—bounding across the lawn
in pursuit of a bird. Both creatures look so clear I want to
reach out and touch them. It looks perfect.

Dad swipes his phone and there's a stunning close-up of a
flower, its orange petals glowing like fire in the sunlight.

The next one catches me by surprise, because it's me,
asleep, and I look so peaceful I almost don't recognize myself.

"Well, that answers your question," Mom says. "It was
Molly."

Dad calls my sister's name until, finally, she waddles in.

"Am I in trouble?" she asks, and Mom says, "No, sweetheart. Did you take these?"

Molly stares at Dad's phone and says, "Yep."

"They're beautiful."

"I know."

Dad is looking at her funny, and I know what he's thinking. He's spent years trying to take the perfect photograph, and his five-year-old daughter is already better than him.

When Molly was younger, I'd sometimes find random videos or blurry close-ups on my phone. Now it seems she's been using Dad's cell when he's not looking—and there's nothing random about these ones.

"Would you mind," he asks, "if we put these online?"

There it is—the look I know so well. He can already feel the glow of another potential star.

He's scratching the edge of the scar on his right arm, the way he does when he's nervous. But this time it's mixed with excitement.

I open my mouth to speak, but the words don't come. Molly is out of bounds. Dad knows that. But he's good at forgetting.

Dad looks at me, like he's reading my mind, and says, "They're great, Sam. You can see that."

Holding up the one of me sleeping, he says, "Obviously, we'd leave this one out."

Why can't he enjoy the moment? My sister made something beautiful, but for him that's not enough. He needs to show *everyone.*

I turn to Mom for support just as Dad does the exact same thing, and she looks at each of us, then down at Molly.

"What do you think, darling? Would you like other people to see these?"

My sister shrugs, then says, "Okay," and Dad beams then goes straight to his Mac.

I love him. I really do. But I wish we were enough.

Back in my room, I google myself, find the photo, and stare at it. It never was taken down, no matter how many times Mom tried.

It's my thirteenth-birthday party but there are no candles on the cake. Next to me, my grandpa grins the biggest grin, and in the background Mom and Dad are hugging the way they did back then, my mother's arms so light around my father that they're barely touching. It was a good moment at the end of a horrible year. And somehow the press got hold of it, twisting it into something it wasn't.

That day was ours, no prying eyes, no filming, no strangers; just my family and two people I thought were my friends.

Haran was there, out of shot, and so was another boy—Dylan. He took the picture and sold it. He stole that moment and I hated him. The last picture of Grandpa before he died.

Dylan was part of our gang back then—the fourth side of a square that was destined to collapse.

No matter how many times Dom mocked him, no matter how often Haran's jealousy turned to spite, Dylan stuck around. In between those times, we had fun, but that's not what I remember.

He betrayed me. Then he moved away. No loss.

Although he did prove one thing—if you try hard enough, you *can* leave Hayschurch and never come back.

Later, I sit on Molly's bed and she rolls over and says, "Are you angry with Dad?"

She's been waiting for me, because my sister can't go to sleep with a question in her head.

Answers are her version of night-lights.

"No," I whisper. "I'm not angry."

"Do you like my photos?"

I brush back her curls and kiss her forehead, then say, "Of course I do. They're awesome."

"Mmm-hmm."

Her eyes are closed and she's already half asleep. I gave her an answer, so now she can dream.

Phone Calls

You can't hide from me.

That's the message I wake up to.

I'm so tempted to reply. To tell whoever's messaging me that I know Sasha isn't real. She's just a figment of Lauren's imagination. I could tell them to stop messing with us. But what will that do?

I focus. It's time to use logic. If it isn't Dom or Lauren sending the messages, then there's only one person it can be.

I call Dom and, when he answers, I say, "Are you absolutely certain Malika isn't behind the messages and the attack?"

He sighs and says, "I believe that Lauren believes them."

"What about you?"

"We have to consider them, right? They're basically the only suspect we have. They're the only one who knows about Sasha. They've also got a motive—revenge. Lauren lied to them and then dumped them . . ."

"Can you get Malika's number? I'll do the talking."

Dom sighs again, deeper this time, then says, "Lauren will be pissed if she knows I went through her phone."

"So, you won't do it?"

I can hear Dom's smile as he whispers, "I didn't say that."

He doesn't send me the number until late. I hide my caller ID and phone right away.

"Hello?"

"Is this Malika?"

"Who wants to know?"

"I'm a friend of Lauren's. She doesn't know I'm calling."

"Is Lauren okay?"

"She's fine," I say. "But I'd appreciate it if we could chat in person."

It's a lot harder to lie when people can see your face. And a lot harder to hide when there's nowhere to run.

"Is this about that thing in the woods? I've already told Lauren that I had nothing to do with it."

"She told you about that?"

Malika goes quiet and I think I've blown it. Then, finally, they say, "I wouldn't do anything to hurt her, okay?"

They sound genuine. I can see how Lauren would believe them, but I'm not so easily swayed.

"Please," I say. "Can we meet? I just want to ask a few questions. I'm scared that if we don't get to the bottom of this, things will get worse. For Lauren."

There's a pause, and then they say, "Okay. But I'll tell you when and where. You could be a psycho for all I know."

I laugh and say, "So could you."

Witness

At school the next morning, I spend my free period in the study center, watching Elisha do what she does best. Three sophomore science kids hang on her every word, and I picture her teaching here one day.

A few times she catches me staring and points at my books, but I can't focus. We've agreed to investigate Sasha, so how exactly do we do that? How do you find someone who isn't real?

I glance over at Chloe—one of the ultra-studious juniors clustered around the corner table. Those are the sort of kids Dom couldn't resist winding up. The irony is, they'd annihilate him in a quiz about literally anything.

I haven't spoken to Chloe since the party and I feel guilty for that. I also feel foolish, because if someone followed us from the house to the woods that night, she might have seen them.

When a couple of her group shuffle out, I wander over and say, "Hey. Do you have a minute?"

Chloe looks me up and down, grins, then says, "No blood today. I take it you don't need to borrow another outfit?"

"I'm good."

She nods at the seat next to her. "Be my guest."

The two other kids still at the table scowl at me, but Chloe calms them with a look of her own. Elisha may be the study center's top dog for now, but my neighbor is a worthy successor.

She packs some past exam papers into her folder and closes it. On the front it says THINK LIKE A PROTON—ALWAYS POSITIVE.

"Come on," Chloe says. "We'll talk outside."

Elisha watches us as we leave, and I mouth *Possible witness.* She shakes her head, then turns back to her groupies.

"So," Chloe says, as the door hisses shut, "what's up?"

"Firstly, I'm sorry about the party. The end, I mean. I know the car journey home was awkward."

She shrugs. "It's fine."

"Something happened. It just wasn't fun anymore, you know?"

"When you vanished?"

"What?"

"You were gone a long time," Chloe says. "I assumed there'd been an argument. Sorry if I'm overstepping but . . . Elisha was so frosty when you got back, and Haran wouldn't sit still in the car. You couldn't get out of there quickly enough."

She's a lot more observant than I thought, which is both a good and a bad thing.

"A few idiots from the Academy stepped up to me," I say,

thinking back to Ghostface and his friends. "It spoiled the evening."

Chloe's stare reminds me of Molly's when she knows I'm holding something back.

"Honestly," I say, "that's all."

"Okay," she says, her happiness snapping back as Elisha walks into the corridor.

"Why are you distracting my protégée?" my girlfriend asks.

Chloe beams. "No distractions. Just a hard-earned break."

"Glad to hear it," Elisha says. "What are you talking about?"

"I was just going to ask Chloe if she saw anyone acting weird on Halloween. You know, after the damage to Dom's house."

"Right," Elisha says, stretching the word a little too long.

"Did you see anyone out of place?" I ask. "Someone there just to cause trouble? Maybe they were acting suspicious?"

"I don't think so," Chloe says.

"Are you sure?"

She looks frustrated, like she desperately wants to help. Usually when someone asks Chloe a question, she answers instantly. But this is a different kind of problem.

"It's okay," Elisha says. "There were so many people. It could have been any of them."

Chloe sighs and says, "Right? I knew it was a big party but . . . seeing is believing, I guess. My friends are super jealous."

My phone vibrates and I glance at it, then freeze.

"Well, I'll see you around."

Chloe nods and says, "I should hope so. You still haven't dropped my clothes back. I *love* those boots."

She heads back into the study center, and then I show Elisha my latest message.

It's another photo from the woods. There are twigs next to the hut, but they haven't just fallen there. Someone has carefully laid them out, forming a stick figure among the crimson leaves, one leg twisted unnaturally to the side.

The caption underneath reads: *We all fall together.*

"How original," Elisha says, glancing back into the room where her phone sits facedown on the desk.

"It's okay to think this is serious," I reply. "It's fine to be freaked out."

"And it's equally fine *not* to be. Why can't this just be a prank that's being stretched out because you keep biting?"

"Do you really believe that?"

Elisha looks through the door at her tutees and holds up one finger. Then she kisses me and says, "Whatever's going on, I need to get back to the real world."

She strides into the room, her smile fixed and her arms outstretched.

"Right," she says before the door closes, "where were we?"

She flicks through a textbook, points at something, then quickly checks her phone, relief washing over her face.

It seems, unsurprisingly, that Sasha's latest message is just for me.

Blood

The following Saturday, I'm sitting in the park with a Starbucks hot chocolate, desperately trying not to look suspicious. About thirty feet away, Haran is doing a terrible job of blending in. He keeps looking over at me and grinning when I catch his eye.

Stop being so obvious, I text, and he replies, *It's not my fault you're a wuss.*

Malika wanted to meet in the open, surrounded by dog walkers and joggers. Fair enough. They don't know I've brought along the world's least subtle bodyguard.

I tried to find Malika on Lauren's Instagram so I could at least check what they look like, but their privacy settings are locked down.

A few times people walk close to me and I try to make eye contact. But no one stops.

"Your friend is acting strange."

The voice makes me jump, and I turn to see someone right behind me.

"Malika?"

"Yeah. I assume you're Sam. And who's that?"

They point at Haran and I say, "Would you believe me if I said he's my protection?"

"No."

Malika sits next to me, points at someone reading a book on the next bench along, and says, "Hey, I brought protection, too."

The man smiles at me, and I laugh. I'd barely noticed him. "Yours is a lot better at blending in than mine."

"So," Malika says, "what do you want to know?"

At first glance they seem legit and I feel guilty for not trusting Lauren's judgment. But a tiny voice at the back of my brain says, *They're the only one who knows.*

"How much did Lauren tell you . . . about Halloween?"

"Someone's sending you creepy messages and they threw blood at your little hut thing. Is that the gist?"

"That's the gist."

"I'll tell you what I told Lauren," Malika says. "I didn't set up a fake profile to haunt you guys. And I didn't go all *Carrie* in the woods."

I smile at the reference, thinking back to the night this all started and Haran covering me in fake blood. We had no idea what was coming.

"Did you tell anyone else about Sasha?" I ask.

Malika laughs and says, "What do you think? Lauren dumped me for her. I told anyone who would listen because I was angry."

I catch their eye before they look at the ground, and I realize they weren't just angry. They were hurt.

"Did you ever try to reach out to her?"

"Sasha?" Malika asks. "No. Well, I tried to find her—of course I did. I looked on social media, but there was nothing. Lauren wouldn't tell me where she lived. Eventually I blocked Lauren. At some point you have to move on, right? Forgive, don't forget, and all that."

They clearly think Sasha is real. It's not my place to say otherwise.

"I appreciate you looking out for Lauren," Malika says. "And I won't tell her about this."

When they see my face, Malika says, "You can't tell me that Lauren knows you're here. Her brother stole my number, right?"

They are smart, and for the briefest moment I think about telling them everything. They might even be able to help. But what scares me is that someone knows Lauren's secret. They know about the Dark Place. And that means they might know *all* our secrets, including mine.

"Thanks," I say, "I appreciate you coming."

"No worries. I had other things to do here, anyway."

"Really?"

Malika laughs and says, "Don't sound so surprised. You're as bad as Lauren. My uncle and auntie live just over there. People can leave Hayschurch and only come back for visits, you know. My parents grew up here and managed to escape. The funny thing is, for a little while, I would have moved here in a heartbeat."

Just as I'm about to leave, Malika says, "Does Lauren ever mention me?"

I hesitate, trying to work out the kindest answer.

"I'm not that close with Lauren," I say. "Only her brother."

I hate myself because that's not entirely true and I can see a little light disappear from Malika's eyes, a little hope. I think that's why they really came today.

"It's okay," Malika says, something hardening in their face, as if they were already prepared for my answer. "Listen, what did the blood smell like?"

"What?"

"Did it smell rancid?"

I think of the thick red oozing down the hut and the stench that smacked me hard between the eyes. "Yeah. It was disgusting."

Malika nods and says, "There aren't many places you can get that much real blood."

I hadn't thought of that before. The fact that the eggs were filled with blood was so shocking I didn't stop to wonder where it came from. I feel foolish for not questioning that sooner.

"If I wanted to get hold of a ton of blood," Malika says, "there's only one place to go around here."

"Where?"

"The slaughterhouse."

Old Times

We drive from the park to Haran's place and he flops on his bed and says, "Remember when life was fun?"

I think back to when it was just the four of us—me, Haran, Dom, and Dylan. We loved spending days at Dom's, because his house was huge and his garden was even bigger.

Back then, Lauren wanted nothing to do with us. She called us "silly little boys" and that was fine because *silly* was all we wanted to be.

This was years before Dom started wearing designer stuff. All of us wore the same combination of T-shirts and jeans, muddied and ripped from untold adventures. Carefree.

Well, the others were carefree. But I wasn't just a kid. I was *that* kid. Any fun I had was temporary, replaced by the fear of another season, another scene, another take . . . until the moment that ended that life forever.

I was jealous of Dom. His parents were obviously rich to own that place, although he never boasted about it. My mom took all the money from *Future Force* and put it in an account I can't touch until I'm twenty-one.

Even when we needed it, when my time on the show ended and we had half a house to rebuild, Mom insisted that *they* top up the insurance money, not me. Sometimes she'd argue with Dad and I'd hear words I didn't like. But, for once, he didn't get his way.

I look around Haran's room, which has barely changed since we were twelve. I'm the only one who comes over. We'd have sleepovers at Dom's and at mine, and at Dylan's before he sold the photo, but Haran always had an excuse.

The others didn't notice, but I did—how Haran flinched when you talked about money; how he went quiet when you reeled off your Christmas list.

That's why I'm the only friend who comes here, because I know what it means for Haran to let me in.

"I miss being a kid," Haran says. "The woods felt a lot less scary. *Everything* felt a lot less scary."

I picture him running into the Dark Place about thirty minutes before things went to shit. He wasn't scared then. He was happy, excited.

"My mom would say we're *still* kids," I reply. "She always says we've got our whole lives ahead of us. She laughs when I say I'm getting old."

Haran grins and says, "You *are* old. Didn't you retire when you were twelve?"

I laugh and then feel guilty for laughing.

The guilt must be catching, because Haran's face changes and he says, "Sorry I . . ."

I touch his shoulder and say, "It's all right to joke about it. That's what friends do, right?"

Haran is looking down at his phone when he nods. I miss his ever-expanding smile whenever he's chatting to Brendan, the way his lips move when he's rereading his favorite messages, how his face would light up whenever his cell did the same.

"How's the boyfriend?" I ask, and Haran raises an eyebrow and says, "How's the girlfriend?"

"Seriously. Is he still enjoying college?"

Haran holds my gaze. "I know what you're doing."

"What's that?"

"You want me to tell you I used to adore this phone because everything on it was Brendan—all the photos and the messages and the voicemails. It was all a reminder of how ridiculously in love I am. And that's all still there. But now it's been tainted because Sasha's messages are there, too. And they keep coming. So yes, Brendan's fine. *We're* fine. But I can't say I'm particularly happy when things like this wake me in the middle of the night."

He tosses me his cell and there's another stick figure, lying amid the crisp leaves. While the picture I received had a jagged leg, Haran's has one arm twisted behind its back. The caption underneath says: *They made me do it.*

"There are two types of killers in the movies," Haran says. "The ones who don't say a word ... and the ones who can't stop talking. This one is taunting us, Sam."

"Except for one thing," I reply. "No one's actually dead. So, they're not a killer, are they? They're just ..."

I struggle for the word, because I don't know *what* they are.

I could show Haran the stick figure I received, but I'm scared of the message that came with it.

We all fall together.

I'm scared because I know what it means.

"Why didn't you show me this sooner?"

"I was going to," Haran replies. "But you were so eager to meet Malika and, I don't know, I was hoping maybe they know something."

"Maybe they do. We need to talk to someone from the slaughterhouse."

"No way," Haran says, and I can see echoes of his old faces—the seven-year-old who looked terrified whenever our parents mentioned that place; the ten-year-old who got morbidly fascinated for one weird summer; the fourteen-year-old who lost a bet with Dom about who could get the closest. "What goes on in there is nasty."

We all know—or *think* we know—what happens in the gray slab of a building that looms over the edge of town like the world's biggest gravestone. It's our campfire classic—decades of lies mixed with uncertain truths. And now it's our only potential lead.

"We don't need to go inside," I say. "But whoever threw those eggs must have gotten the blood from somewhere. It's a clue, isn't it? If we want to stop getting these messages, we need to start digging."

Haran doesn't say anything, but I know we're both thinking the same thing. The blood has to have come from the slaughterhouse—because the alternative is too horrible to think about.

Night

When I close my eyes, I'm back in the woods.

I'm alone in the Dark Place, whispering to myself, the shadows from the candles creeping along the walls and becoming something else; something vast and suffocating.

The shadow creature pushes down on me and I'm not asleep anymore but I'm not awake either. I'm in a horrible in-between and I want to scream but the shape is too heavy. My mouth is a huge hollow O and I can't breathe.

I have always been safe in the Dark Place. But I'm not safe now.

I'm not strong enough to fight back. I push with everything I have but the shape is stronger. It holds my arms and my legs and my throat. It pushes me deeper and deeper into the ground until I know I'm going to die.

Dirt and rotten leaves tumble into my throat, choking me until I force out a cry. But the noise that comes isn't mine. It's someone else's wail ripping through my head. And then I *am* screaming, fighting back against the night until Mom's stroking my hair and whispering, "It's okay. It was just a dream."

I stare at her, trying to work out if she's real. Then Dad is there and his touch brings me back.

"What happened?" he whispers, but I can't tell him that. Not him.

I feel hot and sweaty and my chest hurts. It hurts in the place where the creature held me down.

"You scared us," Mom says.

"I'm fine," I reply, so they'll leave.

I lie awake, picturing dark, sticky blood and fragments of shell.

It was Halloween. That's what I keep telling myself. Scaring people is the norm. But then you stop.

Unless you have a reason not to.

Day

"Dad said people like my pictures," Molly says.

"Of course they do," I say, blinking the sleep away. She's standing by my bed, in the weak morning light.

"He said millions of people like them."

I jump up and follow Molly downstairs, where Dad has the biggest I-told-you-so smile.

"Did she tell you?"

"She did."

Dad thrusts his tablet in my face and says, "One point three million likes. Molly's photos are blowing up."

The Instagram page he set up for her pictures is full of likes and comments and I should be happy but I'm not. If I'm honest, I wanted Molly's photos to be ignored.

Instead, people are calling her a *genius* because of course our father included her age.

"Look at this one," Dad says. "It's an interview request."

"No!" Mom shouts from the kitchen.

"You don't even know who it's with."

"It doesn't matter who it's with. She's our baby. Have you forgotten that?"

Dad gives me a half smile and a shrug, then goes to Mom, where their words shrink to whispers.

Molly sits next to me on the sofa and says, "Is Mom angry with me?"

"Of course not."

"Is she angry with Dad?"

I don't answer that one. Instead, I pick up his tablet, where the notifications are racing, and look at my sister's photographs. They really are amazing.

"I'm so proud of you," I say.

She nuzzles into me and says, "I'm proud of you, too."

If only she knew.

Shopping

I **know what you did!**

I stare at the message until it blurs.

Again.

I know your secret, Sam.

When my phone pings a third time, it says: *Drive to the high street.*

It takes all my courage to write: *What if I don't?*

Then Mommy and Daddy will know what happened.

I try to swallow the sickness surging up my throat, but it fights back and I run to the bathroom just in time.

When my phone goes off again, I wait ten long seconds, imagining a life where none of this is happening. Then I open the text and read: *You've got 15 minutes. The clock's ticking.*

My car keys are hanging in the kitchen, so I grab them.

"Where are you off to?" Mom asks, and without turning around I say, "Just popping into town. Won't be long."

"Could you get . . ."

I'm out the door and away before Mom can finish. Then I drive as calmly as I can until I'm back in the parking lot where we watched Dom and Lauren. That already feels like a lifetime ago.

I'm here, I type.

Okay. Let's go shopping.

This is a joke—it has to be. I walk across the road and stare at the stores around me. When I was a kid, we used to come here all the time. But these days we go to the Riverside mall, because it's ten times bigger and one hundred times better.

Town is mostly thrift shops and banks now, with a supermarket at either end and some coffeehouses in the middle. Half the stores I went to as a kid are either gone or boarded up, and the only busy places are the bars. But the weirdest thing is that no one ever leaves. Like I said, if you're born in Hayschurch, chances are you'll die here, too.

The town center may be on its last legs, but its borders are new and expanding. Housing developments are shooting up everywhere and we're twenty-eight minutes from the city by train. Even if you leave for college, something pulls you home again. Look at Lauren. A summer interning for some tech company, now she's back working in the library.

I walk over to the nearest clothes store, then message Sasha.

What now?

Are you scared, Sam?

Should I be?

I think you've answered your own question.

It's broad daylight. I'm standing outside a boring clothes store. Of course I'm not scared.

Pick something, Sam.

I walk to the men's section and flick through the shirts. There's nothing I like but I don't think we're here for me.

Have you found something?

A shirt?

Perfect. Steal it.

Not a chance. This is some kid messing with me. I hang the shirt back up and walk away.

I said steal it, Sam. You have to do what I say. You know that.

That's when I feel them—invisible eyes. I freeze and look around the store but there's hardly anyone here. There's a woman pushing a stroller while another kid screams at her, and an old man studying the slippers. Two cashiers chat behind the counter. But no one is watching me.

My fingers are shaking so I take a deep breath, steady them, then write: *No.*

Your choice. Nice color, by the way. That blue would look good on you.

I think back to Halloween, the moment I ran out of the Dark Place and back to the twisted elms. I had the same feeling then. Someone was watching us in the woods, and someone is watching me now.

I know what you did, Sam. I know your secret.

I look at the other customers. The woman hushes her kid. The old man yawns. The cashiers laugh.

My phone goes off again.

Do you want me to prove it?

There's a picture message attached. I open it and my vision swims.

They know.

I walk as casually as possible back to the shirts, pick one, and tuck it under my coat just as I get another message.

I've got a better idea. Put that back and go next door.

The shirt I was *this* close to stealing falls from my hands and I hurry out.

There is a store on either side. One has a sign in the otherwise empty window—TO LET. The other is called Bargain Binge. The neon sign above me hums as I enter.

As if she can read my mind, Sasha sends another message.

Why don't we find something good to watch. Something beginning with . . . F.

What would they do if I ran?

Numb now, I head for the box sets.

I know what I'll find and, sure enough, it's there. *The Complete Future Force Collection,* face out on the shelf. There I am. Or should I say: There *he* is. Because the kid staring back at me is from another life.

No one is paying me any attention. There was a time when I couldn't walk into a place like this without getting mobbed. But now I'm just another shopper, except I don't intend to pay.

My phone vibrates.

You know what to do.

I can't see any closed-circuit cameras. If this were Riverside, there would be security everywhere; the ones you can see and the ones you can't. But that costs money, and the stores still open in Hayschurch don't have that to spare. There's nothing stopping me from leaving except the cashier talking loudly with another customer and someone rearranging the anime three aisles over.

I take one deep breath then stuff the box set under my coat.

I dare my feet to take one step, then another, until I can see the doors, hear the outside world, feel the rain on my face.

And then I'm running and I don't stop until I'm at the car, grabbing my keys, jumping in and driving away.

"Fuck," I say, then louder, "Fuck!"

I drive for a few minutes, then pull over, reaching for my phone just as it lights up.

Well done. Now we have another little secret.

I scroll up to the previous message Sasha sent. The one that changes everything.

There it is. Our burned-out house is in the background, two firefighters standing in the space where the front door used to be. And in the foreground, my mother stands alone, staring up at the charred remains of her dream home.

Underneath the photo are three words.

I know everything.

Wunderkind

Who are your inspirations?" the interviewer asks, and Molly closes her eyes, shrugs, and says, "Dora the Explorer?"

The reporter nods and writes that down. His name is Gavin and he's from a prestigious photography magazine that Dad always has copies of lying around. He's also an idiot.

We're in our living room—Mom, Dad, Molly and me, Gavin and a photographer.

This is what happens when Dad gets his way.

"And when did you start taking pictures, Molly?" Gavin asks.

My sister shrugs and says, "I don't know."

"She's five," Mom says. "She has no idea what she did."

"Yes, I do," Molly says, pointing at the photographs spread across the coffee table. "I did that."

"You sure did," Gavin says. "And I'm here to find out how."

"I took Dad's phone and pushed the button," my sister says.

"But what did you feel?" he asks. "Right *before* you pushed it . . . what was happening in your head?"

Molly huffs and reaches for the photo of the flower.

"It looked beautiful," she says. "Dad says every moment is a potential masterpiece and I thought it was one of those so I photoed it."

Gavin is scribbling again. He loves the masterpiece line.

Dad is fidgeting, hoping he gets the credit for it.

"And then?"

"And then we put it on Instagram and everyone liked it."

"What do your friends think about this?" Gavin asks. "Are they jealous? Now that you're famous?"

Famous. I hate him for using that word.

Molly holds Gavin's stare for six long seconds before she says, "I'm not famous." Then she's looking at me and I'm scared of what she knows, because there's pity in her eyes. Just a flash of it, entangled in her love and pride and confusion.

"You're very modest, Molly," Gavin says. "Do you know what *modest* means?"

My sister nods and reaches for her juice.

Turning to us, Gavin says, "She's adorable. I'd like to get some quotes from school friends, teachers . . . to see how they feel about little Molly's success."

"I don't think so," Mom says.

"It's only half a story without it."

"It's not a story at all," Mom snaps, looking at Dad.

Dad turns to Gavin and shrugs apologetically. "The school isn't an option. Molly doesn't want the attention."

Gavin laughs and says, "Maybe you shouldn't have put her

on Instagram then. I notice you're also a photographer, Mr. Hall. Have you taken anything I'd have seen?"

There's a sudden chill in the air as the two men stare at each other.

"Probably not," Dad says at last.

The reporter glances quickly at the photos on the table, then back to our father.

"Okay then."

"Right," says Mom, standing. "We're done. The interview is over. She's just a little girl who pushed a button on a phone." Gavin's scribbling again. "And don't write that!"

"One more thing," he says.

Gavin lifts his photographer's camera off the table and gives it to Molly.

"Take a picture," he says. "It doesn't matter what it is. Just point and press."

Molly fiddles with it then passes it back. "I don't think so," she whispers.

Gavin's eyes meet hers, and I don't like his expression. "Why not?"

"I can't see a masterpiece today."

The Fame Game

How was that?" I ask my sister as we sit in the back garden, and she shrugs and says, "It was okay."

I want to apologize. I want to say it isn't normal for five-year-olds to be interviewed for photography magazines. There's something else, too. I hated the way Gavin looked at us, how he challenged Molly, how he called out our father.

I'm used to being talked down to, ignored in favor of my older costars, but no one could deny my achievements. I can't say the same for Molly. What if Gavin says it was Dad who took the photos? He wouldn't even have to *say* it. Implication is enough. That's how journalists get away with lying.

I wasn't much older than Molly when I filmed the first episode of *Future Force*. To start with, I loved it—because it made Dad happy.

I loved it when he high-fived me after a perfect take. I loved it when he showed off to his friends.

"My son, the superstar," he'd say. And I'd *feel* like a superstar, because Dad's joy came off him in waves.

And then I realized it wasn't fun anymore. Maybe it hadn't been for a long time. Perhaps it never was fun at all. And that's what worries me about Molly.

"You don't have to do this," I say. "If you don't want to talk about the pictures, just say so."

"It's all right," she replies. "It makes Dad happy."

Molly gets it. She's smarter than I was at five. She's smarter than I am *now*.

Mom, Molly, and I—we all know. We know that keeping Dad happy is the most important thing.

I watch Molly playing—always silent, her toys talking only to her. She's so comfortable in herself.

It took me a long time to become the real Sam Hall. For ages I was someone else, then the kid who *used to be* someone else. I don't want my sister being "the girl who took those photos." Or worse, "the girl who lied to go viral."

I want her to be Molly Hall—generous, perfect, one of a kind. I want her to have the childhood I didn't.

I leave her to play, and find Mom, gathering up the dirty cups left behind from the interview.

"I don't want it to happen again."

I see the guilt settle behind her eyes.

"It won't," Mom says. "This isn't like before, like it was with you. Nothing trends for long. Eventually the likes stop."

"Really? Because they're only going in one direction."

Mom sits on the sofa and taps the seat next to her.

"You know what I keep telling myself?" she says. "I keep thinking: At least *she's* not in the photos. She may have taken them, but all people will see is what she captured.

"I hated that you were famous, Sam. I wished every day that I'd talked your father out of that damn show. But you get it, don't you? You could have said no to the documentary and you didn't. You said yes. Because, when your dad looks at you with those eyes, you have to."

I laugh because she's right.

"Molly isn't some prodigy," I tell her. "She's amazing. But not like that."

Mom wipes her eyes and shakes her head.

"We'll let your father have this moment," she says. "He can watch the likes rack up and frame those photos but I guarantee you, Molly will not be used. Not like . . ."

"Like *I* was . . ."

Mom doesn't hide her tears this time. She stares straight at me and says, "I thought it made you happy."

"Sometimes I was."

Mom rests her hand on my leg, right where my scar is.

I don't want to know what she's thinking, because sometimes I'm sure she knows that what happened wasn't an accident.

The Fire

When I'm sure everyone's asleep, I pull the box set out from under my bed. Sasha hasn't messaged me since. She's quiet—for now.

The faces on the *Future Force* collection feel like characters in a recurring dream. Familiar yet strange.

It wasn't all bad. We had plenty of laughs, and most of the adult cast members treated me like their own kid. It wasn't the people I hated. It was the cage we were trapped in.

Technically the show finished with season five. But there were two spin-offs and a movie—and I didn't do either.

Instead of recasting me, the showrunners simply plotted a different course, and my fake *Future Force* family carried on saving the world without me.

I stare at my phone. She knows. She knows everything.

I could bury my cell deep under the bed along with the

box of fan mail. But it would still be there, whispering threats while I lay awake. I need to face this head-on. Finding out who Sasha is—that's the first step.

I can't fight her if I'm afraid. Afraid of the past. So, I need to face that, too.

I open up the photo she sent, staring at it until the image blurs. I'm not here anymore. I'm back there.

Remembering the final quiet moments before our house burned down.

I was twelve when it happened. Just a kid—at least on the outside. Inside I was all grown up, with a script to learn and notes to read.

"Please can I come?"

I hated how desperate I sounded.

"Sorry, sweetheart," Mom said. "You know you need to nail this."

I looked at the script on my lap.

"When I come back, we'll run lines again," Dad said. "This has to be perfect, Sam."

He sounded like the director.

The season-five finale was going to be the biggest episode yet. And my character, Isiah, was integral. I'd prayed every night that they would kill me off. It was clear from the script that wasn't happening.

"We won't be long," Mom said, apologies sewn into every word.

I longed to go with them. It was only the supermarket and the garden center, but those places sounded magical to me. All I wanted was a perfectly normal, perfectly boring life.

Instead, I did what Dad told me to, watching from my bedroom window as they drove away, then going back to my script.

The more I stared at the words, the more they taunted me, dodging my grasp. Finally, I threw them across the room.

I looked at the crumpled pages on the carpet, then up at my poster of Isiah and that painfully fake grin, and I gave him the finger.

"Ten minutes," I said to myself, turning on my games console and getting lost in a fantasy world that had nothing to do with me.

After half an hour, I stopped for a bathroom break. I didn't care if my parents came home to find the game paused. I wasn't bothered if Dad ran lines and I'd forgotten every word. I was sick . . . of . . . everything.

I stared at my reflection in the bathroom mirror for a long time, searching for Sam Hall, but all I saw was Isiah.

"Who am I?" I whispered, then louder, "Who am I?!" The shock of that shout brought Sam back.

I saw him in the anger that rippled across my lips and flared behind my eyes. I saw him in the smile that crept out before morphing into a grimace. The house was full of my school photos but I didn't recognize myself in them.

I shouted again and again, so loud that I was scared the glass would shatter, but with every yell I felt more like myself.

I screamed at my reflection until all Isiah's expressions and emotions were gone, replaced by a twelve-year-old's tears. And then I walked slowly back to my bedroom and ripped that script to shreds.

The pieces fluttered to the floor like dying insects; then I lay on my bed, waiting for my parents to come home.

When Dad asked what had happened, I would tell him. I would scream it in his face. Finally, I felt brave.

But first, I closed my eyes, just for a few minutes, slowly breathing out my worries until I coughed myself awake.

The clock said I'd been asleep for over an hour. The room was thick with smoke. And there were flames snaking across the carpet, pulling the ripped-up pages into their grip and swallowing them whole.

The tiniest voice in my head said, "Run," but the roar of the flames drowned it out. Instead, I watched as the fire crept up the walls, my *Future Force* poster crinkling at the edges, folding in on itself, then vanishing.

The flames licked closer but I didn't move. In that moment, I felt relieved. Happy.

Isiah was gone. The fire didn't scare me. It made me braver. Yet, no matter how hot it got or how thick the smoke felt in my lungs, my legs refused to move.

Fire is ravenous, its hunger impossible to satisfy. That's what I thought as I finally dropped to the ground, coughing out what suddenly felt like my last breaths. Then I heard it—a voice shouting over the crackle of the flames and the screech of the smoke alarm.

"Sam! Sam!"

I was being dragged up and into my parents' room.

Dad slammed the door and pushed towels under it.

"What happened?" he asked.

There's a fire, I thought. That was the easy bit. The difficult part was telling him why I hadn't escaped while I could.

He opened the window as far as it would go, then held out his hand. "Come on." Something in his face made me reach out.

I saw him. I saw someone who was here to save me and I wanted so much to be saved.

"Easy does it," Dad said, as he lifted me onto Mom's dressing table.

She was looking up at me from the driveway, screaming things I couldn't understand. Then one word that I could: "Jump!"

I leaned forward, staring at the ground until it began to swirl, and then I fell.

There was the tiniest moment of unexpected bliss, all my weight left behind; then it smashed back into me as I hit the ground.

The pain was like lightning bolts shooting up my leg, and when I touched it, I felt something strange.

Bone pierced my skin like a tiny white claw and I screamed and screamed. Mom had her arms around me.

"Is he okay?" Dad yelled, and Mom said, "Yes. He's okay."

Only then did I hear the thud as he landed a couple of feet from us, before he rolled over, coughing and crying at the sky.

What Didn't Burn

I can still picture Mom's face when I first woke up in the hospital. She whispered wet words into my ear and said she was sorry and how could this have happened?

I didn't tell her that I could have run. How could I?

"I'm sorry," I whispered, and she said, "So am I."

The space to explain everything shrank a little more each day. But that didn't mean my regret got smaller. If anything, it grew. I had thought I was a phoenix ready to be reborn—no more Isiah, only Sam. Except I'd waited too long, forcing my father into a house he barely got out of alive.

Dad hid his scars from me for a long time. First, they were covered by bandages and then, eventually, by carefully selected clothes. But I knew they were there. I saw it every time Mom looked at him with equal parts sadness and love; every time she hugged him without squeezing too hard, or at all, her arms hovering around his body like a force field.

That wasn't the only thing they tried to keep from me. Unfortunately for them, Haran was useless at lying.

He showed me all the headlines, and all the photographs of our burned-out house that our neighbors must have sold to the press.

Sam Hall's Career Up in Flames
No "Future" for Hall After House Fire
Burned Out at 12: What Next for Sam Hall?

The articles didn't say it outright, because no one wants to get sued. Instead, they mentioned how I was home alone when the fire started. That "unnamed sources" had said I'd seemed quiet, troubled at school in the months before the fire. That I had been struggling on set.

When you put that together, the trolls do the rest.

I thought I knew what gossip was. I'd seen it from my classmates and dealt with my fair share during the show. But this was something else. It was a whisper that grew into a roar.

At school, the mean comments hung in the corridors like nets, forcing me to tread so carefully that, eventually, I hid in the bathroom between periods and arrived late to every class.

All the teachers' responses were the same. No reprimand, no detention, only pity.

"Why do these idiots think you'd burn your own house down?" Haran bemoaned.

"I don't know," I replied, because it was easier than telling the truth.

That was the year I realized that the nastiest rumors are just like the fire that tore through our home, spreading from person to person until reality is nothing but ash.

We stayed at my grandpa's during the rebuild. He said having us around made him feel young again. I think being there made *me* feel young again, too, because there was no pressure.

The face I saw in the mirror was always me. And everything that came out of my mouth was a word *I'd* thought of, not a line from a script deleted and rewritten by ten different people.

When the *Future Force* producers asked to meet, we did it around Grandpa's dinner table. They said I could take all the time I needed and I saw my chance.

"I don't want to go back," I said. "Ever."

Dad fought as hard as he could. But that wasn't much back then. He knew, deep down, that things had changed.

I was relieved and, finally, happy. Yet the night of the fire loomed large over every new day.

I'd hoped that quitting the show would stop the rumors but, for a while, they only grew. Some people claimed I'd been axed. They refused to accept that the decision was my own.

Mom kept her anger hidden for as long as she could. Eventually, it stirred.

She asked Dad why he'd never gotten the fuse box updated, but that was a trick question. She asked him why we'd never had the wiring checked. Her jagged whispers crept through the gap in the door and stung my ears. It had to have been his fault. She just didn't know how.

And, finally, she was proved right.

When the fire brigade had sifted through the wreckage of our life, they determined that it started in Dad's darkroom.

My father had stood soaked in guilt, the weight of it pulling his shoulders toward the ground. But Mom didn't turn on him. She walked away in silence.

We waited for her to respond. It was a long and horrible wait. Words we expected her to say hung on to the edge of every muted conversation. And then, one night, as Grandpa snored and I stared at the ceiling, Mom exploded.

"It serves you right," she spat from the room next door. "Why couldn't you take photographs like everyone else does these days? It's the twenty-first fucking century, Adam!"

Dad said nothing, but I could picture him sinking deeper into the ground.

He was to blame, that was the truth. Only it wasn't. The real truth was more complicated than that. Sometimes no one is to blame. And sometimes everyone is.

School Project

On Monday, Haran and I are waiting for Dom at the school gate. When he arrives, he makes a face and says, "What's going on?"

"Sam has a plan," Haran says.

"Okay."

"We're doing an assignment," I say. "About blood."

"What?"

"You agreed that we have to figure out who this so-called Sasha is, right? This is how we do it."

Dom shakes his head and says, "It's early, dude. I'm really going to need more information . . . and some sugar."

Haran pulls a Mars bar from his pocket and tosses it to Dom, then says, "I supply the snacks. Sam has the info."

"You sound ridiculous," Dom says, but Haran grins back because he's enjoying this.

"The eggs were filled with blood," I say. "And there were tons of them. Lots of eggs means . . ."

"Lots of blood," Dom says.

"Exactly. But where do you get that much blood?"

"You kill someone."

Dom keeps a straight face slightly longer than I'd like, before he sees my expression, smiles, and says, "I'm joking. I give up. Where do you get that much blood?"

"The slaughterhouse."

Dom nods slowly and says, "Okay."

I exchange looks with Haran, then say, "In the interest of honesty, that wasn't my idea. It was Malika's."

"You spoke to them?"

"Yep. I don't think they have anything to do with this. But they *did* tell me to look at the slaughterhouse. I've done some research and they're right. There's a hell of a lot of blood in there. It gets collected regularly, transferred for use in all these other things like medical products and blood meal and black pudding."

"You know a lot about this."

"Google told me. But you know the weirdest thing? If blood isn't transferred quickly, it starts to stink. Remember the blood at Halloween? That smell?"

Dom shudders. "What's the plan?"

"We need to get into the slaughterhouse and ask some questions."

"Which is why," Haran says with his arms outstretched, "we're pretending to do a project on blood."

Dom grins, then goes serious and says, "What do I tell my sister?"

"Tell her exactly the same as we told you—only it's my idea. She doesn't need to know we spoke to Malika."

He thinks about it. "Lauren will be furious if she finds out we lied."

I see Elisha walk through the gates, clock me, and wave; then I turn back to Dom and say, "It's lucky that we're good at keeping secrets."

Where Bad Things Happen

Go through it again," Haran says on Saturday. "I don't want to mess this up."

"We're doing a school assignment about blood," I reply. "That's literally all you have to say."

"So, you're making *me* sound like the serial killer?"

"Look, that's just if we get split up and someone asks you. Otherwise, you say nothing. We'll do the talking."

From the outside, the slaughterhouse looks pretty normal. It's big and gray and boring and I wonder what all the fuss was about when we were kids. But that's the thing about urban legends—fiction kills facts.

There isn't even a sign until we drive through the gates and see a small metal notice that reads HAYSCHURCH ABATTOIR.

A man pokes his head out of a window in a tiny red-bricked booth and snaps, "Are you lost?"

"He's polite," Dom mumbles, but I block him out and say, "We're here to meet Katherine Murphy."

Haran opens his window and says, "We're doing a school assignment on blood."

"Right," the man says, watching Haran for five long seconds before checking his clipboard and then picking up his walkie-talkie.

I watch Lauren trying desperately to hold in a laugh while Dom says, "At least he remembered his line."

"I was trying to be friendly," says Haran.

"I don't think it worked," Elisha says, which makes Lauren crack up until the man is standing by my window and suddenly everyone goes serious.

He has thin gray hair and a patchy beard and I'm guessing he's in his sixties.

"Follow this road to the end then turn right," he says. "Ms. Murphy will be waiting for you by the parking lot. She'll sign you in there."

I watch the man stare at my license plate, then repeat it until he's back in his booth.

"Okay," I say. "Let's go."

"Bad things happen here," Lauren mutters.

A woman in a blue suit is waiting for us when we pull up. She smiles as we get out and shakes our hands. She has a sweet, uncertain smile and dark hair with blond streaks.

"I'm Kat," she says. "Quality control manager. Which one of you is Sam?"

"That would be me." We spoke on the phone. I persuaded her to let us in. I just hope the others stay on script.

"It's great to meet you all. Come this way."

We follow her into the building, then through an open door to a room where she says, "Take a seat, everyone. Can I get you any drinks? Tea? Coffee? Water?"

This room could be anywhere. It's basically the most boring room imaginable. All at once, in a horrible muddle of groans, the five of us say, "No, thank you," and I feel myself start to blush.

"Not to worry," Kat says. "Sam tells me you're doing a school project on blood. How interesting. What can I help you with today?"

"What happens here, exactly?" Lauren asks. "In the slaughterhouse, I mean."

This is *not* part of the script and I shoot her a look.

Kat clears her throat and says, "We process animals."

She doesn't expand on that and there's a weird staring contest between her and Lauren.

There's something odd about this bland little office, like we're in a fake room that will collapse in on itself the moment we leave. A film set. I picture Kat peeling off her business dress, revealing overalls that are stained red.

I can smell it then. The thick, rancid odor of blood.

"Look," says Kat nervously. "We don't get many kids asking to look around. When they do, they usually have a motive. They want to cause trouble. I don't blame them necessarily. They're standing up for what they believe in. But I need to protect my staff. If you want confrontation, you've come to the wrong place."

"We're interested in the blood," Dom says. "Where does it go after . . . ?"

He can't say the rest and I don't blame him.

"*That's* a question I feel more comfortable answering," Kat says, catching my eye and giving me a half smile.

When I spoke to her on the phone, she sounded wary. She said they got a lot of protesters. But I told her that our assignment was purely about the multiple uses of secondhand blood, and her voice changed.

"That's a relief," she'd said.

"We're grateful for your time," I tell her now, and she smiles, a real smile this time.

"The blood collected here is used for a whole host of things," Kat says. "Some of it is used in food products or additives. You know those strange words on ingredients lists—emulsifiers, stabilizers, clarifiers—they all use blood. Then there are fertilizers, pharmaceuticals, animal feeds . . ."

"And how do you transport it?" Dom asks.

"It's collected every day. You can't keep blood for long or . . ."

"It starts to stink," Haran says.

Kat creases her eyebrows and says, "Well, yes. It also becomes less effective in those processes."

"Who collects it?" I ask.

"A tanker comes and takes it away. Then some very smart people work their magic and it's used for all the things I've mentioned and probably a few that I haven't."

I picture the blood-filled eggs and think: *You have no idea.*

"Tell me more about the tanker," I say.

"We're a relatively small plant," Kat says. "Our tanks are emptied by what they call a 'milk round' tanker. Basically, there's a hose and a pump that sucks the blood out and then it's driven away to various locations. Wherever it's needed."

I glance at Elisha, who's been taking notes on her phone, and she nods, then says, "Is there a specific company that collects the blood?"

Kat nods. "Evans-McKinney Haulage. They've been working with us for years."

"What time do they come?" I ask, and then, because Kat suddenly looks suspicious, "I'm assuming they collect it early—or do normal working hours not apply with this kind of thing?"

Kat is giving me a weird look, and for a moment I think I've been rumbled. Then I see it happen like I have a thousand times before. She realizes where she knows me from.

Thankfully she doesn't say anything. Instead, she says, "Nine A.M. on the dot."

I nod, then, as planned, Dom says, "We were scared of this place when we were kids, you know? But it's not that bad once you're inside."

Kat points at herself and says, "You weren't the only one. But we all have to work somewhere."

"Okay," I say. "I think that's everything."

Kat relaxes slightly.

"Do you enjoy being a quality control manager?" I ask, and there's a tiny shake of her head before she says, "It's not the job I dreamed of at school. But I've got responsibilities and it pays the bills."

There it is again—the line Dad uses, the one *all* adults seem to say when they don't enjoy what they do.

"I wasn't sure if it was the right thing letting you come here," Kat says. "But I've enjoyed talking to you all. It's nice to put a face to a name. If you think of any other questions, pop me an email. I'll look forward to reading the finished product."

"Sure," I say, wondering if I now have to write a fake school project about blood.

She guides us out, then waves as we drive away, a slight figure in a smart suit, as Lauren says, "Malika was right."

"About what?" Elisha asks, and Lauren says, "This place is nasty."

"Why are they so interested in it?" I ask.

Lauren glazes over, like she's lost in a daydream; then she says, "Malika is an animal-rights activist. They hate what goes on in places like this."

The gate doesn't open right away. Instead, the security guard comes out of his booth and gestures for me to open the window.

"Did you get your answers?"

"We did," I reply, suddenly feeling uneasy.

"We don't get many school visits," he says, chuckling to himself as he walks away.

His torso leans forward as though his head is too heavy for his body, his arms dangling like broken wind chimes.

He picks something from his teeth, flicks it on the ground between us, then waves as the gate opens.

"So," Dom says when we're back on the main road, "we know the company that collects the blood and when. What now?"

I look at him in the rearview mirror and say, "Now we find out who drives that collection truck."

Breaking News

We drive in silence for a while. I'm thinking that, for all the fuss we make of Dom's house at Halloween, with all its cobwebs and gore, where we've just been is the *real* house of horrors.

"Oh," Lauren says from the backseat, and then, "You should pull over, Sam."

"Why?"

"Because you're all over the internet. It says you shoplifted."

My heart falls into my stomach and I suddenly can't breathe.

Elisha sees my face lose all control, then whispers, "You didn't."

I can't look at her. I can't look at anyone. Instead, I pull over and get out, then walk quickly away from the car, fumbling with my phone.

It's the top story: DISGRACED CHILD STAR SAM HALL CAUGHT RED-HANDED.

But it's not just an article. It's a video.

I click on it and watch. I'm in Bargain Binge, the camera zooming in on the *Future Force* box set in my hands before I take one last look around, hide it, and quickly leave the store.

The emotions of that morning smack me hard between the eyes, and it's not until Elisha is next to me, touching my cheek, that I realize I'm crying.

"Why did you do it?" she asks.

"I had to," I say. "She made me."

Elisha's staring at me, waiting for more, but the rest of the words sit stubbornly at the back of my throat. As much as I've always hoped she would open up to me, there's always been something unspoken from my side, too.

Does she know? Does she care? Today, if I'm reading her right, she does.

Haran, Dom, and Lauren are hanging back. When I turn, they all look away awkwardly, and I feel embarrassed. What must they think of me?

The lies gossip sites used to print had no substance. But here's me, rushing out of the store with stolen goods. Here's undeniable proof that, this time, the horrible headline is true.

"I'm going to be arrested," I say, fighting the urge to retch. I think of my parents—Dad's anger and Mom's shame—and I don't fight it anymore.

I turn away from Elisha and throw up. Then she's stroking my back, saying, "*She* made you—you mean Sasha? Sasha did this to you?"

I nod and suddenly I'm surrounded by all four of them. They pull me into a hug and I focus on my breathing until Haran says, "I bet this looks weird to anyone driving past."

The rest of them laugh and I wish I could join in.

I waited years to be out of the headlines. I thought that part of my life was over. But soon, everyone will be staring at me with those horrible eyes again—the ones that say I'm public property.

And it's all because of Sasha.

History Repeating

When I go home, the house is quiet. For twelve short seconds, I cling to the hope that my family hasn't seen it. That's how long I count before Molly runs into my bedroom and says, "There's a video of you on Mom's phone that made her cry."

I hold my arms out and my sister walks silently into my hug.

"Is everything okay?" she asks.

"Not really. I did something stupid and someone made a video of it."

"Like on TikTok?"

"No, Mol. Not like that. This isn't a funny video."

"Sometimes it is," my sister says, and something horrible stirs in my stomach.

I grab my phone and the footage is everywhere; hundreds of different edits all with one goal—humiliation.

Some people have switched out the box set for other things that I stuff under my jacket before quickly leaving the shop. Others pause on my face the moment before I leave, turning my terror into a joke.

Then there are the memes slamming me, mocking me, intercutting my most triumphant moments on *Future Force* with the few horrible minutes when Sasha pulled my strings.

I hear the staircase creak and I know it's Mom. She walks slowly, whereas Dad bounds. But today she's slower than usual. It's as though she's stopping on every step. Is she wondering what to say to me? Has she already made up her mind that I'm guilty?

"Off you go, Molly," Mom says. "I need to speak to your brother."

She's holding it in, hiding it from Molly. But I can see it. It's the ripples that anger makes in the air; the unfamiliar look Mom's face adopts when she's about to blow.

She closes my bedroom door, then sits on the end of my bed and says, "I assume you've seen it."

I nod. For a moment, I let myself hope she understands. Then Mom says, "Never, in a million years, did I expect this from you."

"I can explain," I say. But can I?

The truth is: I'm being blackmailed over a secret that would break her.

"You'd better," she says, "and I'm expecting one hell of a good reason."

I close my eyes and all I see is that photo of Mom staring helplessly at our burned-out house. All I can feel is shame.

"Well?"

When I don't answer, she says, "I'm embarrassed, Sam. Do you realize that? I had to watch my son commit a crime and I can't for the life of me figure out why."

She doesn't care that I've been humiliated. All that matters is that I've let her down.

Think, think. I need something that is almost the truth . . . but not quite.

"Someone at school," I mumble, unsure of my own lie. "They saw Molly's Instagram. They—they said we're a weird family. They said we're fame-hungry."

Mom's anger softens but it doesn't disappear. She sighs and says, "That's never bothered you before."

"My sister's never been involved before."

I hate myself for using Molly like this. But if there's one way to calm Mom down, it's to redirect the blame.

"They said they'd flood her page with comments about what a freak she is . . . or I could do one dare and they'd leave her alone. They told me to steal that box set. I know I messed up, Mom, but she's so little . . ."

I stop talking because every word is coated in something sharp and nasty—like I had to reach deep into my stomach to pull out this lie.

"I'll talk to the school," Mom says, and, as calmly as possible, I say, "That would make it worse. It's done now."

I think of the discs buried under my bed and say, "How can I make this right?"

"For a start, you go back to that store and apologize. Okay?"

I don't argue. Instead, I stand by the front door as she wrestles Molly into her coat, then sit in silence as we drive to town.

I dare myself to check my feeds, then instantly regret it. Thousands of strangers are ridiculing me, and I slam my phone facedown into my lap.

"You'll be okay," Mom says, her eyes fixed firmly on the road but her hand resting on mine.

All three of us walk into Bargain Binge and up to the counter. The woman at the till, who is about Mom's age, puts down her coffee and says, "How can I help?"

We all stand there in silence. Molly peers up at me, and I don't know how to say this without hurting someone. Why has Mom brought her into this? Is she testing me? Can she see through my bullshit, challenging me to lie about my sister to her face?

I take one last look at Molly, then pull out the box set and lay it on the counter.

"I took this," I say. "I made a mistake. I'm sorry."

The woman looks from me to Mom and back again. It feels like a whole conversation passes silently between them, but Molly is watching even closer.

"Why are you sad?" she asks, and I can't tell which of us she's talking to. Maybe it's all three, because Mom strokes her hair and says, "We're just waiting for your brother to put something right."

"I'm sorry," I say again to the woman.

I stare at her name badge because I can't look her in the eye. It says SANDY (STORE MANAGER).

She looks down at the box set. Isiah's grin taunts me until I look away from his face, too.

There's a horrible moment of overstretched silence as the woman looks at the cover, then at me, then back again. What

must she think—that I'm some kind of narcissist, stealing copies
of my own show for kicks?

We wait. Then the manager sighs, rolls her shoulders, and
says, "Go home."

I can hear the tension leave Mom's mouth as she says,
"Thank you."

Back in the car, Molly stares out the window. Mom and I
sit side by side.

"There are other ways to protect your family," Mom says.
"Ones that don't involve breaking the law. Next time, be
smart."

I nod. I'm thinking that Sasha didn't just hurt me this time;
she hurt my family. Which means that now I have no choice
but to track her down.

Stakeout

At eight thirty on Monday morning, I pick up Haran like always. But today we don't go to school. Instead, we drive back to the slaughterhouse, pulling up three hundred yards short and sitting in silence.

I've turned off my notifications, and I have no desire to search for my latest downfall.

I expected Haran to be a ball of nervous energy, but he's barely said a word since getting in the car.

That's fine by me. It means we don't have to talk about the video, the memes, all the ways people have to turn one horrible moment into thousands. I know stuff like this dies down eventually. But I don't know if I have the patience to go through it again.

I haven't been relevant for years. But that doesn't mean people ignore me when I fall. If anything, they enjoy it more.

To begin with, I thought Haran was being a good friend.

Now I don't think it's just the recording he doesn't want to talk about; it's everything.

"Check the glove box," I say.

"What?"

"The glove box. I've brought something for you."

Haran looks tired and confused. Then he reaches down and pulls out some binoculars.

"You're welcome."

He doesn't laugh. He just turns them over and over in his hands, staring blankly out the window.

"What's up with you?"

"Nothing," he says. "I didn't sleep much."

I get that. My nightmares don't come every night, but when they do, they are savage.

Haran leans his head back and closes his eyes. I hate what Sasha has done to us. When we were following Dom, it felt safe, silly almost. But that's because he had nothing to do with this. Maybe we always knew, and that's why it was easy to follow him into town and spy on Lauren—because it felt like a game.

But *this* isn't. This is real life.

"Have you thought any more about what those twigs mean?" I ask.

"No."

I pass him my phone, open to the image of the stick figure with the twisted leg.

"You got one, too?"

"I did."

I know Haran is keeping stuff from me, because *I'm* hiding stuff from *him,* as well. I'm hiding that I let my house burn. I'm hiding that my dad almost died because of it. And I'm hiding the fact that the stickman with the broken leg is lying in exactly the same position I was after I leaped from the window.

We all fall together.

That's what my message said.

Haran's—under the image of a stick figure with one arm twisted behind its back—said: *They made me do it.*

What is he keeping from me?

"I'm here for you. You know that, right?"

Haran nods and says, "Same to you, bro."

But there's no confession. Only a horrible silence that I've never felt with my best friend before.

At 8:57 A.M. a truck drives past and Haran's eyes shoot open.

"This is it," I say. "Evans-McKinney Haulage."

After a few minutes, I turn the ignition, pull the car around, then put my hazard lights on.

"We should have asked that woman how long it takes to fill the truck," Haran mumbles.

I didn't think of that. A horrible thought occurs to me: What if Kat drives past, on her way to work? What will she think?

I stare at the clock as the minutes slowly blink by.

"Maybe there's another way out," Haran says. "We should probably go."

I look out of my window, focusing on all the little things we usually ignore—the condensation tracing its way down the window, the spiderweb on the side mirror. That's one of Mom's tricks to calm Molly when she's upset: drawing my sister's attention to something so ordinary it's become invisible. She will point at a bug busy going nowhere, or the shifting patterns in windswept clouds, and she'll remind Molly of its magic.

Then I see it.

"Here it comes," I say, as the truck grows bigger in my rearview.

I quickly step out of my car and stand in the road, while Haran slowly does the same.

"They're not going to stop," he says.

For a moment, I think he's right, but then it slows and a man is getting out and walking toward us.

"Okay," I say. "This is it."

"You guys all right?" the man asks.

He looks around forty; his overalls are stained various shades of brown.

I stare at him, trying to work out if he thinks we're suspicious. He frowns, so I say, "The car just sort of . . . stopped."

"No worries. You want me to take a look?"

He walks toward the hood and shouts, "Pop it."

"It's not him, is it?" I whisper, and Haran shakes his head, looking relieved.

I was stupid to think the driver would have had anything to do with this. But he can still be helpful.

There are tons of places you can get blood—the hospital, the morgue, yourself. Maybe they were patient. Maybe they stockpiled the stuff for weeks and then hit us when they had exactly the right amount.

The truck driver waves at me and says, "Try now."

I turn the key, feign surprise when it starts, and shout, "That's it."

The man shrugs and says, "Sometimes you just have to turn it off and on again. Have a good day."

"Before you go," I say, "you transport blood, right?"

The driver's eyes narrow as he says, "I do."

"Does anyone else have access to the tanker? Other than you?"

He looks at Haran, whose eyes are fixed firmly on the ground, then back at me. "That's a strange question."

I find my best fake smile—the kind I used so often on set—and say, "I know. But I've always wondered . . . having this place so close to home. Is blood classed as precious cargo? Or could you, technically, steal it."

I can feel Haran staring at me, but I hold the driver's gaze until he says, "It's impossible to steal. Unless you took the entire truck."

Something about his words sounds like a challenge, but before I can reply, he sees the security guard lumbering toward us and meets him halfway.

"Shit," I whisper.

The two men are talking now, the driver pointing at our car.

"Should we drive off?" Haran asks, but I don't answer. Instead, I slow my breathing and watch as the security guard walks to my window and smiles.

There's no surprise on his face. If anything, he looks too relaxed.

"Here you are again," he says. "Car trouble?"

"Yes," I manage, before he looks back at the driver, who's climbing into his cab, and says, "I assumed Ms. Murphy had answered all your questions."

The truck pulls out and drives past us, blaring its horn as it goes. The men wave at each other. I scan the guard for a name badge but there's nothing.

He turns back to me.

"Sam Hall, isn't it?"

When he sees my face he says, "You signed in when you came last time. I wouldn't be very good at my job if I didn't pay attention to things like that."

"What's *your* name?" I say, feeling simultaneously brave and sick.

He smiles. "I'll cut to the chase. I don't want to see you around here again. Got it?"

I say nothing and his lips curl into a sneer. "That's right. Run off home," he says.

"We should go," Haran whispers. But I can suddenly see all the faces that have looked down at me over the years, all the haters and trolls and bullies.

I think of Halloween and Ghostface. I could tell he was sneering behind his mask. I could see it in his eyes.

I hold the security guard's stare until he's the one to look away. Then I dare myself to say it.

"Do you know a Sasha Craven?"

"What?"

He looks baffled, yet I've seen plenty of good actors in my time. "Have you noticed anyone suspicious hanging around lately?"

He seems genuinely amused now. "Yes. You. We've had a lot of trouble around here with demonstrations, kids thinking they can save the animals, so I want to make sure you're not planning anything. Your cover story about a school assignment seemed pretty fishy to me. And now you're accosting delivery drivers."

"We're not planning anything," Haran says quickly.

"Then I think you should hit the road," says the guard mildly. "And it's probably best if you don't come back."

I watch him for a few more seconds, but all his bravado

has fallen away. He's cocky because he usually has a security barrier and a walkie-talkie, that's all.

"What was that about?" Haran asks. "You don't really think that guy knows Sasha, do you?"

I don't reply.

Eventually, Haran says, "I think you're taking this a bit too seriously. This is just some kid we know messing around."

"Stop lying to yourself!" I shout. "Seriously, Haran, you were the first person to think this was serious. You've seen the films, right? You know what to expect. Don't rewrite things now.

"You don't have to tell me what that message means or explain what secrets you've told the Dark Place. But please don't take me for a fool. I'm trying to solve this. I thought we all were. But suddenly you're acting like it's just a prank.

"You can't always look away from scary things. Sometimes they'll come for you regardless."

The Eyes

Haran walks quickly through the school gates and away.
The rest of the journey was incredibly awkward, but it
had to be said. How can he pretend these messages don't
mean anything?

I have a free period, so I head to the common room, trying
to avoid the smirks and the giggles. *There goes that freak who
stole his own TV show,* I imagine people saying. I shrink into
the corner and wait for Elisha to finish class.

The blood truck is a dead end. The security guard is intense but irrelevant. And now Sasha Craven knows I'll do
whatever she tells me to.

"Hey." Dom slumps down next to me. "How did it go?"

"It was a complete waste of time."

He doesn't look surprised.

"How are you?" he asks, but I don't want to talk about

whatever's happening online. We need to focus on the real world so everything else will stop.

"Look," I say. "Maybe we need to go back there, to the Dark Place. See if there's something we missed on the night. A clue."

Dom shivers. "I still haven't been back. Not even in the daytime."

I think of how we left the Dark Place. If we never return, it will just be another thing abandoned in the woods.

"I get that."

"I used to think it was so cool living in the middle of nowhere, but now ..."

Dom looks at me like he's not quite finished. But the next sentence doesn't come. Maybe he can't admit it—that he's frightened.

I think back to the night we took Chloe. "*Imagine a haunted house.*" That's what I'd said. Being scared is fun—if you know it's just pretend.

"Whoever did this waited until we had all told our secrets," I say. "I was the last one, remember? They were patient. Which means they might have left some trace outside ..."

Dom picks his nails. "Maybe."

"How's Lauren?" I ask.

"She's okay. I think she and Malika are talking again. She's speaking to *someone* a lot, anyway."

I hope he's right and they're working things out. Malika seems cool and Lauren deserves to be happy.

Two senior girls walk in, see Dom, then head straight out again.

He pretends not to notice, but his smile slips ever so slightly. Does he feel guilty? I would, if I'd been as horrible as he has.

I know a thing or two about reputations. Mine is that TV kid whose house burned down in "suspicious circumstances," and Dom's is the onetime bully. It doesn't matter that we're not those people anymore. It's set in stone, until we get out of the town that no one leaves.

Dom walks over to his locker and opens it. Then he cries "Shit!" and slams the door closed.

I jump up. A few people look over. Dom's eyes are wide and he's breathing fast.

"What is it?"

He opens it again, slower this time, then turns and whispers, "Come here."

When he cracks the door a little wider, I see it.

It's a doll's head, battered and filthy-looking. One eye is missing and it only has a few clumps of hair, as if the rest has been ripped out.

Its single blue eye stares at me, daring me to pick it up.

Someone came into school and did this. Someone here, in this very room?

I look around the common area, searching for anyone who looks guilty or entertained. But everyone is lost in their own little world, and Dom says, "What do you think it means?"

I walk to my locker and open it, then pull out another doll's head with the same blue eye and the same scraps of hair. It's only then that I notice what's underneath.

"Did you get a note?"

Dom glances down. "Yeah," he whispers.

The note is typed and I read it aloud.

You're looking in the wrong place.

A Warning

When Elisha walks into the common room I rush over
to her and say, "Please check your locker."

She grins at me. "It's nice to see you, too."

"Seriously. Check it."

Her smile wavers and fades as she looks around and then
says, "Is this about Sasha Craven?"

"Yeah," I say. "I think she—whoever she is—goes here."

"What are you talking about?"

"Please, Lish. Check your locker."

She glances over my shoulder at Dom, then opens it and gasps.

I knew it would be there, but I still feel sick when Elisha
steps aside and another severed doll's head glares at me.

"Did *you* do this?" she asks.

"What? Of course not."

"Then how did you know it was there?"

"We *all* got one," Dom says, and when Elisha looks back at me, I nod.

"Look underneath."

She lifts the head and reads the note.

"Whoever's doing this knows where we've been looking," Elisha says. "So, they *are* still watching us."

"And they have access to our lockers," I reply.

"Not here," Dom says, glancing around. "Let's go and get Haran."

So that's what we do. We wait outside the drama block until I can see Haran at the opposite end of the corridor.

He's with Lottie and Ranvir, throwing his head back and laughing like he doesn't have a care in the world. And, for a moment, I don't want to tell him.

He seems so happy, away from me, from us, from Sasha.

Haran and the rest of his drama class have this bond that, if I'm honest, makes me jealous. They have private jokes and stories about theater trips, and when it's time to rehearse, they vanish for days.

That's the Haran I can see now—the old Haran, with added sprinkles. I don't want to ruin it by forcing him to find a horrible warning in his locker. Plus, he's probably still pissed at me after this morning. No wonder he's happier hanging out with them right now.

When he sees me, his smile doesn't fall but it does falter.

"What are you doing here?" he asks, and then, to the rest of his class, "I'll catch you later."

They glance at me, wait until they are a "polite" distance away, then laugh. It should sting but my head is too full of worries for me to care about assholes today.

"Have you checked your locker recently?" I say, and, when Haran shakes his head, "We've got some bad news."

The four severed heads sit in a row, staring at us like a twisted dolls' picnic.

We're back at the rec, encircling them so no one else can see. What would they think if they could? Maybe they'd assume it's an art project.

Last year, Elisha made a human brain out of papier-mâché social media posts for art class, and when we went to the exhibition, there were all sorts of weird things.

Her teacher gushed over everything but I didn't really get it.

"Art isn't the actual object you're looking at, it's the feeling you get when you see it," he'd said. What I'm feeling now, staring at the things left in our lockers, is terror.

"I need to tell you all something," I say. "It's about the shoplifting."

Everyone's eyes shoot to me. Elisha looks concerned, Dom intrigued, and Haran's face is rippling with too many emotions to focus. He seems worried and shocked and angry all at once.

I take one last deep breath, grip Elisha's hand, and say, "I told you that Sasha made me do it, but I didn't say how. She said if I didn't, she was going to reveal what I said in the Dark Place."

Their expressions all become the same then. They're all afraid.

"What do you mean?" Elisha asks. "How could she know?"

"I don't know how, but she does," I say. "Sasha knows my biggest secret and she's using it to blackmail me. She made me steal that box set and then filmed me. She sent it to the press. She wants to hurt me." I take a deep breath. "Has she . . . done anything like this to you guys?"

"No," Elisha says.

She stares so deeply into my eyes that, for a few seconds, I forget where we are and why. I just watch her looking at me until a smile breaks through the dark and she's grinning back, whispering, "It will be okay."

"Me neither," Haran says, although there's no smile from him. He keeps his head down, pulling up clumps of grass and tossing them to the side.

"What about you?" Elisha asks, turning to Dom. "Are you being blackmailed by a figment of your sister's imagination?"

"Of course not."

I don't know if I believe any of them—except Elisha. I always believe her. "What are we going to do about these?" she asks, nodding toward the dolls' heads.

"We keep them," I say, stuffing them into my bag. "They're evidence. Eventually we have to tell someone about this and, when we do, they'll have trouble believing us."

"Why would we need to tell anyone?" Dom asks, his voice breaking slightly.

"Don't you see?" I reply. "I'd never ask you what secrets you put in the Dark Place. And you'd never tell me, right? But one of Lauren's secrets is taunting us. One of mine is being used against me. It's only a matter of time." I look around at them all. "Whatever you left to die in there, I hope you don't mind it coming back to life."

Pep Talk

Haran and Dom were silent as we walked back to school, and Elisha didn't say much on the way home.

I want to know the secrets they whispered into the Dark Place, year after year. But I'll never ask. I know that some secrets are too dark and too heavy to be shared.

And now I'm home, sitting opposite my dad as he tries to do something that he's never fully understood—parent.

"Mom told me what happened," he says. "If you want me to speak to your principal, I'll . . ."

"No," I say. "It's been dealt with. The person won't bother me anymore."

How easy would it be to replace my fictional tormentor with my actual one? To name them *Sasha Craven* and explain that no, it isn't just a bully bad-mouthing my family and forcing me to steal. It's a made-up girl threatening to shatter everything.

Because we would—shatter. Dad would look at his scars in a completely different way. They wouldn't remind him that he saved his son. They would tell him, every single day for the rest of his life, that I wanted that fire to turn our old life to ash; that I saw it as the ideal way to escape *his* choices. My father is fragile. We all know that.

It would shatter my mother because she would know, deep down, that it was her fault, too.

And it would shatter Molly because it would change everything that she knows about herself. She is the welcome surprise; the final piece of our family; the miracle. While our house was being rebuilt, Mom's pregnancy was a glimmer of light that turned into a sunrise the day Molly was born. It's all true. But I won't be the brother she thought she had. She will never look at me with those clear eyes again.

No. I can't tell them. We'll deal with Sasha on our own.

"Sam? Are you sure you don't want me to talk to the school?"

Dad eyes are pleading. He wants me to make this easy on him.

"It's okay. Tell Mom we talked."

He sighs and says, "Thanks, bud," and I hate him, just a little, for only fighting harder to be heard when it's something *he* wants.

When he's gone, I take the four heads out of my bag and put them on the bed. Then I study the note.

You're looking in the wrong place.

Does Sasha *want* to be found? Is this some twisted version of hide-and-seek?

I pick up my phone and write back.

Where do I look then?

The Watcher

When I wake the next morning, I have a text. Only it's not what I expect. It's from an unknown sender and it's a video message. Blurry at first. Handheld. It takes a few seconds to focus, the camera zooming in on something far away. Not something—someone. Not someone—me.

I'm walking through the school gates with Elisha. Then Haran runs over and slaps me on the back. The sun burns bright in the clear blue sky and this feels like a lifetime ago— the very start of our senior year.

The camera follows us across the playground and the tennis courts, and this should be a perfectly normal scene. But everything is wrong. The colors are off, faded. The noise of schoolyard chatter becomes an incessant low hum.

Then the sounds change—the hum becomes breathing. The sound of someone running, catching their breath, gasping, their heart pounding in their chest.

The video starts to judder as whoever filmed this rushes to keep up. When they reach us, the screaming starts.

The screen fills with red and that's when it goes blank.

I watch the video three times, my hands slippery with sweat.

I try to think logically. Whatever this means, it proves one thing. Sasha, whoever they are, definitely goes to our school. If we needed any more proof after our lockers were broken into, they've handed it to us with a horrible flourish.

I check the username to see who sent this and it says SND99. The profile is blank.

Haran's name appears on my phone, and when I answer, he says, "Did you get one?"

"Yes."

His voice breaks. "Okay. You were right. This is getting scary now, Sam. The blood, dolls' heads . . . now this. What the hell?"

When I don't answer, Haran says, "They go to our school, though, right? Which means we can catch them."

Any bravery he's trying to convey crumbles with the last word. I know what my best friend sounds like when he's unnerved.

"I know about those movies, dude. This is how it starts. It's subtle. It's a warning. And then *bam,* you're being chased through a graveyard and I'm dead."

"Why are *you* dead?"

"Because I'm me."

I want to say, "Welcome back," but something stops me. Because he's not saying these things to be silly or dramatic. He's saying them because they are true.

"I'm sorry," I say. "I'm here for you. You know that, right?"

"I do."

"Look, let me figure out what to do. I'll see you soon. Be ready."

I end the call and watch the video again. Haran is right. One of our classmates did this. That makes me feel braver. It's not some random stranger. They *are* close.

Yet it's not as comforting a thought as it should be. Whoever did this was right behind us. We could have turned and caught them in the act. But they did it anyway.

"What's wrong?" Molly asks.

She's standing in my doorway and I quickly rearrange my face.

"Nothing," I say, scooping her up, flinging her over my shoulder, and carrying her downstairs.

Her laugh used to fill the house when I did that. But now she humors me, staying silent until I flop her on the sofa and ask if she wants toast.

She stares deeper into my eyes and there's no point lying, so I say, "I'll be okay."

That satisfies her enough to look away, and I hope I'm right.

Elisha is calling me now. I answer and she says, "You need to calm your best friend down."

I leave the room and say, "Did you get the video?"

"Yes. Haran thinks it's the intro to his own personal slasher movie. He needs to chill."

I knew he'd call her straight after me. He's panicking and I can't blame him for that.

I've been here before, in a way. Years ago, people would turn up at our door and ask me to sign things or pose for selfies. And I did, because you can't piss off people who know your address. But sometimes people would get angry anyway.

The problem with being watched is you don't know whose eyes are on you. Whether they're the eyes of a curious fan, a fellow schoolkid, a kindly neighbor.

Or whether it's someone else entirely.

School Spirit

We walk through the gates like we did in the video, Elisha holding my hand, staring straight ahead, and Haran looking everywhere at once.

"Calm down," I hiss at him. "We don't want them to know they're getting to us."

"They *are* getting to me," Haran says. "I don't like being spied on."

"*You* spied," Elisha says.

"What?"

"You spied on Dom and Lauren."

She's right.

"It's not the same," Haran says.

Elisha's eyes sharpen and I can see the words before she says them. She's not afraid to tear any of us to shreds if she knows she's right, especially if someone else is being wronged. I'm waiting for her to say it's *exactly* the same. But instead, she says, "Lauren deserves credit for being honest with you. She didn't need to tell you about Malika."

I squeeze her hand but she doesn't squeeze back.

"I'm sorry," I whisper.

The playground fills up around us. The younger kids run past like everything's a game. The older ones hang back, walking as slow as our teachers allow. And we're in the middle, not trusting anyone.

Nearly everyone is holding a phone.

It was easy to film us without being noticed. It could have been anyone.

The nasty comments and jokes break through the bustle but I push them away. A few times I catch someone's eye and I can tell instantly what kind of person they are. The ones who look away are half decent. The ones who grin or laugh are far worse.

Let them mock me for shoplifting. If only they knew what else we had to worry about.

Once we're in the school building—in theory—phones are banned. If the wrong member of staff catches you, it's gone for the day. The rest give a warning or turn a blind eye. But out here anyone can film anything.

I jump when someone behind me screams, but it's just a few freshmen showing off.

Inside, it seems more people are focused on their own thing. There was a time, before all this, when *everyone* was watching me. My first year in middle school was intense. It's scary enough moving up, but when you add in being on TV, that's another level.

Some people wanted to be my friend. Some went for mortal enemy. And one, Dylan, chose both.

"When I catch whoever's doing this . . ." Haran doesn't finish the sentence.

All our phones sound at the same time, and we stare at each other. Haran and I don't reach for ours. But Elisha holds hers high in the air, making a point to whoever is watching.

She reads the new message, then clicks on a video, and the fight falls instantly from her face.

"What is it?" I ask.

Elisha doesn't reply, just hands me her phone.

The video shows Elisha and her granddad. There's no soundtrack over this one. She's walking down the high street, pushing his wheelchair, and they are both laughing. He only likes his wheelchair when she's pushing it. The rest of the time he swears about it.

She's different with her family. They release something in her—a happiness I've never seen around anyone else, including me.

I shouldn't be jealous, because I know what her granddad means to her. But I am, because I want to mean the same.

The camera follows them into a grocery store, where Elisha fills a basket while her granddad points and crosses things off a list. The video has picked up sound.

They are talking about cookies and that's when I shiver, because whoever filmed this was close enough to capture the whole conversation.

They must have been standing right next to Elisha and she didn't notice. Was the camera hidden? Did she look into the eyes of whoever is doing this?

There's a low, static hum that grows. Then the sound

changes to uneven breathing and then, as the screen fills with red, I hear it: a whisper.

"What are they saying, at the end?" I ask. No one says anything. I rewind and play it over and over again but, no matter how hard I concentrate, I can't make out the words. I'm not sure there even are any.

"When did you go to the store?" I ask, and Elisha says, "Last Saturday."

"Did you see anyone suspicious?"

She shakes her head and something crumbles behind her eyes.

"They filmed my fucking granddad," she whispers.

I try to hug her but she steps back and says, "I need a minute."

Elisha walks quickly away and I turn to Haran, who is staring at his own phone.

That's when I remember. We all got messages. Not just Elisha.

"Did you get the same video?" I ask, and he shakes his head.

He clicks play again and we watch as the camera zooms in on the soccer pitch at the rec. A low fog hangs over the night, made thicker by the heavy breaths of constantly moving bodies, and it feels almost magical watching my friend play a sport I've never been interested in.

There are muffled shouts that grow louder as someone walks toward the game. Then Haran is in the shot, sprinting from one end to the other and missing by an inch.

He stares at the sky and yells; then Brendan kisses him and whispers something that makes Haran smile.

Then he's off again, collecting a one-two and smashing the ball into the top corner.

He puts his hands behind his head, catching his breath, and the camera zooms in until Haran is the only person in the frame.

You can see the dazzle from the spotlights in his eyes.

Just like Elisha's video, the sound shifts suddenly—the same sharp, ragged breaths followed by the same nasty whisper.

And the screen floods with red and goes blank.

"That was last weekend," he says.

"Did you see anyone lurking about . . . anyone filming you?"

"No."

I know that place. When it's dark and the lights are on, everything outside is pitch black.

I know what those games mean to Haran. Brendan only comes back from college every few weeks, and they always find time to play. It's where they met and it's one of the places my best friend is happiest.

I'm scared to see my own video, so I pass my phone to Haran and say, "You watch it?"

"Seriously?"

I nod. He opens it and I watch his eyes go wide.

"It is bad?"

"You need to see this."

I feel sick before I even click play because there, behind the thick white triangle, is my house.

I breathe in for four and out for six. Over and over again until my anxiety softens. Then I blow out hard and hit play.

Someone is walking toward our house, the sound of their footsteps changing as they move from the sidewalk to the stones on our driveway.

I want to turn it off. But I need to see what happens next.

The camera is pointed at our front door.

"What the hell?" I say, and Haran says, "Keep watching."

I picture a hand reaching out and ringing the bell, one of my family members coming face-to-face with whoever is doing this. Instead, they step back and walk to the front window.

The image loses focus for a moment. Then it settles and I feel sick.

The camera is aimed at Mom and Molly, the two of them snuggled on the sofa, reading a story.

Mom's lips move soundlessly through the glass while my sister's face glows.

I look past them, trying to spot me or Dad in the background so I can work out when this happened. But it's just the two of them, sharing a moment they had no idea was being stolen.

Whoever is filming this is deathly still, as Mom closes the last page and Molly points at the bookcase.

Our mother rolls her eyes like she's exasperated, but she's only pretending. The truth is, she'd happily read to my sister all day.

Molly chooses another story; then her eyes dart to the window. My heart stops as I imagine her walking toward the camera. Then it beats harder as she slowly turns to Mom and nuzzles back into her hug.

The screen goes red. Then nothing.

Elisha is on the far side of the courtyard, pacing while something grows hard behind her eyes.

She is angry and Haran is scared. And me?

I'm furious.

They came for my sister and that's not an option. If they want to play, let's play.

BEHIND BLUE EYES: PHOTOGRAPHY'S UNLIKELY VIRAL SUPERSTAR

Words **Gavin Green** Portrait **Camilla McGowan**

Molly Hall is not your average viral star. For a start, she is only five years old. When I meet her, the first thing I notice is her stare. She is a watcher, an analyzer. Molly doesn't just use a camera to ensnare fleeting beauty. Her every blink is of a shutter lens. For Molly Hall, her art really is her life.

Photography's latest wunderkind says little during our hour together. But what she does offer is wrapped in a wisdom that belies her years. When I ask what inspired the images that have taken social media by storm, she considers, then strikes me silent with her response:

"Every moment is a potential masterpiece."

I wait for more. But that's it. Miss Hall speaks as she photographs—sporadic, considered, and perfect.

Far from reveling in them, Molly distances herself from her talents, telling me how her father—a photographer with a small Instagram following—has inspired her.

Molly is not the first Hall child to have a brush with fame. Her brother, Samuel, starred in the much-loved science fiction show *Future Force* before a tragic house fire cut his career short.

Humble, gifted, and insightful, Miss Hall is no flash in the pan. After her protective mother tells us it's time to go, I hand Molly a camera and request a keepsake. She considers the camera, then shakes her head and says:

"I can't see a masterpiece today."

Shadows

As I head up to my room, I notice Dad sitting on the floor in his office, his photos spread across the carpet.

I try to sneak past but he catches my eye and says, "Sam. Come here, bud."

I go in and sit beside him.

"I used to love this one," Dad says, holding out a picture of the old hardware store. I remember the day he took it. The sidewalk was filled with homemade ornaments and the owner, Mr. Cotton, let the local kids bid for their favorites. Now the only wood in that place is the boards covering its windows. "I used to love all of them."

"They're still good," I say. "They're still great."

"Thanks, Sam. But that reporter knew it. Molly's already better than me."

"Is that a bad thing?"

Dad looks at me like it's a stupid question.

We used to enjoy flicking through his albums. Every so often, Dad would go in the attic and pass down box after box and our parents would reminisce for hours.

Then there was the fire and he stopped taking pictures for a long time. Most of my father's photos avoided the flames, the boxes they were packed in cowering in the corners of our attic just long enough for the fire department to save them. But Dad had no desire to add more.

One day, Mom handed him her phone as Molly and I played in the garden. I remember the picture—Molly watching me drench our mother with a water pistol, her head thrown back, laughing.

Dad's earliest efforts were reluctant, like a toddler taking their first steps. But soon he was photographing everything and, after a few months, he didn't look guilty doing it. He photographed the after—after the fire. After Molly was born.

I should be able to turn to Dad, I think. I should be able to tell him what's happening to me.

Instead, I say, "I love your photos," and Dad looks up and smiles.

If he's seen the clip of me shoplifting, if his feeds about photography have been interrupted by my memes, he doesn't mention it. And the act itself—Mom dealt with that on her own.

She is in the kitchen but I can't go to her either. Molly is playing upstairs.

I go to the front window and stare out, looking at the path a stranger walked up to secretly film my family.

I don't know how long I stand there. Long enough for the shadows to lengthen and then for darkness to fall. They will come back eventually, and when they do, I'll be ready.

Going Back

We know what we need to do. Everyone agrees—me, Dom, Elisha, and Haran. We need to go back to the Dark Place.

The last time we did this trip to Dom's house on Halloween, we were excited. We knew what to expect, even if there were more people than ever.

This time it's different. The lanes feel darker, the trees taller, the shadows more threatening.

We had Chloe with us that time, and we thought we were so cool, whispering our secrets to dust while a party raged around us.

No one had noticed us slipping off that night. Everyone was too busy. They were getting drunk and hooking up with strangers and making memories. They didn't care about the Dark Place and we didn't care about them.

But what if someone *had* noticed? What if someone *did* care? What if one not-so-random person at that party had followed us into the woods and covered our sacred place with blood?

The blood must have come from somewhere.

I pull into Dom's drive and we sit in silence until a light comes on over the porch. Then he is standing in the doorway, looking all sorts of nervous. We get out and go over.

"Hey," he says. "Quickly. Let's talk upstairs."

A door opens. "Sam?"

Dom sighs and shakes his head but it's too late. His dad has clocked us and he gestures to join him in the front room. He's like an older Dom—tall, handsome, broad shoulders. Everyone likes Steve Simmons.

When we were younger, I thought that Steve was the coolest. He taught me a lot more than my own dad—how to tie knots, pitch a tent. I loved how easygoing Steve was. With him, life was all about having fun. With *my* dad, it was all about running lines.

Dom's dad didn't have a useless hobby like photography. He built things. Go-karts, tree houses, dens, gadgets for show-and-tell.

It's odd, given how much money they have. But Dom's mom was the rich one. She "came from cash" and, sometimes, it felt like everything her husband built was him trying to keep his son humble.

If Dom had asked me, I would have swapped dads in a heartbeat.

In contrast, Dom loved my father's photos, how they came to life as they hung in his darkroom, all those captured moments glowing red in the gloom. A bit like the Dark Place, now that I think of it.

Steve holds out a broad hand.

"Hi, Mr. Simmons," I say. "Mrs. Simmons."

Dom's mom, Hope, stands and says, "Dominic. You didn't tell us you were having guests."

"They're not guests," he replies. "They're my friends."

"Still. It would have been nice to be informed."

Hope's annoyance comes out wrapped in nerves, and I remember feeling sorry for her when we were kids. She's always been like this—uncertain even in her own house, outshone by Dom's dad.

He was the one who built things with us, talked football with us, acted like we were his equals. While she hovered in the background, tentatively stepping into the spotlight just to offer up more treats.

Right on cue, she half clears her throat and says, "Would you like a drink or something to eat?"

The three of us, all at once, say, "No, thank you," and I don't think we could sound any more guilty.

"Okay, well, if you change your mind, you know where I am."

I smile and Dom's mom sits back in her chair. His parents are both facing the TV, the volume low and the subtitles on.

I always thought it was fascinating, how the two of them found each other—one loud and one quiet; one filling every single room with ease, the other most comfortable in its corners. But I think I get it now.

Steve was there the day of that hardware-store auction in Dad's photo, his creations generating the most interest, his enthusiasm electric. But Hope was there, too, making sure everyone in the crowd was fed and watered, ensuring the perfect conditions for the best possible event.

She may be quiet, but she never hides.

Before we go upstairs, I look back and they are still sitting in silence.

I'm used to this house on Halloween—loud and alive and full. Tonight, it feels horribly empty.

Lauren is waiting in her room, listening to music, and I think back to her sitting alone in the Dark Place, Haran charging in and greeting her. It had felt so good.

We thought we were in control that night. We had no idea.

Lauren pulls off her headphones, and we take seats wherever we can—on the bed, the desk chair, a couple of beanbags.

Her bedroom is cluttered—hints of all the Laurens she's been before filling every surface. There are school certificates for 100 percent attendance, photos of when she and Dom were kids, a row of dusty track trophies on top of the wardrobe.

"Now we know how you felt," Dom says to me.

"What do you mean?"

"The shoplifting video—now we've *all* been caught on camera."

I want to tell him it's not the same, because my video is all over the internet. But I realize he's smiling. He's trying to lighten the mood. I wonder just how bad his and Lauren's videos are.

As if she can read my mind, Lauren says, "Let's get this over with."

Lauren hands me her phone, and Haran and Elisha move closer as I push play.

Trees fill the screen. There's the faintest sound of birdsong and someone's soft breathing. Whoever is filming this is calm, still, waiting.

Then there's another noise. A thump, thump, thump, like a heartbeat, then a hammer. As it grows louder, leaves crunch and wings flap. Then a shape flashes past.

"What was that?" I ask, and Lauren says, "You'll see."

The camera moves then, quicker than I expected. It slices through the woods, losing focus as someone hurries after the shape.

Finally, it slows, stops, the breathing steady once more. And then it creeps.

I look at Haran and Elisha but they are fully focused on the screen. When I turn, Dom is staring at me.

The crackle of twigs and dead leaves stops, replaced by an eerie silence. The camera points at a gap between the trees. And there's Lauren, wearing leggings and a sports top, hands on her knees as she catches her breath.

She doesn't look scared. She looks focused. She swigs from a plastic bottle, presses something on her watch, then runs off.

She doesn't know she's not alone.

Whoever is holding the camera doesn't go after her. They walk carefully forward until they are standing where she was. Then they film a three-sixty shot of the huge woods behind Dom and Lauren's house. The rasping breathing begins again, the whispers; then the oranges and yellows of the woods flood with red.

"Holy shit," Elisha says. "Are you okay?"

Lauren nods, then turns to her brother, who, for the first time since we were kids, looks helpless.

"Whoever this person is," Dom says, "we'll catch them."

He reaches out and touches Lauren's arm, and I know

exactly how he feels right now. Someone has threatened both of our sisters—and we hate them for it.

Sometimes I imagine what might have happened if Molly had gone to the window on the day that she was filmed. Would she have come face-to-face with whoever is doing this? What would they have done if she had?

"We need to call the police," Elisha says. "Filming without consent is bad enough but this . . ."

She and Lauren hold each other's stares until my girlfriend says, "Stalking girls through the woods is fucking nasty."

"I know," Dom says.

"Do you? Because you just said 'we' will catch them. That's not our job."

"So, you want to tell the police everything? About the Dark Place and the eggs and the dolls' heads? You want to tell them our secrets?"

Elisha laughs as she says, "Yes. Because they won't give a shit about what we said in that mucky little hut when they see these recordings. Sam . . . you agree, right?"

I squeeze the skin on my upper arms until it stings. Then I look at each of them in turn, trying to find the right words.

"We can't tell the police," Haran says.

He's looking at me and I think of the stick figure and the message underneath: *They made me do it.*

Is it only me and him who got those? If I ask now, will that be more ammunition for Elisha? And just who out of us is being blackmailed?

"We *can* tell the police," Elisha says. "The question is, at this stage, why wouldn't we?"

Her eyes narrow and she moves a few inches away from me.

"We should watch my brother's first," Lauren says.

Dom hands me his phone, then slumps back in his chair. I push play.

The camera is pointing at Dom's house—*this* house—and I shiver. Lauren is sitting on the porch, lighting the pumpkins, while her brother hangs a plastic skeleton beside the front door.

There's movement in the hallway, and their dad walks out holding a suitcase. He puts it in the trunk of his car, then comes over and helps Dom hang the grim reaper from a branch.

The camera cuts off, then flashes back. It's dark now, and whoever's filming this is walking toward the same house.

The front door is open and the music gets louder with every step. There are a few people outside but no one notices the camera. They smoke and laugh and totally ignore the person walking into our party.

They move from room to room and a boy I don't recognize says, "Cool costume," but there's no reply.

Through the crowd I see Dom chatting with two girls from our year—Faridah and Mel; then he smiles, leaves them to it, and walks right past the camera.

I glance at him. His hands are gripped together, knuckles white. "They were here," he says.

The camera blurs, then jumps. Now it films Haran, Dom, Elisha, and me. It hovers behind us as we slip through the back door, down the garden path, and into the shadows.

Then whoever is filming this moves back through the house and into the downstairs bathroom.

The noise shifts—the roar of the party muffled behind the closed door—and the camera slowly moves up from the tiled floor to the sink to the mirror.

Someone in a mask is staring back at us. The yellowing cloth hangs over their entire face, its frayed edges dangling like dried-out worms. The eyes are huge black holes like pits of despair, tempting me to look closer but warning me not to, and the smile is thick and red, like the malicious grin of a killer.

It stares at us for five horrible seconds before the screen goes blank.

Uninvited Guests

What the hell was that?" Haran asks.

We're all shaken. I gather myself. "Sasha was here that night. That's not in question anymore. She wasn't just in the woods. She was in this house."

"So, we're agreed," Elisha replies. "We call the police."

"No," Dom says.

"Why the hell not? Lauren . . . she stalked you. It's time!"

Lauren looks at her brother, then rests her hand on Elisha's and says, "It's not that simple."

Elisha stands quickly, the desk chair bashing against the wall. "You are all so obsessed with the Dark Place. I get it. It's a tradition. But this is serious."

Turning to Haran, she says, "You know all about horror movies, right? Based on what I've just seen, this *is* one. You can't still tell me we can do this alone."

"No one's dead," Haran replies.

"What?"

"Horror movies start with a kill. But we're all still here, so I'd argue this is something different."

Elisha shakes her head and starts pacing. "I don't even know where to start."

"Help us," Lauren says. "Please. Let's do some more digging. We have videos to compare and we've seen who's doing this now. At least, we've seen their mask. Do you want to find the asshole who filmed your granddad?"

Elisha freezes and says, "Of course."

"So, let's do it."

"That place has a horrible hold on you," she says.

Her fight doesn't fade. It hums through her body as she reluctantly takes her seat. I know we've only got so long before Elisha tells someone anyway. But if Sasha is also blackmailing the others, or if she knows secrets that they would do anything to keep, we need to fight while we can.

We watch all five videos over and over again. Every time I see Mom reading to Molly, I want to throw up. And every time that mask fills the screen, I want to reach right through and pull it off.

"I don't remember that costume," Haran says.

"There were a lot of people there," Elisha replies.

She shoots Dom a look, and I know what she's thinking. When you have an open-door policy, anyone can walk through.

I freeze the video on the mask. It does look familiar, I think. I just can't quite remember . . .

"What do we know so far?" Elisha says. I half smile at her intense expression. For so long, she didn't take this seriously. But if you mess with her family, she's your enemy for life.

"If we're doing this on our own, at least for now, we need to work through anyone connected, even tangentially."

Haran nods and types into his Notes app. He writes each of our names and puts an X next to them. "I assume we're all innocent," he says jokily.

Elisha ignores him. "First off—are we sure it's not Malika?" Lauren bristles and Elisha goes on quickly. "They're an obvious suspect. Let's say they found out that Lauren made up a Sasha to dump them—well, there's the motive right there."

"I'm sure," Lauren says.

Haran puts Malika's name down with an X next to it.

"The next lead was the slaughterhouse. There's the security guy, the tanker driver, and the woman we interviewed . . . Kat."

"That's a dead end," I say. "Clearly none of them had anything to do with this and they didn't see anyone suspicious. The tanker driver said it's basically impossible to steal blood without taking the whole truck. And you saw that place. It's locked down tight."

"But it's not the only place that has blood," Dom says. "What about the hospital?"

"We can look into it," says Elisha, and Haran writes it down.

Something keeps tugging at my mind. I haven't wanted to think too hard about where that blood came from, but I have to. Because Sasha is hell-bent on tormenting us and she doesn't care who gets hurt.

"Animals," I whisper. "Not slaughterhouse animals but . . ."

"You mean . . . people's pets?" Lauren asks, and I nod.

"Cats go missing all the time, don't they?"

"That's horrible."

Dom starts pacing, and then he clears his throat and says, "We know something else. Whoever is doing this, they've been planning it a long time. They knew about the Dark Place before we went in that night. You don't just produce blood-filled eggs on the spot. They had a plan."

"They also knew about the party," I say. "Do you know who was there? Maybe we could whittle it down that way."

I know as I ask that it's pointless. I remember that huge crowd of masked partygoers. Dom shakes his head and says, "I could name maybe half."

The best parties are the biggest. At least, that's what Dom used to think. Now I'm wondering if the biggest are the most dangerous, because if there are enough people pretending to be monsters, a real one could creep in unnoticed.

That is just what happened that night.

Now we need to pull the mask off.

Driving Lessons

In the car, everyone is lost in their own thoughts. It seems as though whenever we leave this place, our world has shifted.

Sasha found each of our weak spots. She filmed our homes. She filmed Molly.

She captured Lauren running, thinking she was alone, Haran blissfully happy with Brendan, Elisha with her grand-dad, us walking into school. Dom hanging up Halloween decorations, partying, oblivious.

And, finally, the four of us walking down the path to the Dark Place. It's that last image that I can't shake. With enough time and effort, someone could find out about my kid sister. They could work out that Haran plays soccer, that Elisha shops with her granddad, that Lauren runs, that Dom throws a mas-sive Halloween party every year. But how could someone find out about the Dark Place?

We've always been so careful. It's hidden. We only go there once a year. If anyone had seen us, they would have just seen five teenagers messing around in the woods.

But Sasha knew exactly what that place was.

We all swore to keep the Dark Place a secret. I want to believe the others kept their promise. But there's a voice deep inside me—tiny and fragile—that wonders if one of us isn't telling the truth.

I'd planned to go back there today. But we spoke for so long in Lauren's room that the safety of the sun was replaced by the fickleness of the moon. Sometimes it shines just as bright. Other times, it hides behind the gloom like it knows something bad is coming.

Headlights flash on behind me, catching me by surprise.

"Damn," I say.

"What is it?" Elisha asks, and I say, "Some fool wants to blind me."

This road is normally empty, which is good because it's too sharp and winding for tailgaters. But tonight we've got company, so I push gently on the accelerator, trying to put some distance between us and the car behind.

I focus ahead, trying to ignore the lights that creep back into view.

If they want to overtake on this stretch of road, they've got a death wish. But they don't. Instead, they move steadily forward until I'm dazzled by the lights again.

Haran glances behind him, shielding his eyes with his hand. "I can't see anything," he says.

"Slow down," Elisha says. "That's what my dad does. If someone drives up his ass, he waves it in their face."

I ease off but then the car is almost on top of me.

"Pull over," Elisha says. "Let them overtake."

Haran snorts and says, "Do *not* pull over. We're in the middle of nowhere."

"What do you think—they're going to murder us? It's just some impatient prick desperate to get home."

We're only a few minutes from the main road, so I drive steady and try not to look in the mirror. But the lights burn into the car and my vision starts to blur. I can hardly see the bends ahead. I slow down.

"What are you doing?" Haran asks.

"I don't want to crash. These roads are bad enough when there isn't some maniac on my tail. There's a rest area up ahead. We'll pull in and let them go past."

Haran lets out a whimper.

"There it is," Elisha says, nodding at a bench and a trash can.

I pull over, waiting for the car to drive on. But it creeps into the gap behind me and turns its lights off.

"See!" Haran shouts. "Drive away, Sam. Now!"

"Wait," I reply. "I want to see what happens."

"You want to see what *happens*? It's pitch black and we're in the middle of nowhere and we're being pursued and you want to see what *happens*?"

"He's right," Elisha says, but I don't get the chance to ask if she means me or him because the car's lights flash back on, making us all jump.

Haran leans forward and says, "Please. We need to go."

He's not shouting anymore. He's pleading.

"What if it's her," I say. "What if Sasha Craven is in that car?"

"Why do you think that?" Elisha asks.

"Who else would it be? We're being watched, filmed, blackmailed, and now followed back from Dom's. It has to be her."

"Lock the doors," Elisha says, and the noise echoes through the car as the bolts thud into place.

I stare through my rearview mirror, searching for a face in the vehicle behind, but everything is distorted. Their headlights have turned the space between us into a messy pool of yellow that stings my eyes and bleeds into the black.

"Sam," Haran says. "Come on."

I close my eyes and picture Molly cuddling Mom, Elisha pushing her granddad around while someone filmed her, Lauren running through the woods completely unaware of the person lurking in the shadows, and I unlock my door.

Elisha grabs my arm. "Don't do this."

"I have to. If it's someone at school messing around, they won't hurt me."

"And if it's not?"

"I guess we're about to find out."

I grip the handle, daring myself to pull, just as I see movement in the mirror.

There are three of them. Three dark shapes emerging from the car behind me, stepping into the light.

Haran hits my seat and shouts, "Go!"

He bangs harder and harder but I'm frozen. I want to see them. I need to.

For a moment they are lost in the blaze of their headlights. Then they walk through it and I see them clearly.

I see where their faces should be.

Elisha gasps. "Holy shit."

"Drive the fucking car!" Haran yells, as he kicks my seat so hard that I jolt forward.

I pull away just as the strangers close in.

They don't chase us. They stop and stare, shrinking in my rearview until they are swallowed by the night.

No one says anything until we are on the main road. Even then, I'm convinced the car will appear behind us again, like the killer in those movies who keeps coming back for more. But they don't and soon we're nearing the other side of town.

"Did you see it?" I ask. "Tell me I'm not imagining that."

No one answers. Every now and then, Haran makes noises from the backseat, while Elisha presses her fingers to her temples, calming herself with her own heartbeat.

Any bravery I felt as I psyched myself up to challenge them has gone, replaced by terror.

I wanted to see their faces. That was why I waited. Yet I never saw them.

They were each wearing a mask—the same mask that ended the video of Dom's party. And now we know.

Sasha Craven isn't one person.

She's three.

Insomnia

I **can't sleep**.

I couldn't go home alone, so, after dropping Haran off, I went back to Elisha's.

Elisha's dad is pretty cool. But there are rules here and number one is: I can stay, but only in another room . . . on another floor . . . with at least six creaking floorboards between us.

I keep thinking about the masks and I can't shake the feeling that I've seen them before. Maybe on Halloween.

I think of Elisha lying above me and wish I were with her. I want to fill the darkness with words. To drown it out.

I message her.

Are you awake?

She responds instantly.

Yes.

How scared do you think we should be?

Very.

I close my eyes and am instantly back there, watching the car doors open, seeing the shadows move slowly toward us, their steps in time like they were marching.

"They weren't rushing," I say out loud. "They were taking their time."

My voice sounds strange in the dark and I wonder how we ever found the courage to tell our truths in a rusty hut in the middle of the woods.

Come downstairs.

Seriously?

Please! I've thought of something.

I hear footsteps on the floor above; then Elisha creeps into the spare room and closes the door.

"We've got five minutes max before Dad does his rounds."

I know she's joking but I still worry. She scrambles onto the bed next to me.

"Go on then. What's your idea?"

"They *wanted* us to get away," I whisper. "They weren't in any rush to get to the car."

Elisha shuffles closer. "So what?"

"I don't think they wanted to hurt us. I think it was a warning."

"Or another piece of the jigsaw. We've had messages and dolls' heads and videos. Now we're being forced off the road. What if it keeps escalating?"

She's right. We're playing a game but we don't know the rules. We can't keep letting them win.

"There's something else," I say. "There were three of them . . . and three of us. One for each of us."

"One what? One stalker?"

"Maybe."

"If we each get our own personal stalker, that means there are five different Sashas," says Elisha. "But seriously, when are we going to tell the police? I understand . . . the ceremony, the secrets, it means a lot to you. But you can't keep ignoring the facts, Sam."

"I know."

"You should have backed me up at Dom's place," she says. "I felt so alone. I thought I was over that, feeling like the odd one out with all your 'Halloween friends.' But it came back hard tonight. Maybe it's never gone away."

"I'm sorry. I'll try harder."

"I hope so. Because it won't be long until I tell someone anyway."

I wish I could explain to her what's holding me back. But her steely gaze shuts me down. She's scared of what will happen if we don't tell someone, and I'm scared of what will happen if we do.

I lie back, and Elisha rests her head in the gap between my neck and my shoulder. I love so many things about her, but this is near the top—how we fit together perfectly. If only we could fall asleep like this. If only the tension of the last few days didn't hum between us like an electric fence, making everything that should feel perfect not quite right.

I listen to her breathing soften, and then I whisper, "Lish, you should go."

"Mmm."

A couple more minutes and she'll be out. She can fall asleep almost anywhere and, I'm now realizing, even after the strangest of nights.

I stare at the ceiling while my girlfriend dreams. There's no way I'm sleeping anyway.

My parents don't mind me staying here. I guess they trust Elisha's dad and they can go to bed certain that I'm safe.

It's amazing I'm allowed to sleep over at all, but I have a feeling I can thank Elisha's mother leaving for that. I think her father is afraid he'll lose Elisha, too. So, he says yes, just enough, even if those yeses are framed by noes. Yes, I can stay, but not in the same room, not on the same floor, not if he's away, not more than once a month.

I feel calmer with Elisha in my arms. She makes things a little lighter. But I can't stop probing my worries.

I think of Molly and our parents, asleep in their beds. What if the doorbell goes off in the middle of the night? If I were there, I could tell them to ignore it. But I'm here because I was too scared to go home.

I want to protect Elisha but, truthfully, she's also protecting me.

"Time to go," I say, whispering her awake until she rolls over with a grumble and says, "Why?"

I stand up and walk to the window, staring into the darkness.

The streetlamp outside Elisha's house is broken, but the moon shines bright and everything seems calm.

There are no unusual vehicles, no suspicious shadows, nothing out of the ordinary.

A dog howls in the distance, and the low hum of traffic on the main road fills my ears.

Elisha wraps her arms around me and kisses my neck. "It's fine, Sam. We're safe here."

I desperately hope she's right.

The Morning After

Good morning. Did you sleep well?"

Elisha's dad is in the kitchen making coffee and I feel nervous being alone with him but that's the deal.

I know he doesn't like it if I walk in with Elisha—even if we meet in the hallway. So, I go in alone and try not to feel all kinds of awkward.

"Yes, thanks."

"Glad to hear it."

His name is Marcus but I've never called him that. I don't call him anything, because I'm scared that whatever I say will sound wrong—either too formal or not polite enough.

He sits next to me at the table and sips from his mug.

"How's school?"

"It's fine."

We catch each other's eyes then both look away.

Marcus is as uncomfortable in these situations as I am. I

think it's because I'm his daughter's first boyfriend and everything he *wants* to ask is too awkward.

I can see his anxiety in the moments between his words and his actions; how hard he tries to appear easy. Maybe if I told him that I see it, we'd talk like friends rather than strangers. But I don't.

I've known Marcus for nearly two years, and the only thing that changes our vibe when Elisha's not around is . . .

"Sam!"

Simone runs into the kitchen and beams at me like I'm her favorite person in the world.

If there's one thing I understand, it's little sisters. And Elisha's is almost as cool as mine.

"I didn't know you stayed over," Simone says. "You should have told me."

"It was late," I reply, feeling guilty for not giving Marcus more notice.

"I'm doing karate now," Simone says. "Wanna see?"

"Of course."

She goes super still, then lunges forward with a shout that makes me jump.

Marcus laughs and we share a look that actually feels genuine.

"That's awesome," I say. "No one's messing with you."

"She's obsessed with *Cobra Kai,*" Elisha says, touching my shoulder as she passes.

She kisses her dad on the cheek, then pours some cereal.

If you were watching this, or filming it, you'd think everything was normal. Elisha chats with her sister and answers her father's questions while I sip coffee.

But inside, I'm trying to figure out what's next.

You're looking in the wrong place.

Sasha has been watching us scrabble around for clues. Filming us in the dark. And I've had enough.

We need to go on the attack.

The question is—how?

How can you be on the front foot when you don't know your enemy? They know us. They know where we live and what we do for fun and where we go at night. And they are getting bolder.

If we don't stop this, I'm worried how far they'll go.

I catch Simone's eye and she beams at me with the same pure delight as my sister. Molly isn't always happy, but when she is, it's like an emotional onesie. She's wrapped in it and so is everyone she meets.

I can't have my sister, or Elisha's, or anyone else, suffering because of this. That's why I type the message to Sasha and hit send.

We should meet.

"Where did you go last night?" Marcus asks, and Elisha says, "Just Dom's."

"Another party?"

"Not really. We just hung out."

"Okay," Marcus says. He glances at the wall clock. "Time for school."

Elisha has never spoken to me about her mother. She clams up. I know it's off-limits, but her sister fills in the gaps when no one else is around.

From what I do know, Marcus had a job in the city, wearing, and I quote, "the nicest suits and the biggest smiles." But after his wife left, he started working from home, to be closer to his daughters.

I'll never forget Simone's face when she said, "No more suits and not many smiles."

I follow Elisha back to her room as she grabs her school stuff.

"I'm supposed to be taking my granddad shopping tomorrow," she says. "I'm scared *they'll* be there. What do you think I should do?"

"I don't think they'll film you again. You'll be too alert."

"Damn right, I will."

She used to love taking her grandfather out. They've stolen that from her. Haran won't enjoy soccer anymore, and I won't be able to read with my sister without thinking of that video.

They came for our lives and there's no going back.

My phone vibrates in my pocket, but I don't check it. I wait until Elisha, Simone, and Marcus pull away, and I'm sitting alone in my car.

I take out my phone.

The message is from Sasha.

Whose secrets can you see?

I start typing a reply—*What does that mean?*—then stop. If we keep asking them for the answers, they have all the power. We have to figure this out on our own.

As I turn the ignition, I think of last night—the headlights stinging my eyes; the feeling of dread turning to electric courage.

I breathe in and out, slow and focused, the way Mom taught me.

I'm not going to run anymore. I'm going to solve this riddle and face Sasha head-on.

I just have to see if the others are with me.

The Police

"The school bus is literally a zoo on wheels," Haran says. "Disgusting."

He's pissed because I couldn't pick him up today. Elisha lives in the opposite direction, so, rather than doubling back, I told him it was that or nothing.

"Take your test, then," I say. "I'm not driving you around forever."

Haran doesn't reply, and I can tell by his face that he's thinking about last night.

"We should have taken a picture of the car," I say. "We could have got a license plate."

"Firstly . . . we don't exactly have access to the DMV database. And secondly . . . I was a bit busy being terrified by a bunch of masked weirdos."

"Stop being defeatist. We know something now. We know there are three of them."

"Great." Haran laughs weakly. "I was up all night thinking about it. How's Elisha?"

"She's fine. Her dad dropped her off."

"Was he okay with you staying over? Wasn't worried about you two bumping uglies in the night?"

Haran is dicking around. He knows that my uglies and Elisha's haven't officially met.

He thinks it's simple. If two people like each other, and they want to, they sleep together. That's what he does with Brendan and, last summer, with Holly Fry.

But I'm not Haran and neither is Elisha. We do what we do and we're happy with that.

"I messaged Sasha," I say. "I want to meet whoever is doing this. I've had enough of always playing their game. It's time to take control back."

Haran stares at me. "What did they say?"

I sigh. "Nothing really. Just this."

I show him my phone—*Whose secrets can you see?*—and hear his breath hitch.

"Are you okay?"

"Yes, I . . . What do you think it means?"

"I've no idea."

That question has been racing around my head since I first read it.

I look at Haran and, for a moment, I imagine telling him my secret. Putting it out there between us. It would be easy to tell him the truth about the fire, and I think he'd understand. After I broke my leg, he covered my cast in characters from our favorite anime. Sometimes I could see the thoughts he was too afraid to say—that he was happy I'd survived, that now and again he wondered what it would have been like if I hadn't.

It was years before he told me about the nightmares; how sometimes, when he slept, I burned away to nothing and he woke up screaming.

That was my chance to tell him, "Me, too."

But *my* dreams weren't as simple as that. Some nights it was Dad who turned to ash, other times his scars snaked over his entire body, but the worst nightmares were when Mom ran in to save me.

And I was scared he would ask me why. It would have been easier if I'd wanted to die that day—if the flames were my perfect way out. It's a lot easier to explain than the truth, which is that I wanted Isiah and *Future Force* and my father's ambitions for me to end, leaving the old me behind.

I wonder whether Haran ever wants to tell me his secret.

The bell rings.

"Come on," says Haran. "We'll be late."

Elisha is already in English lit class. She's reading *The Perks of Being a Wallflower* for the hundredth time and, when I sit next to her, she waits until the end of the chapter to speak.

"I missed you," she says. It's not like her to be so open, and I wonder whether being filmed has made her feel vulnerable.

"Me, too," I reply. "How was the drive? Did your dad hear you sneaking around last night?"

"If he did, he kept it to himself. Simone's staying at our aunt's tonight so he was more focused on her."

I think about showing her Sasha's message but, before I do, Elisha says, "You need to see this."

She slides her phone to me under the table, and I glance

down. It's another photo of a stick figure, but this one is different. The arms and legs are all intact but the head is missing, and the words underneath are terrifying.

There's more than one way to break a family.

"When did you . . ."

"This morning," Elisha replies. "It's a threat, Sam. And I don't know what to do."

My body ripples with anger as our teacher, Mr. Moorcroft, walks in and starts the lesson. I only last five minutes before asking for a bathroom break.

"Seriously?" he says. "Am I that boring?"

He's one of the good ones, throwing me a pass as I glance back at Elisha and say, "We'll make this right."

The corridors are eerily empty, the perfect space to fill with a scream, but I hold my rage in until I'm staring at my reflection in the bathroom mirror.

How dare you, I type into my phone. *Don't ever threaten my girlfriend again. If you do, we'll go straight to the police.*

The reply is instant.

You need to keep your head, Sam.

I'm still writing a response when another message comes.

It's simple. If any of you talk to the police, I'll let everyone's secrets run free. If you're happy with that . . . if you are ALL happy with that, try me.

I take a few minutes to try to calm myself; then I go back to class and pass Elisha my phone. Her left knee bashes against the table and her breathing comes out loud and jagged as she reads the message over and over again.

"Have you told anyone else yet?" I whisper.

She shakes her head.

For the rest of the period, I don't hear a word. I'm too busy thinking. I never wanted Elisha to get the police involved, because the thought of my family suffering all over again was too much to bear. Yet now, with Sasha calling the shots, it feels like she's taken away all our power.

What did she mean about families breaking? The more I think about that, the less I want to find out.

Road Rage

Dom is draped over a bench, arms behind his head, feet on the low brick wall that runs the length of the courtyard, while a group of junior girls hang on his every word. It's like that with Dom—people either cluster around him admiringly or, if they've been the victim of his other side, avoid him.

The girls laugh. It comes out shrill and fake, and I wonder if they are always pretending or if they've simply lost the ability to be real.

This is the version of Dom I like the least; the one who holds court over the school gossips, but who can turn fast as lightning.

When he sees me, his expression changes, although he doesn't leave. Instead, he's rolling his eyes, making out that he's trapped when we both know he loves it.

Eventually, Dom says something to the group, stretches, and walks over to me.

"Having fun?"

"You know what they're like."

I do, because he can be the same. Worse. That's why people like Chloe react to his name like a bad smell. But we have bigger things to worry about today.

I check no one's listening, then say, "Was everything okay last night . . . after we left?"

"Of course," Dom replies. "Why wouldn't it be?"

I pause before saying the next bit. I should have called him as soon as it happened but I completely forgot.

"We were followed. Three people, all wearing that mask, tailed us from your place to the rest area."

Dom's eyes widen. "What happened?"

Pain shoots up my arms and I realize I'm clenching my fists so tight that my fingernails are almost breaking the skin. That's how hard I gripped the steering wheel yesterday, in the seconds when I was deciding whether to challenge them or to flee.

"They were practically forcing me off the road," I say. "I pulled over to let them pass except . . . they didn't. They stopped and three people got out. We drove off. I wondered if they'd gone back to your place afterward."

Dom makes the sound of a laugh, although there's nothing happy about his expression. "Yet you waited until now to check."

"I'm sorry. We were freaked out, we didn't think."

He shakes his head. Then he rolls his shoulders back and says, "What type of car was it?"

"I don't know."

"Seriously? What color? What make?"

I'm ashamed to say it again because he's right. We should have taken note of the important stuff.

"You're the one who keeps going on about clues," Dom says. "No. The mystery stalkers—and there are *three* of them now—didn't pop back to my house. We had a perfectly safe evening, thanks for asking. But next time this happens, pay a bit more attention, Sam."

He sounds like the old Dom, mean and cold. But that's not all this is. In the midst of his anger, there's something else.

He's trying hard not to show it, but Dom is terrified.

No Escape

During my free period, I stop by the study center and watch Elisha doing her thing like she doesn't have a care.

Chloe sees me through the window and waves, but I don't go in. It feels like my friends all have worlds that are better without me—Haran and his drama crew, Elisha and her tutees, even Dom and the chosen few he gossiped with rather than bullied. That leaves one other person.

I drive to the town library, head for the front desk, and say, "Do you have any books about blood?"

Lauren's face shoots up, the seriousness disappearing as she realizes it's me.

"Sam! That's not funny."

"I'm sorry. It was poor taste. But I'm serious. I'm back to square one so I thought, why not go old-school?"

I hold my arms out, gesturing to the shelves of books and

the people hunched over the computers in one corner and the newspapers in another.

"Have you heard of Google?" Lauren says. "She literally knows everything."

"You know you're talking yourself out of a job?"

She shrugs and says, "Why are you really here?"

"Honestly, I just wanted a chat."

Lauren grins. "Meet me outside in five. I'm sure I can grab an extra break."

I wait in the same spot where Dom and his sister argued a few weeks ago, trying to piece together all the things that have happened since then. Eventually, Lauren strolls over and says, "Thanks for the fresh air."

I face her. "There's something I have to tell you." Then I unload about the car, the headlights, the three masked figures. I figure Dom would tell her anyway, but I want to be sure she knows.

"Jesus," she says, when I finish. "That must have been terrifying."

"We're fine. I should have driven back to your place. Instead, I hid at my girlfriend's."

Lauren touches my shoulder and says, "It's fine, Sam."

"There's something else. I spoke to Malika."

Lauren takes a step back and her shoulders tense. "What?"

"They seemed worth talking to. Like Elisha said, Malika has a motive."

"So, you didn't trust me?"

"It's not that. I had to see for myself. And, for what it's worth, I think you're right. I don't think Malika has anything to do with this. They seem great."

Lauren's body sags as she says, "They are."

"I wasn't going to tell you. But I wanted to be honest about that because, let's face it, there's a lot we're hiding from each other. I know what you told the Dark Place but everyone else . . ."

"Closed books," she says.

"Something like that."

"You won't find any answers in here," Lauren says, tapping the library wall. "I've already tried."

I should have known that I wasn't the only one looking for answers. The others seem keen to bury their heads in the sand. But Lauren is clearly doing some digging.

"Did you find anything at all?"

"Nope. Absolutely nothing of interest."

Still, it's nice to find a fellow investigator, even if we are as bad as each other.

"How are you?" I ask, and she says, "I'm fine."

"How are you really?"

That's something Mom taught me to say, but I've never used it, because even thinking about those conversations makes me uneasy.

"What do you mean?"

"You said that you broke up with Malika because you were going through some things."

Lauren nods.

"If you want to talk . . ."

I don't finish the sentence because there's nothing more to say. Listening is all I can do.

"I guess, in the cold light of day, it's not that bad," Lauren says. "But it's not always light, is it?"

She stares into the distance for a long time; then she says, "You know what they say about Hayschurch. Even if you leave, you come back. Well, I didn't even get that. All my friends finished school and headed off to college or got a job somewhere else or went traveling and here's me, working at the library."

"What's wrong with that?"

Lauren snorts. "Don't play dumb. You were literally a television star. This is plenty of people's dream job but it's not mine."

"You can still leave," I say.

"I did. At least, I tried to. But my internship came to nothing and so many places don't even get back to you these days. I took this job just to get out of that damn house."

"So, leave again."

"Sometimes that doesn't feel possible. Our mom never left this place and I'm scared it's in our DNA. Hayschurch forever."

Lauren gives two sarcastic thumbs up, then glances toward the door. "I should go."

"You know who else still comes back here? You should call them."

She shakes her head, half smiles, and mumbles, "Maybe. See you, Sam." Then she walks back into the library and I look over to the parking lot.

Haran and I sat there, watching Lauren and Dom fight. Is Sasha watching us now?

The parking lot is silent and almost empty. Today, for whatever reason, they're leaving us alone.

Apologies

Dad's trying to convince Mom that Molly needs an agent. "We should strike while the iron's hot."

"There *is* no iron," Mom says. "I told you—one interview. That's it."

Dad looks like a scolded puppy and I want to scream at him for being so desperate.

He got what he wanted. The photos my sister took went viral, at least on a specific part of the internet. He got her a big interview. But our father always wants more.

After the *Future Force* pilot, all he could talk about was a full pickup. When that happened, right away it was all about season two.

Dad can't stand still. If you do, you might be forgotten, and that's *his* worst nightmare.

"I've set up a meeting," Dad says, and, when he sees Mom's face, "Please don't be angry, Abby."

"What do you mean, you've set up a meeting?"

"I've spoken to an agent. A good one. She'd be delighted to talk to Molly and discuss next steps. Publicity . . . how to monetize her pictures . . . the usual."

Sometimes I know exactly what Mom's thinking, and this is one of those times. She's thinking, *Why? Why? Why?*

Why can't he ever be satisfied?

Why doesn't he listen?

Why did I . . .

She stops herself, swallowing the words I'm scared she'll say out loud one day. Even thinking the whole sentence might be enough to ruin everything. *Why did I marry him?*

My parents met in high school. They were each other's first kiss. Together since fifteen with the photos to prove it.

When we used to look through old pictures, we would laugh at Dad's haircuts and Molly would stare with the widest eyes at Mom as a teenager. And our parents would change in those moments, get younger somehow, as if the greatest memories are time machines.

Could this be me and Elisha one day? And how different will we be? Because our parents aren't those kids anymore. Eventually, when the boxes are back in the attic, they look older again.

"Molly doesn't need an agent," I say.

My parents look surprised. They are used to arguing unchallenged. But there's too much going on for me to stay silent.

Turning to Dad, I say, "Mom's right. You need to stop now. Molly's too young for this. We need to stop before she starts to hate taking pictures, just like . . ."

My heart is pounding because I loathe speaking up. But he doesn't seem angry. His face softens, and then he looks away and nods at the ground.

"All right," he says. "I'm sorry, Sam."

He goes to Mom and hugs her and they don't stop for a long time. She looks at me over his shoulder and smiles and, for the first time in a long time, I see what they used to be.

Did I do this? Is it that easy to make my parents happier, just by stamping out Dad's oversized ambitions? And have I really succeeded—or will my father change his mind?

Molly is in her room, drawing, and I sit next to her.

"Do you know what an agent is, Mol?" I ask. She shakes her head.

"An agent is someone who acts on your behalf. They help you get work and maybe more interviews like you had the other day."

"Okay."

"Did you like doing that interview?" I ask. Molly shakes her head again.

"Well, if Dad asks if you want an agent, and you really don't, tell him no."

My sister stares at me with her brow creased. "Okay."

She's drawn a man holding something shiny and his smile is bigger than his head. I don't need to ask who it is.

"Why are you scared, Sam?" Molly asks.

She's staring at me but, this time, I don't look away.

"I'm not scared."

Her gaze doesn't falter.

"Okay," I say. "I *am* scared. A little bit. But everything will be fine."

Molly smiles then, because she doesn't like being lied to. I pull her toward me in a hug.

"Dad's already talked to me about the agent," she whispers into my shoulder. "He said if Mom says no, he'll take me on his own. That it could be our secret."

Accident

Another day, another smile for Lena, and more shrink-ing small talk until Haran hurries out clutching his back-pack with a worried look on his face.

"Is everything okay?" his mother asks, and he doubles back, kisses her, and says, "Fine. See you later, Mom."

He's silent in the car, constantly checking his phone or turning to look out the back window.

"There's no one there," I say.

I know because I've been watching as well, studying every vehicle behind me, relieved when they turn off or keep their distance.

A horn blares behind us and we practically jump out of our skin.

"Fuck," Haran says. "What was that?"

The car is already in the distance, their beef with someone else, not me. His knee is moving up and down so quickly I want to reach out and calm him. But I keep both hands on the wheel and both eyes on the road.

If they followed us once, they can do it again.

"I want to tell you something," Haran says.

"What."

"I've been thinking about . . ."

I glance at him and, in that moment, something smashes into the windshield.

I brake so hard that I snap forward then back.

My ears are ringing and the glass is a web of cracks.

In slow motion, I come back to myself. The road ahead is empty.

I try turning to Haran, but pain shoots through my neck and I slowly move my upper body toward the passenger seat.

"Are you hurt?"

He shakes his head, then says, "What did we hit?"

I'm terrified and I don't want to get out of the car. Yet my feet are on the road before I can stop them. I look up and down the street but there's no one else here.

A woman is coming out of a house opposite, her mouth moving but her words out of reach.

Haran opens his door and stares over the car at me.

The woman is closer now, touching my shoulder, but it sounds like I'm underwater.

She looks strange, her eyes and mouth too big for her face, her words garbled. Then everything snaps back into focus, forcing me to step away.

". . . you okay?"

"I'm fine," I say. "Something hit us."

There should be another car. We hit something. But the road is empty except for my Honda.

"I didn't see anything," the woman says. "Did they drive off?" When I don't reply, she says, "I'll call the police. Do you need an ambulance?"

I shake my head.

I watch her walk back to her house, then turn to Haran and say, "Did that happen?"

He nods but looks uncertain. "Maybe it was an animal? Can a bird do that much damage?"

I walk to the front of the car and stop dead. A body lies crumpled on the ground.

"What the hell?"

Haran follows me and we stare down at the body in front of us. Except, it's not real, it's a mannequin, lying on its back, one arm bent and its blank face tilted to the side.

I look around. There's a steep slope that runs down to where we are.

I walk to the side of the road, grab a branch and carefully pull myself up, then look down at Haran and the car and the otherwise empty road. Behind me, a field stretches into the distance, and a dirt track creeps off to the right.

"It came from somewhere," I say. "Someone threw it. From up here, maybe."

I look down at the footprints next to mine: two sets that come to the edge of the hill and two more that disappear down the track. They are wide apart, wide enough to let them carry something large and heavy and dangerous.

I take pictures of the prints, then follow them until the track becomes a sidewalk on the next street along. Whoever did this, they are long gone.

I head back. Haran is standing with the woman, who is frowning at the mannequin.

"This wasn't an accident," I say. "Someone chucked that thing at my car."

I lean down and touch the cold plastic.

"Leave it," Haran whispers. "It's evidence."

I *should* leave it. But I don't.

I meet its blank eyes. Then I roll the body over.

That's when I know with absolute certainty that this wasn't the weirdest possible accident. It's another part of the game. Because there are words carved on the mannequin's back, slashed deep into its plastic flesh.

Whose secrets can you see?

Awkward Conversations

The police officers stare at the mannequin, then at me, then at each other.

The woman opens her mouth but doesn't speak. The man shrugs.

"Well," he finally says. "You don't see this every day."

He's trying to make light of things, but it's not working.

The man crouches next to the mannequin while the woman asks questions.

"So, this just appeared . . . out of nowhere?"

"It didn't just *appear,*" Haran says. "It crashed into our car."

"I can see that," the police officer says, looking up as if it fell from the sky. "Do you have any idea what this means?"

She's pointing at the writing, but how do we answer that? Haran shakes his head, and I watch her partner nudge the mannequin with his foot.

We spent so long arguing with Elisha about the police, and

now here they are. It feels a bit anticlimactic, although there's a fear bubbling in my stomach. Sasha told us to keep things to ourselves. Does this count as breaking that rule?

"It came from there," I say, pointing to the hill.

"Probably kids screwing around," the man says.

His partner nods and writes something on her notepad. "I'll be honest. This is a new one for us."

No shit!

They knock on the woman's door and talk for a few minutes, then wait with us until the tow truck arrives.

I think about what Mom said when she first gave me the keys. Two words that are about to haunt me for months—*Be. Careful*.

"We'll look into this," the male officer says, and I imagine them asking every clothes store in town if they are missing a mannequin.

I feel sick the whole way home, and even sicker when Mom stands open-mouthed as my car is backed onto the driveway.

"What happened?" she asks, looking me up and down, searching for injuries.

"I'm fine. There was an accident. But no one else was involved. Honestly, Mom. I'm okay."

She gives Haran a once-over, makes some tea, then sits with us in the living room as we tell the story.

We leave parts out, of course. Most of the parts.

Mom looks confused. "A what?"

"A mannequin," I say. "The police think it was kids being stupid."

I catch Haran's eye then look away.

My phone lights up with a message from Elisha, asking

why I'm not at school. The truth sounds absurd, so I don't reply. Instead, I ask Mom to drop us off.

She sighs and says, "What do I say to your father?"

"Tell him what happened. It can't be any weirder than anything else we've dealt with."

"Someone threw a shopwindow mannequin at the car," I tell Elisha. "It's Sasha—or whoever they are."

I show her the picture I took on my phone of the mannequin's slashed body. *Whose secrets can you see?*

She stares at me in silence, shaking her head, until the bell goes for next period.

"Are you being serious?"

When I nod, she says, "How bad do things have to get, Sam? You could have died. We need to tell *someone*. Even if it's not the police. We can't keep this to ourselves."

"Who then?"

"My dad?"

I try to picture Marcus's reaction to all this. Haran's parents'. Mom's and Dad's.

"We'd need to tell them about the Dark Place," Haran says.

And that's the real reason we don't want to tell. The Dark Place has always felt so special, but have we tricked ourselves into thinking it's still worth protecting? Without us, it's just an empty hut in the woods, its walls echoing with the secrets we shouldn't have been too ashamed to admit.

Elisha's right. We're the ones who need protecting now.

Heart to Heart

Why is the car broken?" Molly asks.

"Your brother had an accident," Mom says. "But everything's fine."

I smile and say, "You have to be careful when you're driving."

"Weren't you careful?"

I guess not. I thought we were safe whispering our secrets into the dark. But someone heard them.

Molly is staring at me.

"I'll be more careful from now on," I tell her.

Dad comes out and pats my shoulder. "It's good that you're safe," he says. And I guess that's it.

But later, after Molly's gone to bed, Dad stands in my bedroom doorway and says, "Can I come in?"

"Sure."

He doesn't usually ask, and I feel nervous until he says, "When your mom called me about the accident, I kept imagining what could have happened. I know you're safe but . . . I never want to lose you, Sam. Be careful, okay? Driving is a big responsibility."

"I know. It wasn't my fault."

Dad smiles and says, "Did they arrest the mannequin?"

I manage a laugh, then wonder what the police did with it. Is it evidence now? Or did they leave it on the side of the road for kids to find and destroy?

"It's been a strange few weeks," Dad says.

He has no idea.

"It really has."

"I know you'd rather Molly stayed out of the spotlight," Dad says. "I know you're protective and that's great. But you have to know I love you both immeasurably."

He looks different—expectant, maybe; open in a way I've rarely seen.

"I know."

"I didn't think I'd ever have this. Your mom is my soulmate and you and your sister—you mean the world to us."

"Is everything all right?" I ask, because Dad never talks like this.

"Everything's fine. I just had a moment today. You hear that your son's been in an accident and you have thoughts, you know?"

I move closer and hug him. He squeezes a bit too hard but I don't mind. While his scars were healing, and for a long time after, we barely touched.

"How's Elisha?" he asks. "We haven't seen her for a while."

"She's fine," I say.

"I can see that she loves you," Dad says. "If that's what you're worried about. Keep the special ones close, Sam, okay?"

I nod. I didn't keep Elisha close. I put her in danger. And now she's trapped keeping everyone's secrets.

"I love you, Dad."

Something strange happens to his face as shock turns to delight, and he taps my shoulder and says, "I love you, too."

"You don't have to worry. I'll be careful next time I drive . . . whenever that is."

"We'll get the windshield fixed soon. Haran needs his chauffeur, after all."

Dad's goofy smile coaxes out one of my own, even if the thought of driving again turns my stomach.

There is a gentle knock at the front door, and Mom comes upstairs and says, "Sam. Visitor."

She doesn't seem angry that it's a late call, which means it's Haran, Elisha, or . . .

"Hey," Chloe says. "What happened to your car?"

"Something hit me. But I'm fine."

"Are *they* fine?"

I picture the twisted plastic person lying in the road and say, "Yep."

"We saw the smashed windshield and . . ."

"Seriously, I'm okay. Everyone's okay."

Chloe nods. "That's a relief. Don't go thinking I was worried about you or anything. My mom's just super nosy."

I laugh. "Of course."

"I wanted to talk to you before . . . about the store thing, the memes. How are you coping?"

"I'm fine," I say. "It's dying down now anyway."

That's not entirely true. If I focus, I can still hear the gossip that follows me down the hall. But it's been buried by everything else Sasha has done, only breaking free when I let it.

"Well, I guess I'll see you at school," Chloe says.

"Wait!"

Her brow creases and I feel awkward for shouting. But I'm getting desperate.

I step outside and pull the door closed. Then I open my phone, paused on the video of the mask in Dom's bathroom mirror.

"Did you see this at the party?"

Chloe peers at the black-hole eyes and the nasty red smile; the dirty cloth that hangs over the stranger's face like saggy skin.

"Yes," she says. "I definitely saw that."

"You did?"

"They were like, everywhere. It was weird because, wherever I turned, I saw them. If it wasn't Halloween, I would have thought they were stalking me. Who is it?"

"That's what I'm trying to find out. Can you remember anything about them? Did you see what else they were wearing . . . who they were talking to?"

"Sorry," she says. "I'm being useless again, aren't I?"

"No, definitely not. But if you think of anything, please let me know."

"Does Dom have a video doorbell? That could help, right?"

"It would," I reply. "But he doesn't have anything like that."

They may be the richest family in town, but Steve and Hope have never tried too hard to protect what they have. They trust the community, and for a long time that trust was well placed.

Chloe's phone vibrates in her hand, and she rolls her eyes. "Patience is a virtue," she says, and then, to me, "Sorry. Dance team drama."

If I'd known we were being stalked that night, she could have been our secret weapon. But whoever is tormenting us, it will take more than that to catch them.

Betrayal

I don't know when I fell asleep, but eventually it came.

In the nightmares, eggs smashed against my skull; the noise like a slammed door inches from my ear, before blood oozed down my forehead, filling my eyes with a sticky, rancid red.

Then there was a softer sound that I had to fight to find in the darkness: a *tap, tap, tap* that grew to a dull, incessant thud. Footsteps. Only then could I sense them—the shapes in the gloom. And beneath it all, the crackle of flames.

The footsteps and the flames grew to a roar. The shadows came closer, becoming one, the same dark mass I dreamed of before. It gripped tight to my arms, dragging me closer, and I knew where it was taking me.

The Dark Place.

Last time I cried out. Not this time.

This time I wake with only a gasp. I don't move for a

while. I lie in bed, my sheets smothered in sweat, and think about everything that comes next.

Elisha wants me to be there when she tells her dad. The thought makes me feel sick. I can imagine him yelling at me for getting his daughter involved in whatever the hell this is.

The Dark Place was harmless. But how many terrible things start that way?

Pale morning light filters through my curtains. My phone buzzes and I check it.

It's an email, forwarded by Sasha Craven. I scroll down. The subject is "Sam Hall Shoplifting" and the message below reads *I thought you'd want to see this.*

I check the email and go cold. The message that Sasha has forwarded to me is from Haran and it's to someone called Jenni. Her email signature says TMZ.

Hi Jenni,

Thank you for the initial bank transfer. I'm attaching the video we discussed so that you can see the whole thing.

  Please keep me anonymous.

H

I jump out of bed and race downstairs before my thoughts have caught up with my body.

"Morning," Mom says. "Is everything okay? You look a bit frazzled."

"I'm fine," I lie, reaching for my car keys before realizing the windshield is still busted.

"Do you want some breakfast?" Mom asks as she pours Cheerios into Molly's bowl.

My sister is watching me, so I walk over and kiss her head,

and then I turn to Dad and say, "Can you take me straight to school today?"

"What about picking up Haran?" he asks, and, desperately trying to keep my cool, I say, "He's coming in later. Doctor's appointment."

"Sure. But there's no rush, is there?"

Everyone is looking at me now.

I catch my reflection in the mirror and quickly rearrange my expression, then grab some muesli from the cupboard and say, "No rush at all."

My family's conversation washes over me and they don't try to pull me back in.

Haran was the one who filmed me stealing, not Sasha. *He* was the one who leaked the video to the media. No wonder he's been so weird lately. That asshole betrayed me, then lied to my face.

He was my best friend. I trusted him. Nothing like Dylan fucking McCabe, who sold that photo from my thirteenth-birthday party to the press. But it turns out that Haran is as bad. No, Haran is worse. He knows how upset I was when that photo leaked, how it broke my family to see Grandpa's last picture plastered over the gossip sites. And now he's tried to break them all over again.

"Earth to Sam," Dad shouts. "You ready?"

I jump up, having barely touched my cereal. My stomach is so knotted that the last thing I want to do is eat.

"Are you sure you're okay, bud?" Dad says in the car; still with the weird empathetic thing he's been doing lately.

"What happened to all your friends?" I reply.

"Pardon?"

"You used to have buddies, right, like Haran's dad. He used

to come over all the time. And you had poker nights and went out drinking. Why did that stop?"

Dad glances quickly at me then back to the road. "What's this about?"

It's about friendships that you thought were unbreakable, I think, *until those friends betray you.*

"We just got older, Sam. Naveen is still my buddy, but . . . when you have kids, your priorities shift. Stuff comes up. And then weeks become months and, before you know it, you haven't seen your best friend for years. Damn, we barely even text each other anymore."

Dad looks sad and I feel guilty.

"But don't worry," he says. "That won't happen to you and Haran. Your bond is incredible. It's been that way since you were babies."

I want to laugh. He has no idea. He might have lost touch with his best friend, but mine stabbed me in the back. And then another thought hits me.

If Haran filmed me stealing, someone had to have told him where I was. And only one person knew.

Sasha Craven.

The Truth

Elisha catches up with me as I walk toward the school gates. Haran is standing a few yards away, completely oblivious to what's about to happen. I messaged him—*No lift today*—and he replied with a single letter—*K*.

"What is it?" Elisha asks. "You look like you want to murder someone."

"It was him."

"It was who?" Elisha says, and I say, "Haran."

"You're going to have to be more specific," she says. "I have no idea what you're talking about."

Memories flood over me then. I stand still as people rush past and I think back to our first day at Stoneleigh Road. Everyone was staring at me—the famous kid they were too scared to talk to but happy enough to point and giggle and smirk at.

Haran's blazer was massive, like *he* had shrunk in the wash.

His hands hid deep in his baggy sleeves, and his trousers rucked up like the saggy skin of an elephant. But he beamed as though he didn't have a care in the world, because we were best friends and we were doing our first day of high school together.

"I've got your back," he said, right before we were washed along on the wave of everyone else. And he always did.

Until now.

"Haran filmed me shoplifting and then leaked it," I say. Elisha recoils. "Only Sasha knew I was there. I think he's Sasha or, at least, one of them."

Three people got out of the car that night. The night Haran pretended to be terrified. I remember him kicking my seat. "*Drive the fucking car!*"

But there could be more Sashas.

"Don't be ridiculous," Elisha says. "Haran would never do that to you."

"You have no idea what he did!" I shout, so loud that the kids in front of us turn and stare. So loud that my girlfriend's face switches in an instant. It goes cold and shuttered.

"Wait, I'm sorry. I'm just . . . a mess right now."

"Don't yell at me," Elisha says. "Ever."

"He leaked it," I say, pulling out my phone. "Look."

Elisha takes my cell and reads the email. Then she hands it back. "If Sasha forwarded this to you, she's screwing with Haran, too. He might have done it—but he's not the one pulling the strings."

"There's only one way to find out," I say, walking quickly toward the gates until Haran clocks me and nods.

But I don't nod back. I stare into his eyes, take one slow breath in and out, then say, "You filmed me shoplifting."

He doesn't deny it. Something shifts behind his eyes and, as weird as it sounds, he looks relieved. He even smiles.

"You think this is funny?" I say, and Haran shakes his head and says, "Not at all."

Someone barges into me from behind and I turn, but they are already lost in the crowd.

"Not here," Haran says, walking toward the athletics field.

I turn back to find Elisha but she's not there. She's not getting involved in this, not right now.

I follow Haran onto the field. We stand there and stare at each other. It's quiet again—too quiet—and he says, "It's not what you think."

I can't reply. I'm scared of what I might say. He sits on the grass and looks up at me expectantly.

"I'll stand," I say.

"I didn't film you shoplifting. I wasn't there. I promise. And I didn't put it online."

"Explain this then." I drop my phone into his lap and study him as he reads the forwarded email.

"I didn't film you," says Haran. "Sasha did. She sent me the video and said that, if I didn't sell it, she'd tell everyone what I told the Dark Place. I thought about it. I really did. But I couldn't betray you, Sam. Not again."

I can feel goose bumps rise up on my arms. "What do you mean, *Not again*?"

Haran turns away from me and says, "That's my secret, Sam. That's what I told the Dark Place. I didn't sell this video. But I did sell the picture."

It takes me a while to realize what he's saying. When I do, everything stops.

"You sold the birthday party photo?"

"Yes."

"Why?"

He looks at me then, with tears in his eyes, and says, "I didn't think I had a choice. You know we don't have much money but, back then, it was really bad. Mom was ill and Dad was really struggling to find work.

"I heard my parents talk about missed payments and eviction. They argued about it every night and then, when the fighting stopped, they cried. I didn't know what to do, Sam. But I had to do something."

"So, you sold the picture."

Haran nods. "Reporters would stop us sometimes. They'd ask about you. Whether you were okay after the fire, whether it was true you'd been unhappy on the show. We always told them to get lost. But one day I had an idea." He swallows. "I told Dad and he said no, over and over again. He said he could never do that to you. Then one night . . .

"I remember he was sitting at the table, surrounded by all these letters with red writing. He hadn't found any work for months and the bills kept coming. So, I did it on my own. I called one of the journalists and said I had a photo. It wasn't much, but they wanted it.

"I was so naïve, Sam. I thought we'd pay off all our bills with that cash, but do you know how much I got for it? Two hundred dollars. That's it. They gave it to me in a brown envelope like it was some kind of crime. They paid one kid to betray another. That's what kind of people they are.

"I was so embarrassed that I didn't want to give Dad the money. I kept it for weeks then told him I'd been car washing on the weekends. He still wouldn't take it though. Even after all that, they put the money in *my* bank account."

I've always wondered what Haran's biggest secret is. But I never once thought it had to do with me.

"I've been so ashamed for so long. When Sasha started messaging me, telling me she knew . . . I thought I'd lose you. But I was never going to sell that video." He hands back the phone. "That's not even my email address."

When I look closer, I can see there's an extra *r* in his first name. I should have noticed that but, in the heat of the moment, I saw what Sasha wanted me to see.

And I rushed off to confront Haran, just as she had known I would.

"They're trying to turn us against each other," Haran says.

I think back to Dylan—the boy I've always blamed for leaking my photo. He'd denied it and I hadn't believed him. I'd told him I would never trust him again. I was so sure, because I knew that no one else in that room would ever have done that to me. He was the only suspect because he was the one person there I didn't love. But now I know love isn't an alibi.

"You could have told me," I say. "We would have lent you money."

Haran huffs out a laugh and says, "My dad would never have taken it. Do you ever wonder how hard it was growing up with a TV star and Dom as best friends?"

"I didn't realize it was 'hard' being friends with me."

"That's not what I mean and you know it."

I stare across the field, trying to pick some sense from all the thoughts crashing through my mind. Then I turn to him and say, "You told me you'd always have my back."

"I did. I do."

"Maybe. But you also stabbed me in it."

I walk off before he can reply.

Haran might not have filmed me for Sasha, but he kept that secret for five years. Every time I cried about it, every time I called Dylan a snake, my best friend had sat there and nodded. And then he'd walked into the Dark Place and whispered his betrayal into the shadows.

Elisha is standing in the courtyard, waiting for me with a concerned look. "Well?"

"How many secrets have you told on Halloween?" I reply.

"What?"

I have a theory and I need her to prove it.

"I have one big secret," I say. "So does Haran. What about you?"

Elisha frowns. "I thought we don't talk about that."

"We didn't. But things have changed."

She doesn't answer. Instead, she backs away. "I've got to get to class."

"Someone was listening to us," I call after her. She stops and I add more quietly, "I don't know how, but things we told the Dark Place years ago are out there."

She knows what I'm going to say before I say it. "We need to go back."

Loyalty

I was used to seeing my face in the newspapers and online. It was, rightly or wrongly, part of the job. But my grandpa didn't deserve that.

My thirteenth birthday felt like a promise that might actually be kept; a sign of better things to come.

As we crowded around my birthday cake—the absent candles flaring in our minds, Dad's scars still healing under light clothes and a lighter touch—my life felt almost good.

Grandpa's patchy stubble tickled my cheek as he whispered, "It will be okay, kiddo. The worst is over now."

As with everything he said, I believed him.

A week later, he was dead.

A month after that, the last photo of us together was published above a story that reignited all the old rumors. I was home alone when the fire started. I'd been sad and withdrawn on set. The blaze started in "suspicious" circumstances.

This time, my grandpa was tangled up with those lies. His unbreakable smile, his warm eyes, the tattoos that covered his arms in a story I found more fascinating than one hundred fairy tales.

That photo should have been a good memory. Instead, it was tainted by the press's horrible desperation to break me over and over again.

It had felt healing living with Grandpa, for all of us. At least our house could be rebuilt. When *he* was gone, it was forever.

He used to give me advice when I was on the show. I would never ask for it, but he knew exactly what to say and when. He gave me guidance when others gave me grief.

Yet, what he gave me most was his voice.

I didn't realize at the time, but he would fight for me. He would argue with my father when no one else would, telling him that the show was wrong, that I was a kid, that I was unhappy.

The fact that he did it in private, never showing me how upset the situation made him, never turning *his* argument into *mine,* tells you everything you need to know about my grandfather.

It's why I hated Dylan so much. And why I hate Haran now.

My grandpa fought so hard for me to escape *Future Force.* But, in the end, his last photo got trapped in there with me.

I will always feel guilty for that.

Better in the Light

On Saturday, Elisha picks me up and the two of us drive to the Dark Place.

It feels so different in the daytime, and I wonder which is the lie—how safe we feel when the sun is up or how scared we are in the shadows.

"Have you spoken to Haran?" Elisha asks.

"No. What else is there to say?"

"You could make up. Try to see it from his point of view. His family was broke and desperate. He was trying to help them."

"He could have done it differently," I reply, because I've been thinking about it constantly and, yes, he felt trapped. He needed to do *something*. But why did it have to be that? He knew how important that day was to me—my first birthday since the fire; Dad's scars still stinging; Mom's sorrow still raw. But somehow, against all those odds, it was a good day. Haran took that from me.

We park along the side of a lane, farther up than usual. There are other ways to get to the Dark Place. Ways that don't involve Dom's back garden.

Elisha and I walk through the orchard where we picked apples as kids, then the field where the farmer would scare us away with his shouts. This is where Dom, Haran, and I enjoyed our summers.

"Here it is," I say, leading Elisha into the woods.

I pause and rest my hand on the trunk of a broad elm. The tree Dom once got stuck climbing. He sat there for hours, whining while we giggled until, eventually, his father convinced him to jump.

This place has so many memories; not just of secrets whispered away, but of childhoods we expected to keep forever. Correction—*parts* of childhoods.

Without the adults, without the cameras, without the expectations, it was perfect.

"Why couldn't you have done this alone?" Elisha asks.

"Because I wanted you to be with me."

She turns her head but I can still see her eyes roll.

I've been thinking a lot about what Dad said, how he knows Elisha loves me and how my friendship with Haran is unbreakable.

He's already been proved wrong about one thing. I can't bear it if he's wrong about the other.

When I asked Elisha out two years ago, I knew she'd say no. I did it anyway. Haran convinced me—through a mixture of ego stroking, hard truths, and ridicule—to take my shot.

"What's the worst that can happen?" he'd said when I admitted I liked her. There were too many worst things. So, I did nothing for months.

Then, for a few strange seconds on an otherwise ordinary day, I found the courage to talk to her and, unbelievably, she talked back.

I watch Elisha stomping ahead through the woods and worry that we're not those people anymore. She feels distant. Is it because we refused to call the police? Or because of the message about broken families? Or is it not one thing but *every*thing?

Our world feels so uncertain. Even the parts I used to rely on are either lost or slipping away.

When we reach the Dark Place, I stop and study it from the opposite end of the clearing. Sunlight falls through the leaves of the twisted elms, creating beautiful shapes on the ground, and I think of all the people who've come here by accident.

It looks stunning; the perfect place for a picnic or a first date. If you ignore the bloodstained hut in the corner.

I walk slowly over to it, then touch the outer wall. The last time I did that, my fingers came away sticky. But the blood has dried to a crimson brown, the eggshells crushed even smaller by whatever walks the woods at night.

The candles are still inside, and Haran's words flash through my brain. "*I think someone blew them out.*"

I close my eyes and try to remember. The eggs came first, then the scream. When we came back, the hut was pitch black. We know now that Sasha is three people. One to throw the eggs, one to wail deep within the gloom, and one to leave the hut in darkness.

I turn to see Elisha hanging back. "Can you see anything weird?" I ask her.

"This isn't normal, Sam."

"What do you mean?"

"I mean *this*. What are we doing?"

I don't like the look in her eyes. She seems angry with me, and I wonder if this is it—the moment she tells me it's over.

"Someone heard us in here," I say. "How is that possible?"

She doesn't answer.

"I'm sorry," I say. "I know this isn't what you wanted. But there's a reason we're being tormented and I think the answer might be here."

She offers me a half smile and says, "Maybe the problem was that, instead of talking, we dumped our secrets here. We shouldn't have needed this place."

She's right, I think. But we still don't talk. The space for those words is too big now, or too small.

I push the door open, go in, and start picking my way through the hut, searching for anything suspicious. But there's barely anything here as it is. That's the joy of the place—it's empty, at least physically. It's full of what we've told it, but those things exist on a different plane, layers of memories and confessions hanging on top of each other, as thin as air.

I lift the candles one by one, then stare at the box they are sitting on. It's been here as long as we've been coming, our initials carved into the dark brown swirls, and I run my finger over the jagged letters—*SH, HS, DS.*

Elisha's initials aren't here. She wasn't around at the beginning and we never thought to add her. I remember Dom carrying the box into the clearing as we sat eagerly with our penknives. Ceremonially carving our initials into the wood, one by one.

The box once felt huge but now I can lift it easily. When I knock it with my knuckles, it sounds hollow. And that's when something clicks. Not a feeling. A noise.

I push on a section that suddenly seems loose and it pops out, revealing an empty drawer.

"Lish," I shout. "I've found something."

"What is it?" Her voice is thin and anxious outside.

It's another secret, in a place already full of them. A hidden compartment.

Elisha joins me inside. I show her the drawer. "It's the perfect size for a phone."

"Why would someone hide a phone in there?" she asks, then shakes her head. "To record us."

"Exactly. That's how Sasha listened to us. I don't think we were ever really alone in here."

"But you found this box, right? It was just trash in the woods."

"No," I say. "This was made for us."

I picture all the wood piled up in Dom's father's shed, all the times he turned it into something amazing. Skateboards, mud kitchens, tree houses, assault courses . . . and this box.

Steve built it for us to play games on or as a place to rest our drinks while we bounded across the lawn. One day, Dom brought it into the Dark Place.

When all this first happened, Dom was the obvious suspect, because the Dark Place is right on his doorstep. But he's not the only person who lives here.

Why would Steve want to know our secrets? It doesn't make any sense. And yet . . .

I watch Elisha turn the box over in her hands and then say, "I think we have a new suspect."

Surprise Visit

Y ou're going *now*?" Elisha says, as I push through the undergrowth. "Shouldn't we call first?"

"We've spent enough time waiting," I reply. "I need to speak to Dom."

This is the walk we did on Halloween, back to a house that was heaving, the scream still ringing in our ears and everything washed in uncertainty.

Today, that same house looks unrecognizable, its doors closed, its soundtrack muted.

I march up the garden path and look through the back door. When we were kids, I'd run in without thinking. Dom's house was never closed to us and his parents always made me feel welcome. But now Elisha and I walk around to the front and I ring the bell.

Lauren looks out of the living room window, smiles, then opens the door. "Hey. What are you doing here?"

"Is your brother here?"

"He's upstairs. Dom!"

I tense, waiting for Hope to appear and offer us tea and cake or, so much worse, Steve to smile like everything's fine. But the only sound from inside is Dom yelling "What?!" through the floorboards.

Lauren opens her mouth to yell back, then grins and says, "You should probably come in. We can talk like this for hours."

I look at Elisha and say, "I'll be back in a minute." Then I run upstairs and bang on Dom's door.

Dom's reading on his bed and he tosses the book aside when he sees me and says, "Samuel. What's happening?"

He looks pleased to see me and I don't want to ruin that. But we can't keep hiding the truth from each other, not if we want to figure out who's tormenting us.

"You told me your parents don't know about the parties," I say. "But in the video Sasha sent you, your dad was helping set up."

Dom's smile doesn't falter. If anything, it widens as he says, "Oh they figured it out years ago."

"But they still go to a hotel?"

"Yeah. They love it. It's about the only thing they get excited about these days."

I watch Dom closely. His face is open, sunny, cheerful. I'm about to ruin that.

"Come with me," I say. "There's something you need to see."

Dom stands reluctantly. "What is it?"

"You don't know everything about the Dark Place."

I walk back downstairs and out the front door without stopping. If I know one thing about Dom, it's that he hates being left out.

Then he's behind me, followed by Lauren and Elisha, and we walk back into the woods.

"Sam," Dom says. "I'd rather not . . ."

His voice cracks, as if he's scared. Has he even been back since we were attacked?

I stop then, look past him and focus on Lauren. "You don't have to come. If, you know, after the jogging . . ."

"It's fine," Lauren says, and when I glance down, I notice she's holding Elisha's hand.

I turn and head straight for the clearing, then through the open door of the hut.

Dom follows me inside and I point at the box. "Who built this?"

He shakes his head and says, "You know who built it."

"Your dad, right?" I push on the wood, and the secret compartment clicks free. Then I stare at Dom and say, "Why did he put this here?"

Everyone stares at the hidden section.

"It's the perfect size for a phone," I say. "Or something to record us."

"And you're saying *Dad's* the one doing that?" Lauren says, watching from the doorway. "That's a pretty big accusation. Did he stalk me through the woods, too? Is he Sasha? Is . . ."

"Lauren, stop," Dom replies.

"Why? He's accusing our father!"

"Lauren . . ."

"No! I get that this is horrible. We've all left secrets in here thinking they were safe. But I won't have you accusing one of my family—"

"It was me," Dom whispers.

Lauren's eyes snap to him as she says, "What did you say?"

"It was me. I hid a phone so I'd know what you said in here."

He's staring straight at me with tears in his eyes. Slowly, I take this in.

How could Haran and Dom both betray me?

"You spied on us?" Elisha says, and Dom mumbles, "It's not that simple."

"Either you did or you didn't." I've never heard Elisha sound so harsh and cold.

Dom turns and pushes past Lauren and Elisha, out of the hut, and starts pacing the clearing. Then he stares into the sky, his fingers locked behind his head, and breathes out.

"I didn't listen to everyone," Dom says at last. "I only listened to Sam."

The Second Truth

Dom can't look at me and I don't want to focus on him either.

"What the hell are you talking about?" Lauren asks.

He turns to her, his eyes pleading, and says, "I didn't listen to a word you said. You have to believe me."

"And yet my secret got out anyway," Lauren spits.

"Because someone stole the phone."

I think of Halloween, the minutes after the scream when we walked back to the Dark Place. I remember Dom running into the hut, then coming out looking angry. Was that when he realized the phone was missing? All our secrets, recorded one after another, in the hands of a stranger?

"Why?" I ask, and Dom looks at his sister and says, "I'll explain everything. But can Sam and I have a minute first?"

Lauren stands firm, defiance in her eyes; then I turn to Elisha, who looks as angry as I feel.

"Can you take Lauren back to the house? I want to hear what he has to say."

"So do I."

The girls don't budge and Dom crumbles under their gaze, sitting on the muddy ground and wrapping his head in his hands.

"I'm sorry," he says. "It's not how it sounds. I had a reason."

"Then tell us," Lauren says.

He meets my gaze. "I needed to know if it was my fault."

My temper flares. I need answers, not more riddles. I crouch next to him and say, "Haran was the one who sold that photograph of my birthday party. All these years and *he* was the one who betrayed me. Did you know that? Did you hear it on your secret phone?"

Dom looks genuinely surprised as he says, "What? No, I . . . I only knew *your* secrets." He swallows. "The fire. I needed to know if you suspected me."

"Why would I suspect you?"

"Because I . . ."

Something breaks inside him and he's suddenly sobbing. Painful, hard sobs. I don't think I've heard Dom cry since he was six and fell in the poison ivy.

I turn to the girls, and Elisha shrugs. Lauren walks forward and rests her hand on her brother's shoulder.

"What did you do?" I ask.

Dom peers up at me and there he is—the nervous little kid he used to be. The years fall away. His features rearrange in front of my eyes, all the sarcastic sneers and cocky looks replaced by one overriding emotion—fear.

He looks at Lauren, then Elisha, and then, finally, me. His shoulders sag, the last fleck of fight seeping out of him, and then he speaks.

"I was there," Dom whispers. "At your house. That day."

"No, you weren't. I'd remember."

He stares at the ground and says, "Not if you didn't see me."

Elisha takes my hand and squeezes it. I don't break Dom's gaze.

"I'm so sorry, Sam."

"Sorry for what?"

"Your dad left a key for his studio in the garden. He said if I ever wanted to come over and work on my own photos, I should let myself in."

I try to remember if I knew that. But so much of those days was taken up with rehearsals and filming. Between that and school, I didn't pay much attention to what Dad did in the garage.

I know Dom went in sometimes, visiting me then fanboying while my father developed his latest batch. But did I know Dom was an aspiring photographer? Did I care?

I can see the desperation in his eyes. He doesn't want to keep talking and yet, he has to.

"I didn't think anyone was home," Dom says. "I just wanted to try a few things, without anyone watching. I was . . . embarrassed to tell anyone. I was shy."

I stifle a laugh, because the thought of Dom ever being shy is hilarious. At least, it *would* be, if he didn't look so serious now.

"I knew everyone would say it was a dorky hobby but I loved it," he says. "I was fooling around; doing what I'd seen your dad do. But something happened. There was a spark by the wall and it smelled weird. I panicked."

"What did you do then?" Lauren asks.

I close my eyes and remember. Where was I when the spark caught in Dad's studio? I was *there*—screaming at my reflection in the bathroom mirror, then glaring at the ruined script until exhaustion dragged me into a sleep that could have been my last.

"Nothing," Dom says. "I locked the door, put the key back, and ran." He stares hard into my eyes and says, "I had no idea you were home, Sam. I swear. I thought everyone was out. The car was gone."

I think of the tears, the recriminations. Mom whisper-screaming at Dad into the night.

"*You* started the fire?"

"No! I told you . . . the spark came from the wall. I didn't know it was going to catch fire. But I was there and I could have saved you. I could have raised the alarm. Instead, I . . ."

The tears come for him again.

I've seen plenty of good actors in my life and, if you look closely, you can always see the joint between who they are and who they're pretending to be. But not here. Dom is telling the truth—about everything. If anything, *this* is the truth and everything else was the lie.

"We always thought it was an electrical fire," I say. "But the fire department wasn't sure. Then they found out it started in the darkroom, so we thought it must have been something Dad did wrong."

Either way, Dad was to blame in Mom's eyes. He should have had the ancient fuse box checked, updated the wiring. Not left out dangerous, flammable liquids.

"I know," Dom says. "Maybe it was. But maybe I did something. I was there, wasn't I? Messing around, using the chemicals. It wouldn't have happened if I'd stayed away."

"*Might* not have happened," Lauren says, rubbing her brother's back.

"That's why you invited me to the Dark Place," I say. "You said it would help me get over the fire, but you just wanted to hear what I was thinking."

He nods and I step forward, picturing the punch I'm this close to throwing. But he looks broken, the mirror image of Haran when *he* was the one confessing.

"I didn't suspect you for one second. I never even mentioned you in there. So why did you keep recording?"

Dom shrugs and says, "Sometimes you don't realize the truth until you're older."

"I know exactly how that feels," I reply, because I can suddenly see all the lies that were right in front of me. All the times Haran claimed he had my back; all the times Dom told me the Dark Place was helping me cope when he was only looking out for himself. They both used me.

"What would you have done if I'd said your name in there? Would you have gone on the run or something? You were thirteen."

Another image crashes into my head—a collage of all the younger kids Dom tormented back then. His way of dealing with it, I suppose.

Dom made people's lives a misery, while I tore the guilt I felt whenever I saw Dad's scars or heard Mom cry into smaller and smaller pieces until, eventually, I could scatter them unseen.

"I don't know what I would have done," Dom mutters. "I just wanted to know. Sometimes it's better to know what you're up against. Every year you didn't suspect me, I felt a bit less afraid."

"Oh, well that's okay then," I say. "Do you know how many

times my parents nearly broke up because of that fucking fire? Do you know how it feels to see your dad's arms covered in scars or watch your stuff get carried out of a smoking house?"

I open my mouth to say more but something stops me, because I'm no better than Dom. He saw the flames and ran. I saw them and didn't. Neither of us called for help. And he knows that. He heard exactly what I said in the Dark Place, but he's not fighting back with it.

"I guess everything's a lie," I say.

I realize I'm still holding Elisha's hand. Together we turn and walk out of the clearing. We leave Dom slumped on the ground, Lauren's hand on his back. For the final time, we walk away from the Dark Place.

If Sasha Craven wanted to break us, it's worked.

Alone

"**W**here do you want to go?" Elisha asks, and I say, "Home."

Elisha follows me in, and when I see our reflection in the hallway mirror, I realize she hasn't been here for ages. Dad was right: our old routine has fallen away, and I need it back.

"Where have you been?" Molly asks.

For the weirdest moment, I'm convinced my sister knows we went back to the Dark Place, but she's not looking at me. She's staring at Elisha, who kneels down, grins, and says, "I've missed you, Mol."

"I've missed you, too."

We go into the living room. I sit at one end of the sofa while Elisha and Molly cuddle together at the other, my sister whispering about all the things she's done since they last saw each other. Sometimes I hear snippets of things she's never told me, but I'm not jealous. I love that they are close like this.

I've taken Elisha for granted, and I hope there's time to put things right.

Eventually, Mom gets home from the store and Dad comes in from the garden. They start bickering about all the things she forgot to buy until they notice Elisha and Dad says, "Oh, hi."

"Hey, Adam," she replies. "Hi, Abby." Unlike me, my girlfriend doesn't have any issues calling people by their first name.

"It's wonderful to see you," Mom says. She glances quickly at the two of us, then says, "Come on, Molly. Do you want to see what I've bought?"

Molly jumps up and rushes out of the room because she loves going through the food shopping. It's my sister's job to write the weekly meals on the chalkboard. I smile at Mom, then slide closer to Elisha.

When we're alone, she rests her head on my shoulder and says, "Do you think Dom really caused the fire?"

"He was there. No one else was. And he definitely *feels* guilty."

Elisha is quiet for a long time; then she sighs and says, "Feeling guilty isn't a bad thing. Not if you've done something wrong."

"I know. But he could have just spoken to me. Why did he have to record me in secret?"

"Kids do stupid things."

That's true. But we aren't kids anymore. If Dom wanted to hear my thoughts when I was twelve, I get that. But why did he record us for the next six years? Did he really think that, one day, I was suddenly going to think it was his fault that Dad's studio caught fire?

I know why, because I know Dom. He likes to be in control. He doesn't like people to know what he doesn't. Which makes me wonder—was it really only my secrets he listened to in the dark?

As though reading my mind, Elisha lifts her head and says, "Do you believe him . . . that he only listened to your confessions?"

"I don't know what to believe anymore."

We fall back into silence.

We all played our part in what happened at my house that day. Dom could have stopped it the minute he saw that spark. Dad could have checked the wiring, like he promised. My parents could have taken me shopping with them instead of leaving me alone. And I could have run, raised the alarm. Instead, I let the flames roar, hoping for a new beginning, staying silent when most would scream.

We were all guilty.

If I push past the pain, I can see that clearly. And yet . . .

"Is it bad?" I ask.

Elisha stiffens and says, "Is what bad?"

"Your biggest secret."

I watch her reflection in the television, the way her mouth shifts and her brow creases, until her eyes catch mine and she says, "Don't worry. It has nothing to do with you."

And I know that's all she'll say.

A Normal Night

nything?" Molly asks, and Mom says, "Yes, sweetheart. Anything."

"Fancy pizza!" my sister shouts.

Dad grins and says, "Fancy pizza it is."

Molly's choice of dinner is a reward for her photos going viral. But it's something else, too. It's my parents patching the cracks caused by the shoplifting and the crash, because they are still looking at me differently—fear mixed with love and relief.

They want an old-fashioned family night and I'm happy to play along because, honestly, so do I.

It's starting to feel like the three people in this house are all I've got.

There's still Elisha. But even she left with something unsaid.

Tonight, for a few blissful hours, I'll try not to worry about any of it.

When Mom comes downstairs, she's wearing a blue dress and Dad says, "Wow." Then he passes his phone to my sister and says, "Molly. Would you do the honors?"

The first picture is nice but it's the second, when Mom and Dad don't realize they're being photographed, that shows just how good my sister is—accidentally or otherwise.

In the second picture, Dad's smile is smaller but more real and Mom isn't looking at the camera anymore. She's watching my father like she did in their wedding photographs—like he's her favorite thing in the world.

"Is that okay?" Molly asks, and Mom wipes her eyes and says, "It's perfect."

I can't remember the last time we went out as a family. But we haven't forgotten how to enjoy it.

This is the restaurant we go to for special occasions. It's where we went for Grandpa's sixtieth birthday. It's where my parents took us when they first met Elisha. And now we're back—not for anything specific. Just because.

"Can we order one each?" Molly asks, and Dad says, "Same as always."

The pizzas are huge and my sister can only manage a few slices. But Molly always says she wants to enjoy it as long as possible—which means tonight's dinner for tomorrow's lunch.

"How was the drive here, Sam?" Mom asks. "Were you nervous?"

I sat in the back of Dad's car with Molly, but Mom kept glancing around like I was going to have a panic attack.

"It was fine."

Another chance to be honest that I deflect with a lie. Because it wasn't fine. I don't want to drive anymore. I don't think I ever will.

Dad's smiling, and I wonder if it's because Molly hit some new level of viral. But it's as if he's a different person. No ... not different ... just the version I like most.

"Remember the first time we came here?" Dad says. He's looking right at Mom.

She grins and says, "You were trying very hard to impress me."

"Did it work?"

"Nope."

My parents laugh so loud that it fills the restaurant. For the tiniest moment I'm embarrassed, because people are looking, but then I'm not. I'm just happy that we're the ones laughing.

"Tell us about the flowers," Molly pleads, and Mom shakes her head and says, "Those damn lilies."

Dad snorts. "I was trying to be romantic."

I've heard this story a thousand times but I never tire of it.

"Okay," Mom says, focusing on my sister. "I think we all know your father was enamored with me. But he'd never actually asked me out."

"Because you liked somebody else," Dad says.

"Well, so the story goes. But when he did finally pluck up the courage, I said yes."

Our father coughs and says, "Actually, you said, 'Why not?'"

"Anyway, he turns up at the restaurant with this ridiculous bouquet of lilies. I mean, huge. It must have cost him a fortune. There's nowhere to put it so I leave it on the floor, and it keeps tripping up the waitress and staining everything it touches. People keep sneezing. Your dad was mortified but I couldn't stop laughing."

Mom goes quiet, and she and Dad just look at each other

for a moment. Then she says, to all of us, "So I guess 'Why not?' was the right answer."

Three years later they went off to college, did the long-distance thing; then, like everyone, they came back to Hayschurch, and the rest is, well, us.

While my parents talk quietly, and Molly stares at them like she's watching a rom-com, everything that's been happening lately slithers back, twisting around my happiness until it's all I can think about.

I want to ask Dad about him leaving the key in the garden, if Dom really could have come and gone on the day everything changed for us. I want to tell him his guilt was misplaced all these years, that it wasn't just *him* at fault for the fire that left its mark on his home and his marriage and his body. It was my fault and Dom's fault, too.

But maybe now that I've lived for so long with one version of the truth, it would be wrong to reveal another. Because they are happy and, tonight, that's all that matters.

"You've been coming here a long time," Molly says.

Mom holds Dad's hand across the table. "Twenty-three years."

My sister grins, and I wish it could always be like this.

I wish my friends hadn't betrayed me. I wish I'd driven everyone here tonight because my car wasn't wrecked. I wish the Dark Place still felt safe. I wish Lauren and Malika were still together, and I wish Elisha still looked at me the way she did when we came here two years ago.

She laughed at all my dad's jokes and talked quietly with Mom. Every few minutes Elisha would glance at me and smile and I wondered how many times we'd come back here.

But this is my parents' special place. As soon as they walk through the door, I see echoes of who they were before us.

Elisha and I don't have anything like that. I thought it might have been the Dark Place, but now I realize how twisted that was. I should have listened to Dom when he said no to her joining us. And I should have walked away, too.

Molly makes a point of rubbing her tummy, like she's got a stomach ache; then she reaches for another slice of pizza.

She smiles and takes one tiny bite, then passes it to Mom, who does the same. And me and Dad.

This is how we finish the meal; the four of us having one last piece. Then they pack up the rest for us to take home.

Molly falls asleep in the car and I stare out of the window, as our parents whisper about the past.

I want this moment to be every moment, but I know life doesn't work like that. So, I focus on the late-night love songs on the radio, the sight of my sister dreaming, the sound of Mom and Dad when they are lost in each other's words.

And I keep my own eyes open, because I don't want to miss a second.

Family Portraits

Mom unlocks the front door while Dad tries to get Molly out of the car without waking her. He scoops her up with practiced ease.

Over his shoulder, I see my sister open her eyes, work out where she is, then fall instantly back to sleep.

When she was a baby, my parents tried everything to soothe her. There was a sweet spot, halfway between the kitchen and the living room, where she would sleep for hours, but only if Dad stood and rocked her. Now she'll crash anywhere.

"Hot chocolate?" Mom asks, but she already knows the answer. It's a family tradition. The perfect end to a great night.

Dad comes downstairs, then stops before he gets to us, a strange look on his face.

He turns, unhooks a photo from the wall, and says, "Did you do this?"

"Do what?"

"This!"

Dad passes me the frame, and I make a noise that sounds like a whimper. Mom stops making the drinks and stares at me.

"What's wrong?" she asks.

I look at Dad, then back to the photo.

"There are more," he mumbles. "I think it's all of them."

Mom comes closer and gasps.

I know every single pixel of this photograph. It's been hanging above our fireplace for years: the four of us smiling real smiles, wearing our best clothes, the perfect family portrait.

Except, it's not that anymore, because my sister's face has been scratched out.

I look at the bookcase, where Molly's school photo has pride of place. But all I see is a mess of jagged paper and holes where her innocent face should be.

Mom pulls the curtains back and grabs a frame from the windowsill. We're on vacation, me, Mom, and Molly all squeezed onto a sun lounger while Dad pokes his head in from the side. That picture wouldn't win any awards or get many likes, but it's one of my favorites.

Except now, Molly's face has gone.

The room starts to spin and I sit down before I pass out. Then I breathe in for four and out for six, but it isn't helping.

Dad comes back with the canvas that usually hangs halfway up the stairs. It's me holding my newborn sister, only, she's not there anymore.

The sickness comes so quickly I almost vomit on the rug. But I push my hand against my mouth and swallow the sting until I'm in the bathroom.

They didn't just stare through our window this time. They came inside and . . .

"Dad!"

"What is it?"

"What if they're still here?"

Fear and rage flicker across Dad's face and he marches toward the stairs. We go straight to Molly's room and stand over her but she's fast asleep.

Dad quietly opens her wardrobe then looks under her bed before I check the other rooms. Together, we comb the house. There's no one here, just the damage they've left behind.

Every single photo of Molly has been ruined—hacked to pieces while everyone else is untouched.

When we're certain the house is safe, we go downstairs to where Mom is holding my sister's school photograph and crying.

Dad wraps his arms around her and she sobs.

"Maybe it was someone who's jealous of her talent," he says.

"It's not," I say.

My parents look up at me. This is it.

"I haven't been honest with you," I say. "The car crash wasn't an accident—someone threw that dummy at the car for a reason. And I didn't shoplift because I was being bullied. It's bigger than that."

Mom and Dad look at each other, but they don't speak.

"Someone has been stalking us—me, Elisha, Haran, Dom, and Lauren. First, it was weird messages. Then they filmed us. And then, it got worse."

"Worse how?" Mom whispers.

"They followed us home one night. Three of them . . . all wearing these horrible masks."

Mom frowns. "A mask? What sort of mask?"

"Yellowing cloth, with dark holes for eyes and a red mouth. I was finally going to tell you, but you seemed so happy. I wanted tonight to be normal."

I stare at the ruined pictures of my sister and feel relieved that she's asleep. I hate the thought of her seeing this.

"We should call the police," I say. "Whoever did this might come back. I'm sorry. If I'd told you sooner, this wouldn't have happened."

Mom nods and reaches for the phone. I go into the hallway and I see Dad joining her.

Sasha warned me. They sent me that video of Molly. I should have told our parents then and they could have done something.

We were so close to the perfect night. Instead, it feels like a horror movie.

A floorboard creaks in Molly's room and I freeze.

I walk up the stairs. *No one's here,* I think. *We checked.*

On the landing, I stop. The air feels different, like the silence is holding its breath. And then I see it. Our attic hatch isn't quite level, the thick slab of wood that usually covers the hole raised on one side so a slice of darkness creeps through.

I quickly push Molly's door open and there's a shape standing over her, holding something.

The shape turns and charges at me before I can move, pushing me against the wall and darting onto the landing. They are dressed all in gray, a hood pulled low over their face, and their mouth and nose covered by a plain black mask.

"Dad!" I shout. "They're still here!"

I'm running down the stairs as fast as I can but they are already at the front door, flinging it open and sprinting out.

"Sam!" Dad yells. "Stop!"

I keep running. I can hear his footsteps slapping on the pavement behind me. The shape turns left at the end of our road, flinging a garden waste bin into my path that I dodge at the last moment.

My legs are burning and my heart is racing, but *they were in my house.* They were in my sister's room.

Whoever it is, they're fast, their outline fading into the black until I stop, hands on my knees, panting into the cold night air.

"Which way?" Dad asks, and when I point, he charges after them.

Someone peers out of their front window, while curtains fall back into place two doors down. That's what happens when there are late-night noises around here. People check for answers and those answers are usually grocery trucks or wailing cats.

Now, though, no one comes out to ask what's wrong.

I could shout into the emptiness, pleading for help, but the longer I wait, the farther my father disappears into the gloom. That's why I burst forward again, until the gaps between the streetlamps widen and the noise shifts, from the hum of sub-urbia to the buzz of the wild.

I see Dad standing in the road next to the kindergarten. He whispers, "I think we've got them."

Before I can answer, he puts a finger to his mouth and points at the kids' playground.

I stare into the shadows. The swings Molly used to love, the jungle gym she hated, the merry-go-round that's always broken. And then one of the shadows moves. It's barely a flicker but it's there—a shape creeping through the black.

A low iron fence surrounds them, and Dad starts creeping right.

"Stay here," he whispers, and for a moment I'm frozen to the spot. Then, something snaps me into action. I can't let him go in alone, so I approach the playground from the other side.

Can they see us as clearly as I can suddenly see them? Because that's all I'm focused on—a shape that doesn't quite fit the pattern around it.

There are two gates into the park, but I don't risk making a sound. Instead, I gently climb over one while Dad eases his open.

I brace myself for the shape to move, because it has to. They can't simply wait to be caught. Not after all this. But there's nothing.

Dad gestures to me to wait. He creeps closer and closer. Slowly, slowly, feet soundless on the ground. The shape doesn't move.

Dad is so close now. He lunges, grabs it, spins it around, and the mask that's been haunting us stares deep into my soul.

Its eyes look deep enough to fall into and its grin is written in blood, but the body doesn't move. Because it's not a body. Not a real one, at least. It's plastic. A mannequin; like the one thrown at my car.

It's leaned up against the back fence, its face terrifyingly real despite everything below.

Dad peels the mask off and holds it in front of him and I can't read his expression. The dirty fake skin looks so lifelike in the gloom, hanging in the space between us, forcing me to look away.

"I'm sorry," I say. "I'm so sorry."

They were hiding in the attic, I realize. Watching through the crack while we convinced ourselves that our home was safe again.

"It's not your fault," Dad says, and that's when I fall apart.

"Of course it is. This is *all* my fault. Why are they doing this to me?"

He puts his arms around me and I cry into his sweater for a long time.

Eventually, he steps back and says, "Let's go home."

He stares at the mannequin one last time, then tucks the mask under his jacket.

I look back at the school and the main road, searching for eyes in the darkness; then I follow my father to a house I couldn't protect, to a sister I failed, to a mother standing under the porch light with Molly's tiny arms wrapped around her neck.

"We lost them," Dad says as he walks past, straight up the stairs and into my sister's room.

I follow in silence.

He flicks on the light and five dolls' heads smirk at me with one-eyed faces.

I stand behind Dad, watching as he untangles the string hanging over Molly's shelves and her headboard.

"We got these in our lockers," I say, and Dad's shoulders tense.

He doesn't reply until all the heads have gone and Molly's room looks almost normal again. Then he stands in front of me with his hands on my shoulders and says, "It's not your job to protect this family, Sam. It's mine."

"But . . . but we need to tell the police," I say.

"I know," Dad replies. "We'll call them first thing tomorrow."

All the times I stopped myself from telling him what was going on, and this is what would have happened if I had. His face would have flickered with the rage of a protective father. He would have stepped up.

"I'm sorry," I say—for tonight, for hiding the truth, for doubting him.

"No need," he replies, squeezing my shoulder on his way back downstairs.

Molly is asleep on the sofa, Mom stroking her hair while cartoons play quietly on the TV.

"It's done," Dad says, before he carries the box of heads to the garage and then stares at the smashed pane of glass in the patio doors.

Tiny shards glisten on the conservatory tiles along with dirt, and he brushes them up, then drops them like dust into the trash.

"Shouldn't we leave that?" I ask. "For when the police get here?"

With his back to me, his shoulders stiffening, Dad says, "Leave it to me, Sam. Like I said."

"But . . . it's evidence."

"It's dangerous."

Dad does one final sweep, then walks past me with his eyes to the ground. Is he angry that this happened on his watch? Does he believe all the superhero movies and think he's the one destined to end this?

Through the doorway I watch as he goes to Mom. "You need to see this," he says quietly.

He pulls the mask from under his jacket and she flinches.

Slowly, reluctantly, she reaches out and touches it. Then a tear creeps down her cheek and she pushes it away.

I hate myself for putting them through this. They've suffered so much through the years and most of it is because of me.

I go into the garden and look at the fences that I always assumed were too big to climb.

Then I watch from outside—my parents and Molly framed by the arch that separates our living room from our kitchen, the light amplified in the dark as if they are on stage and I am the audience.

Something cracks underfoot. I crouch down and fragments of glass glow in the moonlight. I hold the biggest piece carefully between my fingers, then study the hole someone made to break in.

There are no bricks or rocks or obvious weapons lying around. "What did they use?" I say to myself.

I run my hands gently over the ground, and tiny shards stick to my skin.

The glass Dad swept up had specks of dirt mixed in, as if it had come from the garden. But that doesn't make sense.

Unless the door was smashed from inside.

Crime Scene

Mom spends the night in Molly's room, easing her cries with that voice I know so well; the one that kept me company after the fire.

Sometimes Molly talks back, her words fragile and full of fear, and I want to go to her. I want to lie with them but something stops me. Maybe it's shame. Maybe it's my own fear that swells in the darkness but feels more manageable on my own.

I stare at the ceiling, convinced sleep will never come, then jolt awake each time it pulls me under.

In my nightmares, I'm back in Molly's room, watching the shape standing over her bed. It looms over her, the single eye from the dangling dolls' heads lit by the glow of my sister's night-light. Then the shape bends down and picks Molly up. I try to tear my feet from the floor but they are frozen, and all I can do is watch as the shape carries her slowly away.

My head is aching when I finally go downstairs the next morning, the walls and shelves filled with freshly printed copies of my sister's pictures.

Dad's been busy. If you didn't know better, you'd think nothing happened last night. But his face tells the truth, his eyes red and puffy, the darkness below them seeping into his cheeks, the lines on his forehead carved deeper.

"Morning," he says. No "Good" today.

"How's Molly?"

The landing creaks and something icy and sharp slithers up my spine. Then my sister is walking down the stairs while gripping Mom's hand, like she's a toddler again.

I crouch and hold my arms out until she walks silently into my hug.

"I love you so much," I whisper, and something like a smile comes out as she says, "More than ice cream?"

"Well, maybe not that much."

She doesn't giggle like normal. But I feel her soften against me and I'm grateful that she didn't see what I saw.

When she woke up, she was surrounded by those horrible dolls' heads. But she never saw the person who put them there.

"Molly would like pancakes for breakfast," Mom says, her voice only breaking on the last syllable.

"I'm sure we could rustle something up," Dad replies, offering a hand that my sister takes after a smile and a nod from our mother.

When they're in the kitchen, I turn to Mom and say, "When are the police coming?"

She looks away, picking something from her fingernails, and says, "I don't know yet."

"Did you call them?"

She glances up, and I think I can see the moment she decides not to lie to me, because her lips open then close twice before she says, "No."

"What are you waiting for? I told you they've been tormenting me for weeks and it's getting worse. What if I hadn't gone into Molly's room? They could have hurt her."

Mom wipes her eyes, but I don't feel guilty. We need to *do* something. I've waited long enough and, whatever reason Sasha has for targeting me, it's time we fought back.

"We won't be calling the police, Sam."

Mom still won't look me in the eye, and I don't understand what she's saying.

"Why not?"

She stares past me, then sits on the bottom step and says, "Do you really want that? Do you want the press knowing what happened?"

"I want the police to know. That's different. They can help us."

Mom shakes her head. "You know as well as I do that there can't be one without the other. Not with us. If you want a quiet life, you keep quiet."

I can't believe what I'm hearing.

"What happened last night is serious, Mom. Whoever is doing this, they're getting braver. Next time, I'm worried it won't just be dolls' heads. They threw blood at me. They know everything about me and it's not stopping."

Her eyes go wide. "What do you mean? What blood?"

"It was Halloween. Someone threw eggs at us but they weren't just eggs. There was blood inside. Now they've got into the house!"

"We're getting a new security system," Mom says. "This place will be like Fort Knox by the time we've finished with it."

"I don't understand."

"Just trust us, Sam. We'll deal with it, okay?"

"You're supposed to protect us."

Mom steps even closer and says, "Speak quietly. We don't want to worry your sister. We're doing what we think is right for this family. Trust me."

She kisses my forehead, then goes to the kitchen, her voice changing as she chats to Molly about what she wants in her pancakes. It's too high, too fake, but my sister doesn't seem to notice. She's too busy playing let's-pretend with our parents.

New copies of Molly's photos fill the house, and the way the dolls' heads have been hidden, and the hole in the door has been boarded up, it's as if last night was a horrible dream. If only.

I go upstairs and look at the attic hatch. It's resting perfectly now, but I get the ladder from the hall closet and stand on the top step, pushing the wood up and then reaching for the switch.

The thick neon striplights don't come on right away. They tinkle, buzz, then stutter to life. I put my hands on either side of the hole and pull myself up.

There's no elegant way to do this. There are no drop-down rungs for safety. Sometimes we don't even use a stepladder. We stand on the wide wood railing that runs the length of our landing and climb up that way—just like whoever broke in last night.

I look around for any sign of clues, but nothing has been disturbed. All the boxes are piled high in the corners, black bags full of Molly's old clothes next to deconstructed baby-bouncers and walkers.

I remember us coming home from dinner. Did the intruder hear us and quickly hide in the attic, then come back down and carry on with what they had planned?

We willingly handed Molly over to them, sleeping and helpless. If Mom doesn't want to call the police, I'll do it. I don't care if the reporters come. I don't care if there are more headlines and more lies.

There will also be the truth—that Sasha Craven is out there, all of them, and they must be stopped.

I see it in my mind—that grimy face with its horrible red grin as it sat on the mannequin, as it marched toward my car, as it stared through the bathroom mirror after walking un-challenged into Dom's party.

I know that mask. I saw it that night, just like Chloe did—a flash of something truly sinister in a collage of harmless cos-tumes. And yet I can't remember the exact moment. What room were we in? Did they say anything to me? Did they stare directly at me while I looked around, oblivious, search-ing for a familiar face?

They must have, because the image is burned into my subconscious.

I close my eyes and focus on it, the piercing stare as black as oil, the smile carved out of blood.

The mask is as mysterious as whoever was wearing it. And yet, the faces that are buried deepest in my mind are all in one place.

I listen carefully at the hatch, focusing on the low rum-bling of my parents talking and Molly's favorite soundtrack coming through the speaker.

They are doing everything they can to make this morning perfect, planning a trip to the big park on the other side of town, then a stop-off at the ice cream parlor, which gives me time.

I walk slowly across the boards, careful to avoid the gaps between them, and then I push the boxes aside until I find the right one. It's marked *Old Times* and I quickly lift the lid and see the moments we used to spread across the carpet every Sunday.

Dad's photos send a thousand memories through my mind; not just mine, but his and Mom's and our grandparents'. Every picture has a story attached, and I wish they still told them. But those tales are dusty now, hidden away rather than displayed with pride.

I flick through the photo albums, the feel of the green and red leather a memory in itself—of all the times I sat holding these collections while Mom and Dad laughed about their past.

Every single face in every single photo feels familiar, every captured second so much more magical than the countless ones Dad let go. I lose myself in those moments, then pull a plain white envelope from the back of the last collection. It's yellowing at the edges and it smells musty, the opening making a cracking sound as I peel it back.

In the photograph inside, Mom is a teenager, her legs dangling off an upturned tree stump. Haran's dad Naveen is there, too, giving peace signs to the camera, along with another boy I don't recognize.

But it's the fourth person I'm interested in; the one sitting on the other side of my mother.

I don't know why I didn't realize before—why I couldn't

remember this image that I must have seen every time my parents unpacked their memories.

There are four people in this photograph, but only three of them are smiling real smiles. The other is staring out of the image with eyes as black as coal and a grin like a knife slash, because they are wearing a mask.

The same mask that has been haunting us for weeks.

The Enemy Within

My heart is racing. Is that why Mom and Dad won't call the police—because they're part of this somehow?

I tuck the photograph in my jeans, quietly slide the boxes back into place, and lower myself down from the attic.

The hatch slides back with a thud that I'm sure they can hear downstairs. But their voices continue undisturbed.

I stare at the picture again, at the girl who became my mom and the boy who turned into Haran's dad. They look like actors playing the people I thought I knew.

The other boy looks familiar, but I can't put my finger on it. There's something sharp in his stare, like he's unhappy with whoever took the picture. But I know who took it. It's the same person who took every photo—my father.

Someone else is wearing the mask.

I practice looking relaxed in the bathroom mirror. Mom

knows my face too well. She'll see straight through me, because I don't think this is something I could hide even if I wanted to.

In my mind, I charge downstairs and slam the photo on the dining table, demanding an explanation. But that scenario fizzles and fades, replaced by a tightness in my stomach that twists until it feels like I've swallowed needles.

I spent so long protecting my mom from the truth because I didn't want to upset her. It never occurred to me that she might have a truth of her own—one that was much worse.

Pressing my fingers against my mouth, I stare at my reflection until the ripples of fear settle. *I can pretend,* I think, *just long enough to get out of the house.*

Then I go downstairs, grab my house key from the hook, and walk back into the hallway.

"Where are you off to?" Mom asks.

When I turn, she's standing with her arms crossed.

"I'm going out."

"Molly wants to eat pancakes with you."

I quickly glance up. Mom isn't even attempting a smile. She's blank-faced, like she's posing for a passport photo.

"I'm not hungry."

"Can you at least pretend?" she says. "We're trying our best here and your sister needs some normality."

I stare past her into the kitchen, where Molly is looking expectantly at me. I imagine grabbing her and getting out of here.

But I can't. I need time.

"Okay," I say. "I'll do it for Molly."

As I walk past, Mom catches my arm. I flinch.

"Please don't do anything silly," she whispers.

For a moment, I think she's talking about the police. But

then another thought strikes. *Does she know what's hidden in my pocket?*

I've never been afraid of my mother before, but I am now.

"Here he is," Dad says, so loud and so fake that my sister scowls at him.

She's not stupid. She knows exactly what this is, and she's happy to go along with it, provided we don't take her for a fool.

Focusing solely on my sister, blocking everything else out, I say, "Are you okay?"

Her nod is small but forceful and I'm proud of her.

I sit quietly as Mom dishes out the pancakes, then eat as much as I can, every swallow a battle with my desert-dry throat.

Mom and Dad make small talk.

Then Dad turns to me and says, "We're having the windshield fixed today. You'll be back on the road tomorrow."

That's good, I think. If I'm going to leave quickly, I need the car. I take one long drink of orange juice before kissing Molly's forehead and grabbing my stuff.

"The security system is being fitted soon, too," says Mom. She looks at me and I look away. "There's no need to worry."

After what I found in the attic, they suddenly seem a lot harder to believe.

I stand at the bus stop with the younger kids who live around here. I edge away and take out the photo. It feels more than important. I think it's vital. An answer staring me in the face.

Except, I can't quite translate it. I know Mom and Naveen are in the picture, and I'm sure Dad's behind the camera. But that still leaves two strangers—the boy with the intense stare and whoever is wearing that mask.

I think about texting someone—but who?

I have tons of messages from Haran—lines and lines of sorrys said in a hundred different ways. Dom only sent one message—*I wish you knew how guilty I felt*—and that's him all over. Even now, in the midst of all this mess, he's centering himself. And nothing from Elisha.

I think about our secrets. We all did bad things—but we all had a reason.

Lauren had a reason to conjure up a fake girlfriend.

Haran had a reason to sell that picture.

Dom had a reason to sneak into Dad's studio that day and then run off.

And Elisha—what is her secret?

I watch four younger kids laugh so hard that one spits his drink across the ground, while another doubles over in pain. We used to laugh like that, ignoring the world around us and thinking only of ourselves.

It's not until one of them looks straight at me that I realize I'm smiling.

He nods, then turns back to his friends just as the bus pulls up.

I hang back, typing three messages that all say the same thing. Then I take a seat and wait for the next stop.

Haran gets on and sits next to me without a word. Then he pulls out his phone, types a message, and my own phone vibrates with his reply.

What now?

No Stranger

Haran is nervous. We both are. Our words sound fragile, like we are passing them to each other for closer inspection. But by the time we get off the bus, things feel a bit less spiky.

Elisha is outside Slice of Life, the dust from her morning doughnut falling to the ground like snow. When she sees us together, her mouth stays open until Haran says, "It will fall out if you're not careful."

She finishes her latest bite, then puts the rest back in the bag for later. Another thing we have in common is needing to enjoy our food. Every single bite is a moment to be cherished, and it's clear Elisha has other things on her mind.

"When did you make up?"

Before I can reply, Haran says, "It's a work in progress," and I can't help grinning at that.

"What does this mean?" Elisha asks, showing me my own message.

We're not the only ones who've seen the mask.

That's what I sent to Elisha, Haran, and Dom.

Whatever is happening between us, however things might carry on, or end, this is more important.

"It means I have a proper, one-hundred-percent, actual clue," I say.

"That's what you said about the slaughterhouse," Haran replies.

I want to show him the photograph, but we're surrounded by Stoneleigh Road kids and Dom's not here yet. When I do this, I want to see everyone's reaction.

I need to know if they are as shocked by the picture as I was.

"Trust me," I tell Haran. It isn't the best choice of words—it's not meant as an insult or an olive branch—but he nods like he understands and says, "I do."

We don't say anything else until we're inside the school gates and Dom is sauntering toward us.

He can't look any of us in the eye. He looks even more sheepish than Haran, but that's not a bad thing. If we're going to get over this—if only for long enough to unmask every Sasha—I need to know he's genuinely sorry.

If Dom's willing to keep all his masks in reserve—all the faces he puts on to play the role of teacher's pet or sassy rich kid or gossip queen—our friendship might mean something to him after all.

"Come on," I say. "I've got something to show you."

They follow me across the courtyard and into the main block. This early in the morning, no one's in the silent reading room next to the study center, so that's where I go, sitting with my eyes on the door and my hands on the photograph that changes everything.

Dom clears his throat but doesn't speak. Everyone looks uncertain, like this is a trap and I'm the ringleader.

"Sasha broke into my house," I say. "She scratched my sister out of the family photos. We thought she'd gone but I found her in Molly's room. She'd hung dolls' heads in there. Five of them."

Elisha stares at me in confusion. "Are you being serious?"

I stare back at her and say, "I don't joke about my sister."

"What happened?"

"She got away. My parents won't call the police. But then I found this."

I unfold the photo and lay it on the table.

"That's my dad," Haran says, pointing to Naveen, and I say, "Look closer."

"Fuck," he whispers. "It's the mask."

"I don't know who's wearing it," I say. "But our parents do."

"Have you asked them?" Dom says.

"Not yet. I wanted to talk to you first. I need your help. I know we all have our secrets but, compared to this one, they're small. I get that now." I tap the photo—my finger resting on the boy with the sharp face. "Do any of you know who this is?"

I glance over at Elisha. A tear is creeping slowly down her cheek.

"What's wrong?" I ask.

"That's *my* dad."

A Lifetime Ago

Marcus knew my parents.

In a town like this, that's no surprise. Like I said, people rarely leave, and even when they do, something always brings them home again. It makes sense they would have been friends once. What's weird is that we never knew that.

"Did you know they were friends?" I ask.

Elisha shakes her head. Then she points at the figure in the mask. "Who's that?"

"I don't know. But we know four people who do."

"Then let's ask them," Haran says.

"No," I say. "We need to do this differently."

Elisha looks shaken and I reach across the table and squeeze her hand. She squeezes back, then sniffs and says, "They keep coming for our families. This has never been about just us."

She's right. First it was her granddad, then my sister, and now my parents.

Haran pulls a notepad from his bag and says, "What do we know?" Then he's answering his own question, writing down names and events, the paper becoming an elaborate doodle of all the things that have happened since Halloween.

The blood-filled eggs, the scream in the darkness, the messages from Sasha, the blackmail, the dolls' heads, the videos, the car, the mannequin, the break-in. With every new thing Haran writes down, it feels like a tsunami rising from the deep.

"Nothing points to our parents," he says.

"And yet," I say, "*everything* points to them."

Principal Milano walks past and stares at us. If she's surprised to see so many of us in the silent study room before first bell, she doesn't show it. She just smiles and disappears down the corridor.

"I know we've been through a lot," I say. "And I know we're not exactly the best of friends right now. But I think this is bigger than us. This must have something to do with our parents. So, who's up for spying on them?"

All three of them stare at me until the faintest flicker of a smile dances across Dom's lips.

"I'm in," he says.

"Me, too," Haran says. "Whatever it takes."

Elisha is staring at the photo, at a teenage Marcus.

She's quiet for so long that I think she'll never answer. Then, finally, she clears her throat and says, "Sure."

Elisha is not like Dom and Haran—so eager to appease me that they'll do whatever I ask. I can see that she's uncertain about something.

I think back to the first time my parents met her. Did they

give any clues that her father was their friend? I don't think so. They were playing the role of perfect parents, but *I* was playing the role of shit-scared boyfriend, so who knows what their faces actually looked like, how many silent signs passed between them.

There must be a reason they kept it quiet. If there wasn't, they would have told me. They would have laughed at the coincidence—that their son's first and only girlfriend is the daughter of someone they grew up with. Instead, they acted like it was nothing.

"Does this mean you are friends again?" Elisha asks as she stands. There's no smile on her face and no one replies.

Dom's and Haran's eyes shoot to mine and I shrug. Then I say, "Let's get to the bottom of this first."

After that, we'll see.

Secrets and Lies

My house is never empty.

The day it was emptiest is the one I will never forget—when my parents left me alone and then came home to a burned-out shell and a son stained by secrets.

Maybe that's why it's so hard to find a quiet moment now.

Even in my room that evening, with the door closed, the sound of someone else drifts through the floorboards or the walls. The jumble of Mom's long sentences and the low groan of Dad's short replies. The singsong of Molly's play as she slowly feels safe again.

There's no new security system. Not yet, anyway. The windshield *has* been fixed, but my car key remains on the hook because I haven't found the courage to drive yet.

The evening drags itself reluctantly toward the night until, finally, Dad puts Molly to bed and my parents fall asleep in front of the TV.

I watch them from the hallway, wondering how they can be so calm.

The baby monitor crackles on the table beside them. They dug it out of the cupboard tonight and set it back up in Molly's room.

She's not asleep. She's facing the ceiling, as still as the mannequin that was thrown at my car, her eyes glowing in the dark.

I'll go to her, but not yet. First, I pick up Dad's tablet and click on his emails, searching for anything suspicious. He files everything into separate folders—*work* and *bills* and *family*—but there isn't one marked *Sasha* or *Halloween* or *The Mask*. If there was any evidence in here, it's been deleted.

Dad's phone sits on the arm of the sofa, tilting to the side like it's about to fall.

I quickly grab it and type in his code—Molly's birthday—then search his messages and his texts. But there's nothing—absolutely no suggestion that our home was targeted, zero evidence that he's scared. It's only work stuff, a message from the garage about the windshield, one from Naveen about catching up that he still hasn't replied to.

I look around for Mom's phone but I can't see it; then Molly rises from her bed and stares directly into the camera.

Her face looks distorted in the infrared light and I wonder what she's thinking. Does she feel safer knowing she's being watched? Or is it a reminder of that night?

I've been playing it over and over in my head, wondering how much my sister actually knows. Because it all happened so fast and she woke up in such a daze. Did she see the person standing over her?

I gently lean across my parents and mute the monitor. Then I head upstairs and sit on Molly's bed.

"Hey," I say. "Can't you sleep?"

She shakes her head, then rests it on my lap. "Mom and Dad are acting weird. Dad's looking at me funny and Mom's pretending to be happy."

Nothing gets past my sister. If she were a bit older, she would probably be the one to solve this. But I can't drag her any further into things than she already is.

"Is that bothering you?" I say, pointing at the tiny orange light on the baby camera.

She glances up, then gently places her head back on me and whispers, "No."

For the briefest moment, I want to ask her what she knows about that night. The words are there, almost beyond the tip of my tongue, but in the next instant, I snatch them back.

"Go to sleep, Mol," I say, tucking her in, and then I stand on the landing.

I stare at our parents' bedroom door, slip inside, and lift Mom's phone off the floor where it's charging.

I push the home button, but I already know what will happen. Nothing. The only way in is my mother's fingerprint.

Dad's phone and his tablet are dead ends. This is the last chance to find something. Is it any coincidence that it's also the hardest to open?

I unplug the phone and creep downstairs, half expecting my parents to be awake, the baby monitor switched back on, my whispered conversation with Molly playing loudly from a floor away. But Dad is snoring and Mom looks dead to the world.

If I do this, and she wakes up, what then?

The fear of her eyes flashing open stops me. Then the finality of never knowing propels me forward.

I hold the phone in one shaking hand and reach out for Mom's with the other.

Her fingers are warm, limp. I gently lift one. Mom lets out a sigh and, in my panic, I almost let go. Yet something stops me, steadies me, and I gently push her thumb onto the phone until it lights up. Then I lower her hand, unmute the monitor, and back out of the room, one painful step at a time.

My heart is racing, and I wonder when I started seeing our mother as someone to fear, because I'd had a lot of thoughts about what would happen if she caught me, and none of them were good.

I quickly head to my room and scroll through photos that are mostly of Molly being cute, then emails that are all just shopping orders and review requests.

It feels weird reading Mom's text messages, because she talks differently to her friends. She sends memes and chats about shows I didn't know she watches. She talks about us without being specific—how everything is "good" and "fine" and "nice"—and that makes me happy.

I know she doesn't always believe those things, but I'm glad we're not something she gossips about.

There are a few random numbers and spam texts, but I go through them anyway, and that's when I find it.

The message is to an unsaved number, from Mom's phone the night of the break-in. Six words.

I told you it wasn't over.

The Call

I stare at the message longer than I should. At any moment, Mom could wake up and find me. But the words hold my gaze like a tractor beam, pulling me into them until my eyes sting and my brain aches.

I grab my own phone and quickly make a note of the digits. My finger hovers over Mom's cell, daring me to push call. But I don't.

She can't know that I've unlocked her phone and seen this. At last, I'm ahead of something. I just need to figure out what.

First, I plug Mom's phone back into the charger. Then I check on Molly, whose soft breathing through the door crack tells me she's finally dreaming. And then I go to my room and stare at the numbers that could reveal everything.

Who was Mom texting that night and what did she mean? I think back. Mom sent the message just minutes after Dad and I chased a monster out of our house.

I click on my phone settings and hide my caller ID; then I type the number and call it without hesitating.

It rings and rings but I don't hang up. It feels like I'm banging on a door, over and over again, forcing someone to answer. I can be brave here, alone in my room, waiting for a stranger who can't hurt me.

Eventually the ringing stops and the line goes dead, but I try again and, this time, a man answers immediately. I'm so shocked by his voice that I jump, because it feels like he's here with me, his "Hello?" resting horribly in my ear.

I press my other hand to my mouth, nervous that my breathing will give me away.

"Hello?"

There's another voice in the background, high-pitched and muffled, then a rustling as though someone is covering the mouthpiece.

A sharp noise, followed by silence, tells me the man is alone again. But he doesn't speak. He listens to me listening to him for fifteen long seconds before the line goes dead.

My bedroom suddenly doesn't feel safe, as if calling the number invited him in. I take the photograph I found in the attic and stare at it for a long time. Mom looks about fifteen, which means this was taken twenty-three years ago.

That thought pushes another toward me like a domino. Not a thought, a memory, of the night we went out for pizza, unaware of what was happening back home.

"You've been coming here a long time," Molly had said, and Mom had replied, "Twenty-three years."

Twenty-three years.

I think this picture was taken the year they got together.

This image is a time machine, transporting me back to

when my parents weren't parents at all—just teenagers without a care in the world. That mask has been around for over two decades—and so has the person who's wearing it.

I look closer at the image, of Mom with her arm around someone unknown, and wonder if I'm wrong.

What if Dad didn't take every picture back then? What if he's not the one behind the camera?

What if he's the one in the mask?

(Un)Known Numbers

This is our headquarters now—the silent study room that isn't silent and where we definitely aren't studying. Well, not schoolwork, at least.

Three sets of eyes are on me as I say, "My mom's involved somehow. And I think Dad might be the one behind that mask."

The photo stares up at us—a portal to another world—and Haran says, "What do you mean, your mom's involved?"

"She sent someone a message right after the break-in. It was an unknown number. She said, 'I told you it wasn't over.' I called it last night and someone answered."

"Really?" Elisha says, and I say, "Yes. A man picked up but what could I say? 'How do you know Abby Hall?' I just listened until he hung up."

Dom pulls the photograph toward him, points at the mask,

and says, "Let's say that's your dad in the mask. Then who took the picture?"

He's right. One way or another, there's still one person hiding from their history.

"I've been watching my dad," Haran says. "I can't say he's been acting any weirder than usual."

I turn to Elisha, wondering about Marcus, but she's staring off into space with concern in her eyes.

"It feels like we're close," I say. "Maybe I should call the number again and just ask outright—'Are you Sasha Craven?'"

The door to the reading room swings open and Principal Milano strides in like she owns the place. I guess, in a way, she does.

"I've been seeing a lot of you lately," she says with a smile. "Working hard, I hope."

She looks down at the table, which is suddenly empty. But she's not looking for the photo. As her brow creases, I know she's wondering why there are no textbooks or past papers laid out.

"You don't share any classes, do you," she says. It isn't a question and nobody answers.

The edge of the photograph pokes out from under Elisha's hand.

Principal Milano sighs and says, "I don't mind you being in here before school. You're not bothering anyone but, please, at least *look* like you're studying."

"We will," Dom says, waiting until she's walked past the long window before adding, "Is it weird how suddenly I don't trust anyone?"

I try to hide my loudest thought, which is *No, it's not weird. Because I'm not sure if I trust half the people in this room.*

"What's the number?" Haran says. "I'll call it."

"No," I say. "It's going to look suspicious if they suddenly get lots of missed calls."

"Who knew your mom had a secret life?" Dom says. He's trying to lighten the mood, but some moods are destined to be dark.

"It's not only my mom," I reply, looking from Haran to Elisha, just as she stands and starts pacing the room.

"What's up?"

"What time did you phone that number?" Elisha asks.

I check my call log. "Ten thirty-three."

She nods, then says, "My sister's ill. She couldn't sleep last night so Dad and I were taking turns trying to calm her." She swallows. "His phone rang."

I think back to the call last night. The noise in the background. Could it have been Simone? The higher-pitched voice could have been Elisha.

"Show me," she says.

I pass her my cell and her head drops. I don't have to ask if it's her dad's number. The mess of emotions on her face is my answer.

I told you it wasn't over. That's what my mom sent to Marcus. But there was no reply.

So Marcus is involved. We know that.

But everything else is a mystery. Marcus and Naveen love their families. I'm sure of it. And my mother adores hers. She would do anything to protect us. Yet someone broke into our home to destroy my sister's photos, and Mom's only action was to text someone?

"We need to check their phones," I say. "All of them."

I make sure I look at everyone, even though it's Elisha I'm talking to. Her dad's messages may be the missing piece, connecting my mom to the exact reason she's involved.

"Even me?" Dom says. He smirks for a few seconds too long, then says, "It's kind of funny how you all suspected me, but it turns out your parents have some kind of twisted history."

"Who says it's twisted?" Haran replies.

Dom huffs out a laugh, points at the mask in the photo, then says, "*You're* the movie nerd. Of course it's twisted."

The Dead of Night

You know you don't need to get the bus anymore," Dad says, and Mom rests her hand on his leg and whispers, "Adam. Stop. He'll drive when he's ready."

She looks at me with what she thinks is understanding. But all her expressions are illusions now.

"I'm sorry," Dad says, which is weird in itself because there's no "but." Every time I think my father is going to revert to *before*—fighting back against every little thing or pressuring Molly to take another photo—he doesn't.

Was it me standing up to him that changed things? Or the car crash? Or when he dropped the ripped-up images of my sister into the trash?

Whatever the reason: Dad is being the best version of himself and I wish I could enjoy that. I wish I could tell him how proud I am.

Our relationship is complex, unique, weird, but he's still

my dad. For all the moments he pushed me further into a life I hated, *he* has the scars from the day I broke free.

My thumb and forefinger rub the edge of the photograph that is always in my pocket now. Partly, it's to protect it. But it's also because there's a voice in my head, daring me to place it on the table and ask what it means.

The same voice chitters behind the hum of my parents' conversation: *Did Dad take this photo? Or is he the person in the mask?*

I know the answer I want, even if it won't help. I want my father to be behind the camera, like always. I want whoever is behind that thick red smile to be unknown . . . at least for a little longer.

I imagine showing my parents the picture—but I can't. I hold on to it, because it's the only thing I have that I am certain of right now. It's an answer in a world of questions—incomplete, confusing, but real.

Every night, Molly gets a bit braver. She still needs someone with her before she can fall asleep, but I can see how quickly the emotions of that night are fading.

It took a long time for the ravenous roar of the fire to leave *my* nightmares. It was years after the rebuild when I first woke up from a completely undisturbed sleep, no longer exhausted as if I'd run a marathon in my dreams.

And yet Molly sleeps better now. I think the horror of the other night will be with me long after it's left my sister.

I stare at the bold numbers on my bedside clock until I'm sure I will never sleep again.

The house is quiet, my sister dreaming, the low hum of the TV in our parents' room replaced by the sound of taps, the flush of a toilet, and then . . . nothing.

I've always tried my hardest not to think about what goes on in their bedroom. But tonight, I imagine them sleeping with a secret between them.

I turn the clock over in my hands, remembering all the times I woke up to its bright red stare when I slept at Grandpa's place.

When we took things away from that house, deciding which parts of his life were important, I held the clock as tight as I wish I'd held him.

He was the only person who really got me. He could sense my sadness before I'd walked through the door, the right words always on the tip of his tongue. My anxiety was bubbles he liked to pop, my growing frustration with my father a storm he could always subdue.

A wicked smile would tickle his lips whenever he saw a giggle brewing, because there was nothing Grandpa liked more than laughing. And that's what I remember most—how everything was, in one way or another, happy.

I wake with a jolt, the clock telling me I've been asleep for nearly two hours. Muffled voices drift up from the floor below.

My whole body stiffens when I think: *They're back!* But, as the sound settles in my ears, I realize it's my parents talking.

The clock jumps another minute—2:17 A.M.—and my heart jumps with it, because I can hear the briefest tinkle of Dad's keys as he unlocks the front door.

I get out of bed as quietly as I can, avoiding every creak on the landing until I can see Mom sitting on the bottom step, pulling her high-tops on. She hasn't worn them in years, and I slip into the dark as Dad waits in the doorway.

"Are you sure they'll . . ."

"We don't have any choice," Mom whispers. "We won't be gone long."

For a moment, all my thoughts collapse in on themselves, blocking my path. Then the only thought that matters barges through: *Follow them.*

I dart back to my room, pull on some clothes, then run to the landing just as the door closes. But someone is in my way.

"Shit," I say out loud, staring into Molly's wide eyes as she says, "What's happening?"

She doesn't look like she's been asleep and I wonder how many nights she's spent awake until exhaustion finally took her.

"Where did Mom and Dad go?" she asks.

"They just popped out," I reply, even though lying to my sister feels like a waste of time.

"To the shops?"

"Yes."

"Aren't they closed?"

She's laying traps that I'm stumbling into because I'm half asleep and half frustrated and one hundred percent confused.

"Not all of them," I say. "Some stay open late."

"Okay. So where are *you* going?"

I picture the car keys on the hook and wonder who I could leave Molly with.

The closest people are Chloe and her mom, but it's nearly half past two in the morning, so I can't wake them now. Besides, Dad's car is long gone.

"Don't worry," I say. "They'll be back soon."

It's my job to keep her out of this; to pretend that our parents and everything that happens here is totally normal.

Who am I kidding? She'll find out the truth eventually. Whatever that is.

"I'm thirsty." Molly waddles back into her room and stares at the stars on her ceiling while I go downstairs to get her a drink.

There's a slip of paper on the countertop: a note in our mother's handwriting.

Went to the store. Back soon x

I shiver at the similarity of our lies. Because why would *both* our parents leave in the middle of the night just to buy something? Wherever they've gone, it's something they can only do in the dark, together.

I leave the note where it is, because they don't want me to see it. It's a safety net, a just-in-case that will be balled up and thrown away when they come home.

Maybe I should wait for them, sitting in the shadows like they do in movies. Aren't I supposed to be the one who sneaks out at night? They are meant to catch me, not the other way around.

Then another thought splits from that one: What if they've done this before? How many notes have been written and then thrown away over the years?

I put the glass of water on Molly's bedside table, stroke her eyes until she closes them, then go back to my room. My phone is full of messages and missed calls from Elisha and I quickly call her back.

"What's wrong?" I ask, and she whispers, "Where are you?"

"I'm at home. Where do you think I am?"

"Come to the Community Center near Haran's house now."

"Why?"

"Stop asking questions, just come. Avoid the parking lot. You'll need to bring Molly."

How does she know my parents aren't here? "How do you . . ."

I don't finish the question because the answer suddenly hits me hard.

"You're with my parents," I say, and Elisha whispers, "Hurry up. Things are getting interesting."

Intermediary Spying

Change of plan," I tell Molly. "We're going out for a drive."

She doesn't ask any questions. She just clambers out of bed, pulls her robe on, and mumbles, "Adventure."

I wish it were that simple. An adventure, just me and her. I wish I were the kind of brother who filled his sister's life with magic moments. Playful. But whatever this is, it's not a game.

I take the keys and make sure Molly's wearing shoes, and then we head out to my newly repaired car. I put the key in the ignition but don't turn it. Instead, I stare at the new windshield and try to tame the rising rumble at the back of my head, the one that will turn into a crash if I let it. I hear the thud of the body hitting the car, see the glass shatter. I remember how the world sped up and then slowed right down, adrenaline washed away by confusion and then, finally, fear.

Molly grins at me in the rearview mirror and I start the car and carefully pull away.

I drive slowly. I'm waiting for headlights to flash awake behind me, or something to splinter the pristine glass, or my parents to drive back the other way and see us.

Why is Elisha with them and what does it mean?

I remember what she said about avoiding the parking lot, so I pull up on the road opposite the Community Center and search for any sign of life.

A fox scampers along the sidewalk opposite, turning to look as my lights dim, then carrying on its way.

My phone vibrates with a message from Haran.

Don't freak out.

Someone taps on the window and I jump out of my skin. But Molly is giggling, because he's standing there with both hands out in front of him.

When I open the door he says, "I told you not to freak out."

"That message could have used a few extra words."

Haran looks serious and says, "I'll stay with Molly. Elisha's waiting for you."

"What is happening?"

He shakes his head and says, "You're wasting time, that's what's happening. Just go."

I get out of the car and see my girlfriend standing at the end of the road.

I give Molly a thumbs-up, tell her I'll be back in a minute, then walk quickly to Elisha. "Are you okay?"

"I'm fine. Come on. And don't talk."

Elisha strides forward and I have to jog to keep up; then

she turns in to an alley between the center and an abandoned bar.

The buzz of streetlamps fades the farther we walk into the gloom, until the only sound is my pulse throbbing in my head. I want to ask her what's going on, but she's focused and silent, and I know to stay quiet.

Finally, Elisha stops and ducks down, gesturing for me to do the same. Then she holds a finger to her lips and points to a gap in the chain-link fence.

The weeds are overgrown, but there is a space, and then suddenly it expands, because I can see my parents standing in the Community Center parking lot. Mom is gesturing, talking to someone, and Dad is standing with his head down, and they're not alone. I edge slightly closer.

Marcus is there, too, and Naveen, along with another person whose back is to us.

Elisha taps me on the shoulder, then points to her ear before mouthing *Listen*.

I hold one hand to my mouth, trying to calm my jagged breathing, then focus on my mother. The night is still and she's upset. Her voice carries.

"... told you already ... they came to our house. They are messing with our children."

Her face looks fierce but her words sound fragile as she wipes her eyes with her hand.

"What do you want us to do?" Naveen asks. His voice is calm, reasonable, like always, but there's an edge of fear in it. "I'm assuming no one wants the ... traditional solution?"

Dad's head shoots up as he says, "We're *not* going to the police."

He glances at my mom, and then I look down and see that they are holding hands.

Marcus clears his throat and says, "Do we know for certain it was them?"

"Of course it was them," Mom spits. "Who else would it be?"

Naveen says, almost apologetically, "I don't think Haran has been impacted like this. He hasn't said anything. They certainly haven't come to our house. And Elisha . . ."

Naveen turns to Marcus, waiting for him to finish the sentence. But Elisha's dad ignores him, focusing instead on my mom as he says, "My family has been through enough. I won't let anyone else hurt them. We're ending this, one way or another."

"Then we're agreed," says the other person, the one with their back to us. "We'll deal with this ourselves."

I turn to Elisha because I know that voice. She nods, puts her finger to her lips for a second time, then stares back at our parents.

All this time I thought *I* was the reason we were being tormented. All these weeks I was certain the Dark Place was the key. But the fear on Mom's and Dad's faces tells a different story.

The photograph was the key. Those past friendships between my parents and Marcus and Naveen—and someone else. The same someone who stares at each of them now and says, in a low, urgent voice, "Remember what we promised."

"I know," Dad says.

Mom nods at Marcus. Then Naveen steps forward and awkwardly shakes my father's hand.

"We need to get back. We'll fix this, I promise," Mom says.

They're getting ready to go, but I need to know more. This is my chance for answers. I won't leave with even more questions.

I start to stand and Elisha grabs my hand and pulls me back. Her eyes are wider than I've ever seen them. "No," she breathes. "No, Sam."

But I have to. The answer is right in front of us and we can't let it escape.

I push myself up and pull the weeds back, the eyes of every adult shooting toward me when they hear the noise.

"What the . . ." Naveen says, as Dad stares, confused, into the alley and Mom gasps.

"Sam," she says, "what are you . . ."

No one can finish their sentences now.

No one except Dom's mother, who turns to face us and says, "Sam. Elisha. Lovely to see you again."

Maskless

Come on over," Hope says. "It feels like we're talking through prison bars."

She's acting strange, at least compared to what I usually see. Dom's mom has always seemed so small and nervous, so much in his father's shadow, with her platters of snacks and quiet fretting, but now she stands with her shoulders straight and an expression like she's the one in control. She looks cool and self-possessed, whereas my parents look lost and confused.

Now I'm wondering what was fake and what was real.

"Why did you do that?" Elisha asks as we walk out of the alley.

"Because they would have left and we wouldn't have known anything. This way, they have to explain."

Elisha's voice is strained as she says, "What if I don't want them to?"

I hadn't thought of that. I hadn't thought of anything except working out what the hell is going on.

"I'm sorry," I say. "I have to know."

I think of how fractured her family was when her mom went away and how her dad is all she has left. "I'm sorry," I say again, "I know this is a lot for you."

"You have no idea," Elisha says.

She's right. I don't. She's never told me what that part of her life is like. Just as I've never told her about the fire.

"I know you're upset that your dad's involved," I say, stopping and facing her. "But at least this way we can stop it. I don't want them coming for you or Simone like they came for my sister."

I think of Molly sitting in my car with Haran. I hope whatever we find out, we can protect her from it.

We walk on and close the distance between us and our parents.

"What are you doing here?" Marcus asks. He's looking at Elisha with a mixture of shock and shame, and she runs to him, gripping him tight around the waist.

"Sam," Mom says. "Did you follow us?"

"No," I say, because I didn't. Elisha did. And Haran. I realize now why we're here—because they listened to me. I asked them to keep a close eye on their parents.

But will they be happy with what we find?

"It's no coincidence though, is it?" Dom's mom says. "You've been spying on us. Snooping around."

"Hope," Naveen says. "He's just looking out for his family."

"Aren't we all," she replies.

Naveen gives me a weak smile and I feel guilty, because he has no idea his son is here, too.

"Since we're all here," Hope says, "what do you want to know?"

I stare at her, this tiny, quiet woman who suddenly seems to be in charge. Someone we never paid much attention to—and now we're hanging on her every word.

But I look past Hope, directly at my parents, and say, "I want to know everything."

A tremble dances over Mom's lips, while Dad refuses to look at me. Elisha is standing next to Marcus and it feels like it's me against them all.

No one else wants to either tell the truth or hear it, but that's all we've got left.

"We have a problem," Dom's mom says. "And there are two possible solutions. We could get the authorities involved but, to be honest with you, Sam, no one wants that. There are doors we don't want opened . . . explanations we'd rather not give . . . trust issues, shall we say."

Hope looks at each of our parents in turn, and maybe it's my imagination, but they all seem to cower.

"What's the other solution?" I ask. "You deal with it yourself?"

Hope smiles and says, "He's smart."

Hatred flickers over Mom's face, while Dad's right foot makes the smallest movement forward before settling back on the ground.

"Before you judge," Hope says, "you should probably know what we're dealing with."

Then she turns back to Mom, Dad, Marcus, and Naveen and says, "It's time."

Twenty - Three Years Earlier

October 26, 1999

Abby and Marcus should get a room. There, I said it. They've been making eyes at each other for months and, frankly, it's gross. And don't get me started on Adam. He's like a lovestruck puppy, following her around with that damn camera. He says he wants to be a photographer but, personally, I think he'd make a better stalker.

I don't know what's so special about Abby. Maybe she has a nice face and she's definitely not dumb, but are those really reasons to snag all the attention?

Everyone is stoked for Halloween and I'm assuming that's where Marcus will make his move. It's not everyone's idea of romantic, although it would definitely be memorable. I wonder how Adam will take it. I don't think anyone else sees how he feels, but I've always been good at noticing things.

October 27, 1999

Naveen literally won't shut up about his costume which, his words, is going to be "fucking amazing." He's bugging me to show him my sketches, but I won't, because my surprise should be as big as everyone else's.

He thinks if he nags me enough, I'll just give in when, actually, it has the opposite effect. The more someone bothers me, the more I hate them.

I wonder if it's all right to think those things, because you shouldn't hate your friends. But maybe it's okay to just hate bits of them—like Abby and Marcus's terrible flirting and Naveen's nagging and Adam's damn camera.

October 28, 1999

It's ready three days early. The paint has dried and it's hanging on the mannequin Mom uses for dressmaking.

When she came into the garage and saw the mask, she screamed like they do in the movies. It was hilarious and weird at the same time because, seriously, who does that?

Overreacting is my mother's favorite hobby. If she finds something funny, she does this thing that I had to look up because it was way bigger than a laugh and turns out it's called a guffaw.

If she dislikes something, she'll moan about it for days, and I wonder if she'd be a lot happier if she just learned how to shut up and moved on.

And when something scares her, like the mask I made, she'll scream bloody murder.

October 29, 1999

"Are you going to ask her out?" Naveen says, and Marcus gives him the death-stare.

I watch Adam pretending not to care and imagine another piece of his heart falling out. He's got it bad and I actually feel sorry for him, because unrequited love must suck. It's like starving and someone tipping your dinner in the trash in front of you, over and over again until you die of hunger. Except Adam won't die because you don't die from a broken heart. Besides, he thinks, eventually, she'll look at him the way she looks at Marcus.

So, he's not only lovesick. He's also stupid.

October 30, 1999

Everyone is talking about Scott Brathwaite's party but we've never been "everyone." We listen to the over-the-top excitement then feel relieved that we didn't get an invite because, if you look up cliché in the dictionary, you'll probably see Scott Brathwaite's face and his horrible frat-boy party.

We like to do our own thing.

"How's the costume coming along?" Abby asks, and I say, "I finished it early and it scared the crap out of my mother. Hopefully I'll give some kids nightmares."

Abby's laugh sounds like it got lost halfway and tried to crawl back in. She's never known how to take me and that's fine. Sometimes I'm not sure how to take myself. We don't really do best friends but, if we did, Abby would probably top the list because she annoys me less than the others.

I like that she doesn't talk about boys all the time. Even Marcus. Her eyes talk about him a lot more than her mouth does but she's always been like that. She's not quiet but she's not loud either. She says what needs to be said, whereas the boys are on a three-person mission to use up every word ever invented.

It's also obvious that Abby hates Hayschurch Academy as much as

I do. Maybe even more because, when the boys talk about Stoneleigh Road, you can smell her jealousy.

"You know what would be cool?" Naveen says. "You should host a party one day, Hope. Not on Halloween . . . obviously . . . but your house is huge. You could be the new Scott Brathwaite."

I put a finger in my mouth and pretend to be sick and everyone laughs.

"Never," I say, because you wouldn't dig a hole you knew you couldn't fill, and that's basically the same as me having a party.

October 31, 1999

I pull the mask over my head and stare at my reflection. This is a Hope Belling original, created from a sketch I drew last year, and I love it.

Most people don't like nightmares but I think they're important, because that's when your brain is honest. There's no one to distract it, nothing to remind it what you should or shouldn't be feeling. Your nightmares are you with all the doors and windows open. People wouldn't be so scared if they realized that.

"Where's the rest of it?" Mom asks, and I say, "This is it."

"Just a mask?"

"It's creepier this way, don't you think?"

"Yes."

Mom thinks we're going to the party because, well, who isn't? She doesn't think there's an alternative and I don't correct her.

Dad's traveling for work again so Mom's home alone this Halloween. She pretends she's cool with that but I know she isn't.

When she drops me off at Abby's, I wave and say, "Check the peephole before you answer the door."

She smiles and shivers at the same time and I can't help a little grin.

"Jesus!" Abby shouts. "That is scary."

She can't see my smile under the mask, just the one I painted in my favorite shade of red.

"You look great," I say.

We have a rule—never ask who someone is because it's rude—so I wait for Abby to say, "I'm evil Alice in Wonderland."

"I love it."

My words feel hot under the mask and I pull it off because I don't want to hyperventilate. But Abby is so keen to leave that it's back on again in minutes and we're out the door. I want to scare as many trick-or-treaters as possible.

The road is full of little ones with their cute costumes and candy-filled buckets. When they look at me, I tilt my head and hold my hands out like I want to snatch them, and they scream or whimper or cuddle into their parents.

The adults laugh because this is just a bit of fun. But I wonder why it's okay to scare the shit out of your kids one day a year and then protect them from it for the other 364.

Marcus and Adam are standing at the end of Sycamore Street, waiting for us—or waiting for Abby, really. I imagine what it's like to be the object of two people's affections. Does it make Abby feel amazing or uncomfortable? I'd definitely be the latter but that's because I don't find anyone attractive really.

I'm attracted to books and songs and music. There's no way a person will ever compete with those.

"Hey," Adam says. He's dressed as Leatherface with a chain saw strapped to his back.

"Is that real?" I ask, and Adam says, "Of course not. I made it."

I'm impressed because most people these days buy stuff and I could if I wanted to but where's the fun in that?

Marcus has come as a zombie, his real arms tucked deep in his costume while fake ones jut out at horrible angles. But it's his belly that I can't tear my eyes from. Guts soaked in blood hang out, leaving pools of red on the pavement.

"That is disgusting," I say, and Marcus grins and says, "Why, thank you."

"You're going hard early though. What happens when all that's gone?"

He wrestles with his costume until one hand pokes out and pulls back his top. Underneath, stitched into the lining, are rows of crimson vials. "I came prepared."

Naveen runs up behind us, double-takes when he sees me, and says, "That's creepy. You win." But he looks good, too. His mask is framed by thick black hair like an oil spill and there are holes where his eyes should be. When I look closer, I see that he's put candy inside, and I wonder if any kid will be brave enough to reach into his face and pull some out.

"Ready?" he asks, and we follow him toward Scott Brathwaite's house. But there's no twist here. We aren't suddenly the cool kids or even the not-cool kids who sneak in anyway. We're the other kids, who walk past the house pulsing with music and spewing out teenagers, and head for the Hayschurch woods.

"The first dare," Marcus says, "is for Hope."

He grins at me and I pull off my mask and say, "Bring it on."

"Close your eyes," he says. "No peeking."

I do. My friends' voices suddenly stop and all I can hear is the slow sway of trees above us and the crackle of leaves underfoot.

They are abandoning me, slowly creeping into the distance until I'm sure they've gone. Then I feel hot breath on my ear and my body goes stiff as I fight the urge to scream because that's the challenge. I need to stay cool. Whatever they do, I mustn't react.

"Have you ever heard of the Snappers?" Marcus asks.

His voice is so close to my ear that I can almost feel his lips on my skin, but this isn't a game for replies. I stay silent and wait for Marcus to continue.

"The Snappers creep through these woods at night," he whispers, "looking for victims. The only way to escape them is to stay . . . completely . . . still."

There are more footsteps as Marcus leaves me in my own darkness. For a long time, there's nothing except the ringing in my ears and the sound of tiny, clawed feet hurrying through the undergrowth. And then I hear it. SNAP!

It's far away, somewhere to my left, and I fight the urge to open my eyes. I've completely lost my bearings but I think calm thoughts, because I've never lost a dare and I won't start now.

SNAP!

My eyes shoot to the right but I keep them closed. Then there's another SNAP! straight ahead. It's getting closer with every sound. I know it's only my friends but the terror boils anyway. That's part of the fun.

SNAP!

It's right by my neck, catching me by surprise, but I stay statue-still until Abby giggles and says, "You win."

Only then do I open my eyes and see the four of them scattered around the woods, all with broken twigs in their hands and smiles on their faces.

"Come on," Adam says, "you know the drill."

Naveen sighs, like this is the last thing he wants to do. Then he grins and jumps up to sit on the fallen trunk, patting the space next to him. Marcus joins him and Abby slides awkwardly along, leaving me to sit on the end.

Abby puts her arm around me and I don't know if it's just because she likes me or because she's conscious of Marcus on the other side. But I roll with it, slipping my mask back on just as Adam holds up the camera and says, "Say Halloweeeeen."

"You know what I'm going to say."

Naveen shrugs, like, we can't blame him just because he's predict-able. But I guess we also can't blame him because this is the only dare that we've never managed to do.

"Really?" Abby says. "Every single year?"

"Every single year until someone does it," Naveen says, jumping from one tree stump to another and back again.

I've already done my dare, partly because I'll never do this one. Don't tell anyone but, if you always go first, you can generally avoid bad ideas, and Naveen's is up there with the worst.

"I'll do it," Adam says. He's obviously joking, he must be, but he looks serious and, when we laugh, his lips stiffen along with his shoulders. "Seriously. I said I'll do it."

"You don't have to," Abby says quietly, and he says, "It's fine."

That's when I get it. He's doing it to impress her.

"Okay," Naveen says. "We have a challenger. Do you want me to go over the rules?"

"No!" we all say at once, because the "rules" are burned into our brains. Every single year Naveen explains the impossible dare. No one tries it—except this time, Adam does.

Adam starts marching deeper into the woods and we follow him until we can see the caravan through the trees. There's smoke blowing out of the top and the smeared square windows glow orange.

If you don't know, this is where One-Eyed Patrick lives. He doesn't actually have one eye. Well, he does. But he has another one, too. Not all nicknames are literal.

I look up at the trees above us and that's when I see them—hundreds of dolls' heads hanging from the branches. Every face staring back at us has a single eye and they are all a warning.

They mean stay away, beware of the owner, leave while you can. But we don't leave. We crouch in the bushes and stare at the rusty green caravan until Naveen whispers, "You know what to do."

Adam lets out the biggest sigh I've ever heard, then steps into the clearing.

He looks back at us and Naveen gives him a thumbs-up, but no one else is happy. This is a dumb dare and we should scatter, because Hayschurch only has one urban legend and this is it. One-Eyed Patrick.

Adam is about to knock on the door of the man who steals children. The one who hangs a new doll's head in the trees for every kid he takes. And here's one serving himself up because he's doing it for love, confirming my suspicion that love is really, incredibly stupid.

Adam steps nervously onto the first step, then the second, and even from here I can see his hand shake as he lifts it up then knocks.

The sound is heavy in the darkness, shocking the birds above us into flight, and Marcus mumbles, "This isn't good."

But you know what? I'm proud of Adam, because I like it when people shake things up. Marcus hasn't really done anything to impress Abby. He's just been Marcus. But Adam is trying something different. He's literally willing to get himself killed if it wins him a few points, so kudos for that.

I glance over at Abby and there's the faintest smile on her face; then it gets swallowed by her fear because Adam looks back at us, shrugs, and lifts his hand to knock again.

"Shit," Naveen mumbles. "He's got guts."

Then the door swings open and Adam falls backward onto his ass. A figure stands over him and shouts "Will you kids stop bother-

ing me!" and the woods vibrate with the noise. Something cold shoots up my back and I'm thinking: This is why no one's ever done the dare.

The Snappers aren't real. They're just my friends cracking twigs in the dark. But One-Eyed Patrick is real . . . and he's pissed.

Adam jumps up and darts past us without stopping. It's less cowardly than it seems. As far as the angry dude in the woods is concerned, there's only one kid dumb enough to bother him and that kid has bolted. So, we sit in silence until the caravan door clanks shut, then slowly sneak away.

We find Adam back in the clearing, sitting on a tree stump with his head in his hands. When we get closer, he looks up with this weird smile on his face and says, "I did it."

Naveen slaps him on the back and says, "That was awesome," and Marcus nods, which is basically his version of a two-minute hug with both arms. Abby whispers something that makes Adam blush but I hang back because, honestly, someone needs to keep his ego in check.

It's nights like this that can turn underdogs into dickheads.

"He was angry," Naveen says, dragging out the last word before doing a little jig in the clearing. He's hyped because that's what fear does to you. When you're in it, it smothers you but, if you're lucky enough to escape, it makes you feel brave enough to be stupid.

I can see it before it happens. Naveen wants a piece of this, so he unzips his bag, pulls out a pack of eggs, and says, "Let's go back."

"No, thank you," I say, but Adam nods and Abby follows him and Marcus follows Abby, so I tag along because they've basically given me no choice.

Naveen hands out the eggs, then throws one at the caravan. The thud sends more animals skittering into the shadows just as the door crashes open and Patrick's silhouette swallows the light.

Adam stands, chucks his egg, then ducks as it strikes the metal, while Naveen stifles a laugh. Then Patrick stomps down the steps and stares at the yolk dripping down the outside of his home.

He turns and stares straight at us, rage roaring in his eyes, and then he marches forward.

"Shit," Marcus whispers, and Naveen says, "Run."

Everything is a blur as we bound into the shadows. The noises are scratches in my ears and my heart pounds like a drill, but I don't stop.

"I'll kill you!" Patrick shouts, and I believe him because that's what bogeymen do. I've heard the campfire stories. I've seen the movies. So, I run and I run and I run.

I smash headlong into a tree, the air knocked out of me as I stumble backward and fall, something sharp poking into my leg as I hit the ground.

"Come back here!"

The angry voice in the darkness forces me to my feet until I'm climbing, higher and higher into the sky. The mask slips from my fingers and I watch it float toward the ground.

Then I stop . . . and I listen.

Even up here, the crunch of the leaves below feels like someone twisting my insides in their fist.

"Why won't you leave me alone?!" Patrick yells, but no one answers.

Where are my friends hiding? Or are they still running? My legs feel like they're on fire as I try to get comfortable without making a sound.

I can see the top of his head as he slowly stomps back and forth like he's sniffing me out. Then his eyes shoot up and he says, "Bingo."

He's climbing after me and I try to pull myself higher but there's nowhere to go.

I move to the edge of the branch and think about jumping. I kick out at his hands as they move closer and he laughs. Then his foot slips and his hand flails for something that's not there.

I see his face the moment before he falls, the anger in his eyes replaced by horror, and then he's back on the ground, his limbs twisted, the light in those eyes blown out.

Covering Your Tracks

Hope shrugs and says, "So now you know."

After a story like that, I'd expect her to look sad, but she looks proud. Her stare is ice-cold. She was never fragile, I realize. And yet, there's something further back—a glimmer of who she's always been to me.

I turn to Elisha, hoping she knows how to respond. But her mouth is hanging open and I imagine tiny question marks swimming in her eyes.

Mom touches my hand, her skin so cold I pull back, and says, "I'm so sorry, Sam."

"You killed someone."

"No!"

The word comes from everywhere at once—my parents, Marcus, Naveen, and Hope.

"We didn't kill anyone," Dad says. "He was chasing Hope and he fell."

"So, what did you do next?" Elisha asks.

Anger is coming off her in waves.

Quietly, Marcus says, "We didn't do anything. We were scared."

"So, you didn't help," Elisha says, and her dad whispers, "It was too late for that."

He looks ashamed. They all do. But that's not enough. The blood-filled eggs, the dolls' heads, the messages.

Whose secrets can you see?

We all fall together.

I've spent weeks thinking *I'm* the reason for this, but we're just collateral. Sasha didn't want us. She was using us to get to *them.*

I pull the photograph out of my pocket and throw it into the space between us. It flutters to the ground and lands faceup, and my father slowly crouches and stares until Naveen asks, "What is it?"

Dad stands and shows them, then says, "How long have you had this?"

"Long enough to know you were involved," I reply, and then, turning to Dom's mom: "What happened to the mask?"

Hope touches her face, like she's remembering it; then she shakes her head and says, "I lost it in the woods that night."

"Well, now it's back," I spit, watching every word hit my parents like bullets. "People wearing that mask have been tormenting us for weeks."

Marcus stares into the starless sky. Then he shakes his head, like he's having a silent conversation with himself, and says, "I told you he wasn't dead."

"You think One-Eyed Patrick is terrorizing our kids?"

Hope says with a smile, and Marcus says, "Who else would it be?"

"He was dead," my mom says at last, but Dad says slowly, "They never found a body."

"You know why that is," Mom replies. "No one reported him missing. They left the weirdo in the woods to himself and there are enough animals in there to . . ."

Tears pool in my mother's eyes as she steps into Dad's embrace. She says something indistinct against his chest.

Naveen steps toward me. He looks desperate and I feel guilty that we're hearing this before Haran, waiting patiently in the car with Molly. What kind of a twisted dinner table chat is that going to be?

"We were scared, Sam. We spent months waiting for someone to find the body but they never did and . . . eventually . . . things got easier. I've never forgotten but, at some point, you have to move on. We were fifteen. We did something stupid. But it wasn't our fault that he fell."

They truly believe that. They think they're innocent just because no one pushed him. But he only fell because he was up there. And he was only up there because of them. They could have helped him, could have called an ambulance. Now someone is getting revenge—on all of us.

"We've been followed and filmed and blackmailed and scared by this creep," I say. "So, what are you going to do about it?"

They look at each other and I can see hundreds of silent words pass between them. Then Dad says, "We'll deal with it our way."

"If we call the police—" I start.

Mom says, "If we call the police, we tell them we're guilty of murder. What happens to Molly? What happens to you?"

"Whoever is doing this broke into our house and scratched my sister's face out of every picture. Do you really think they'll stop there? They were in her *room,* Mom!"

I can feel it rising—my sadness and shock and horror—but I don't try to stop it. I let it wash over me until I'm crying hard and loud.

"They won't stop," I say, and Dad pulls me into a hug that I fight, his arms tensing, his own tears merging with mine until, eventually, I'm done fighting. I sag against him, spent.

"We know how serious it is now," Dad whispers. "I'm sorry you had to go through that but, I promise, we'll stop him. Whoever this is."

"Them," I reply, thinking back to the night we were followed by the car. "There are three of them. At least."

There's silence. Then Dad steps back and looks at his friends. Mom takes Elisha's and my hands in hers and says, "Well, there are a lot more of us."

Aftermath

Where's your sister?" Mom asks, like it's literally just entered her mind.

"She's waiting with Haran in the car," I reply, and Naveen looks worried as he says, "Haran's here?"

I nod, then watch Naveen's face rearrange a hundred different ways as he tries to figure out what he's going to tell his son.

"We'll drive you home," Dad says, and I say, "No. I'll go with Molly. We'll meet you there."

They don't argue because they can't. They've lied to us for too long. They've put us in danger and I won't let that happen again. I'll keep my sister close until I figure out what the hell is happening and, more importantly, how we're going to stop it.

I take Elisha's hand so we can talk in private. Then I say, "Thank you for following your dad."

She looks like she's going to burst into tears before she

composes herself and says, "When you don't . . . sometimes they never come back."

There's the gap in a door Elisha has never opened before; not with me, anyway. She's talking about her mother. But, just as quickly, she slams that door shut, because Marcus walks past and mutters, "Let's go."

"I'll drive myself home," she replies, and he says, "We'll come back for your car tomorrow."

If I couldn't see his face, it would sound like an order. But Marcus is pleading with her. He's already had to rebuild his family once. If he loses Elisha as well, it will be beyond repair.

At least this is the night Simone stays at her aunt's house. Elisha and Marcus have a lot to talk through. We all do. And yet, everything feels like such a mess, and I want to go with Molly, Elisha, and Haran, meet up with Dom and Lauren, and figure this out on our own.

This isn't my fault. None of it. This is *their* fault—with a secret so big it could crush us all.

They were good at keeping it. I'll give them that. But I've learned that secrets can come back from the dead no matter how deep you bury them.

Hope walks over to me, that cocky smile still on her face, and I can suddenly see a lot of Dom in her. I thought he took after Steve—I was wrong.

"I admire you for wanting to protect your family," she says, "and mine."

I glare at her until she looks back at her former friends and says, "I didn't kill him. But I watched him die. I've always felt guilty for that."

"Good for you."

Hope chuckles, steps closer, and whispers, "This is how I

cope now. I've tried a lot of things down the years, Sam. Some traditional, some not. And this works for me."

She holds my stare until Mom comes over and says, "We're leaving."

I walk to the car. Molly is fast asleep and Haran is wide-eyed.

"What happened?" Haran asks, and when I turn, his dad is lurking awkwardly behind. "Dad?"

"We've got some things to discuss," Naveen says, and Haran tilts his head at me, but how can I fill him in?

Instead, I say, "I'll see you tomorrow."

I sit in the car, watching Molly snoring in the back as Haran and Naveen walk off.

I don't want to go home, but where else is there? My sister murmurs something and I wonder what she's dreaming. Then I think of the last time we carried her out of the car, when the ghost from my parents' past was creeping through our house.

There's still so much I don't know. Is it really Patrick who's doing this? Some strange man from the woods who waited two decades to get his revenge? Or is it someone else, seeking revenge on his behalf? Because three people marched toward our car that night, all wearing copies of the mask Hope created for that one fateful Halloween, twenty-four years ago.

I think of Dom and Lauren, because they were the only ones not here tonight. It was *their* Dark Place, *their* party, *their* home, and, as it turns out, it was all because of *their* mother.

Remember Me?

Our house is cold and tense and my head aches from lack of sleep. Only Molly brings any warmth, temporarily defrosting whatever room she's in or whatever chat she instigates. Then she leaves and the chill returns to my body.

All morning, our parents watch me, uncertainty on their faces and doubt in their words. They are desperate to make this better, but I'm in no mood to help.

I *want* them to feel bad.

I message Elisha—*Are you okay?*—and her typing starts and stops over and over before, finally, she replies—*I'm fine. I need some space from Dad though. I'm going to escape as soon as he stops apologizing.*

I'll come over whenever you need me, I write back, and she says, *I need to be alone for a while. Clear my head. I just need air.*

I wonder what things are like over at her house. Marcus is a big talker, Elisha says. So, I can imagine he's trying to repair things before they spiral out of control, sitting down with her and talking it through.

It's the complete opposite of this house—Mom and Dad tiptoeing around me, their shame coming off them in waves.

Of everyone, I can imagine Haran and his dad making up first. Naveen was the only person who looked truly sorry for what they'd done. Everyone else looked scared that they'd been caught. Everyone except Hope, who seemed to be enjoying it.

What has she told Dom and Lauren, if anything? Dom hasn't messaged me—and I haven't contacted him because I don't know what to say. And what does Steve know? Does he still think his wife is timid and helpful? Has she been lying to him most of all?

I keep thinking about what Hope said about coping—how she'd tried so many things and settled on "this" to keep the guilt at bay. Is she playing a villain because she feels like one?

In a way, I understand that. I felt guilty for Dad's scars for so long that I've changed how I look at them. I used to stare at his flame-ravaged skin until my head pounded and my heart screamed. Now I see the scars but distance myself from the memory of what happened.

Hope watched a man fall to his death, then smiled as she told us the story.

But she was only a kid, I think. Just a couple of years older than I was when I let our house burn around me.

My phone vibrates and I grab it without thinking. When I see Sasha's profile picture, my throat fills with sharp bile, and I swallow it down, then compose myself.

There is no video this time, no sound effects. Just an address, a name, and an order.

Nightingale House. Do you know Patrick Whyte? Come alone.

I know Nightingale House. It's the old people's home on the edge of town.

Do you know Patrick Whyte?

One-Eyed Patrick.

I google "Patrick Whyte Hayschurch" and there's nothing.

There is no evidence that anyone with that name ever lived here, so I try something different—"One-Eyed Patrick Hayschurch."

Again, a dead end. If it was an urban legend around here, no one was talking about it online.

I read the message over and over, searching for a hidden clue that clearly isn't there. If I want to know the truth, I need to do as Sasha says. Last time I did that, I ended up shoplifting. But what choice do I have?

Come alone. I could ignore that part, but something tells me she has eyes everywhere. Why else is she messaging me now, just hours after my parents came clean?

And what happens if I *do* bring someone with me? Call me paranoid, but I don't want to find out.

Molly is watching TV in the living room while Mom sits in the kitchen with her laptop. I don't know where Dad is and I don't ask.

I open the front door as quietly as I can and leave without saying goodbye. It feels good being out of there, even if I have no idea what I'm heading into.

The air is crisp, but it's the nice kind of cold; the kind you can enjoy rather than endure. I reach for the car handle, then stop, because I suddenly feel safer in the open. Besides, the address Sasha sent me is only a few minutes away.

At the bottom of the hill that leads out of town, between

a newsstand and a fast-food place, is Nightingale House, its gold gates and polished sign glistening in the December sun.

I remember how hard it was to get into the slaughterhouse as I walk up the pebbled path and into their reception.

The lady behind the desk smiles and says, "Hello. How can I help?"

"Patrick Whyte?" I say, unable to hide the doubt in my voice.

The woman's face lights up as she says, "Really? Wonderful. He doesn't get many visitors. How are you related?"

I stutter and the lady's brow creases. Then the words fall out before I can stop them. "We're not related. Patrick was friends with my grandpa."

The lie sticks in my stomach.

"Excellent," she says. "If you can please sign in, then I'll take you through. Just so you know, Patrick's memory isn't what it was. And like I say, he doesn't see many people. But your visit will mean a lot to him."

I stare down at the paper and write a name: *Isiah Craven*. Then the receptionist pulls off a visitor sticker and I press it against my coat.

"Right this way," she says, and I follow her down a long corridor with doors as far as I can see.

I flash back to when we visited Grandpa in the hospital, all the rooms we passed that I tried so hard not to look into; all the other patients and their families having private moments in public spaces.

Just like then, my eyes are drawn to the open doors. Some of the residents smile at me, some stare into the distance or call me other people's names. A few are lost in the television or their own thoughts, but the farther we get, the more I can see the difference—between those who see me and those who don't.

How many worlds are in this place? How many stories that I'll never know? That's how I felt after Grandpa died, when we were clearing out his things and I saw parts of a life that he'd never talked about.

When I mentioned it to Mom, she said, "You didn't ask."

Then slowly, reluctantly, she revealed all the times he'd fought for me; all the arguments he'd had with her and Dad, about a show he knew I hated and a life that wasn't mine.

The receptionist knocks on a door and sings, "Patrick. You have a visitor."

She gestures for me to go in, but my legs feel stiff and she smiles and says, "You'll be fine."

"Thank you," I say, my throat dry and my heart pounding. Then I walk in, imagining a room full of masks and severed dolls' heads when, in fact, it's only an old man lying in his bed.

"I'll leave you to it," the lady says. "If you need anything, you know where I am."

She's nice. But she's too trusting. I could be anyone. Although I guess you could say the same about the person I'm looking at.

I stand a few feet away from him, listening as his breathing rattles through his chest. He is gaunt, his skin almost see-through, and it scares me to look at him for too long.

I shouldn't be here. And yet, it's exactly where Sasha wants me to be.

The radio plays softly in the background and, when I focus, I can hear the sixties and seventies tunes that filled my grandparents' house every Sunday.

I edge closer, each step a dare that feels harder than the last.

But Patrick Whyte doesn't move a muscle. If this is the man my parents thought they'd killed twenty-four years ago, he can't hurt them now.

"I'm Sam," I say. "It's nice to meet you."

I pull the seat closer to his bed and sit. Then his head moves slowly to the side until he's facing me.

What do I do now? Do I just come out and say it? *Are you One-Eyed Patrick? Did kids used to torment you in the woods? Did you come back from the dead?*

His eyes look strange, like the bulbs inside have blown. And there's something else—a fear, like when Molly was younger and she couldn't find us. Even when she had, for a moment there was a terror that slowly faded. But Patrick's terror sits like a curtain over his stare.

He looks lost, and I imagine touching his hand, because Mom said sometimes that's enough. But I didn't touch Grandpa at the end and I don't touch this man, either. Instead, I lean in and whisper, "I'm sorry for what happened that night. It was Halloween, do you remember? I'm sorry."

There's a moment of focus in his eyes that sends me backward in my chair. Then it's gone just as fast.

"Everything okay in here?"

I turn and the receptionist is back. Maybe she's not as trusting as I first thought.

"Fine," I say. "I don't really know what to say but . . ."

And then I see something.

I quickly stand and walk over to the chest of drawers, then point at the photograph staring back at me. "Who's that?"

The lady looks suspicious, because surely I should know that, if I know Patrick. But I don't care if my story falls apart now. I just need to know who's in the only framed picture in this room.

"That's Patrick's daughter," the receptionist says. "Katherine."

I stare at the image, of the man who looks nothing like the person fighting for every breath behind me and the girl next to him. She's younger, probably mid-teens, and her hair is a few shades lighter, but it's unmistakable. Her smile is exactly the same—nervous and half formed; a reluctant kind of happy.

"Malika was right," I whisper, and the receptionist says, "Excuse me?"

"I have to go. But thank you. And Patrick—I'm so sorry."

Then I turn. I rush past all the open doors and the front desk, not stopping until I'm out of the gates and back on the street.

Only then do I call Elisha, desperate for her to pick up.

Her phone rings and rings. When it goes to voicemail, I say, "One-Eyed Patrick is still alive and he has a daughter. We've met her, Lish. We literally sat in the same room as her. Call me when you get this."

Then I crouch on the sidewalk with my head in my hands and think back to that day at the slaughterhouse. A woman in a smart suit, an uncertain smile, a neat haircut. Wary but pleasant.

Kat Murphy—that's what she called herself.

I thought we'd tricked her into giving us that place's secrets, into telling us everything she knew.

But she's been playing us since the beginning.

So Close

need to get home as soon as possible. Patrick is alive, which means my parents didn't kill anyone. Once they realize that, we can tell the police what's been going on and no one else needs to get hurt.

Mom and Dad have been carrying this guilt around with them for more than two decades and it was all for nothing.

Kat is involved—she has to be. I don't know why. But that can wait. Telling my parents can't.

I start to jog, then to run.

My phone vibrates and I'm relieved to see Elisha's name on the screen.

"Hey," I say. "Did you get my voicemail?"

"I did," someone says, but it's not my girlfriend.

"Who is this?" I ask, and the voice breaks in and out as it says, "I think you know . . . pretty clever . . . but . . ."

"Hello? Hello? Elisha?"

The line goes dead and, when I call back, it goes straight to voicemail again.

As I start typing out a message, I can see her phone is doing the same so I stop and wait. A picture message comes through.

Elisha is in the Dark Place, her hands tied, candles lit all around her.

And the caption.

I think it's time we heard your girlfriend's secret, don't you? You know the drill. Don't. Tell. Anyone.

I start typing: *If you hurt her . . .* but even the thought sends panic crashing through my skull. Instead, I sprint home as fast as I can.

I'm done with this. No more games. No more doing Sasha's bidding. I'm telling my parents and we can rain ten tons of crap down on Kat and her twisted friends.

My legs are burning and a stitch cuts deep into my side but I keep going. I run until I see my house. The phone rings. I answer it, gasping for breath. If I can stall them, I can buy some time.

They speak before I do. "I'd stop right there if I were you."

I stop dead. I can see my house. Someone is standing outside the front door with the mask on.

If I want to get to my family, I need to get past them. But that's not even a challenge. I march toward the figure, ready to kick the shit out of them. I'm not afraid anymore. Or maybe that's all I am. Maybe there's so much fear inside me that it's turned to anger.

The voice says, "We got into your house once and we can do it again. If you want to make sure your sister is safe, do as you're told. Come straight here . . . and don't tell anyone."

I take two more steps forward before the voice says, "This is your final warning, Sam."

It's not until they've hung up that I realize it's a different voice. And a different number.

The reception is always bad in the woods. That's where the first call must have been made. But this one came from somewhere else. The initial voice could well have been Kat's, whereas the second was much deeper—stirring a distant memory that I can't quite reach.

I know that voice. I just don't know where from.

I stare at the masked figure in front of me and wonder how many there are. I could still take this one out. But can I risk someone hurting Molly? Especially when Elisha might be running out of time.

I go to the car and pull out my keys, then I creep away as the figure watches me.

I drive as calmly as I can, ignoring the voice that is screaming at me to go faster. As I approach Dom's place, I make a decision. This is the quickest way to the Dark Place, and every second counts, so I pull into his drive, then run straight down his garden and into the woods.

I charge deeper into the trees, desperately trying to pull a plan from my panic. But I'm in the clearing before I know it, opening the door to the Dark Place and staring at Elisha, a dirty rag stuffed deep into her mouth.

"I'm sorry," I say. "I'm so sorry."

She makes a noise when I reach out to help her; then her eyes go even wider as she's cast in shadow and something hard smashes against my skull.

The End

Slices of light and slivers of sound flash through my head as the woods slowly come back into view.

Something sharp digs into my wrists, and when I look down, I see my hands are tied together, blood creeping out and dropping on the leaves at my tethered feet.

"Wakey-wakey," someone says.

I stare at Kat and she looks nothing like the woman who told us about the slaughterhouse. That woman was kind, polite, almost nervous. But it was all an act, because fury now fills her face, her eyes dark, her voice taunting.

"So, you met my father," she says with a horrible grin. "He doesn't say much these days but I hope you got along."

She's almost snarling at me, like a tiger eyeing its prey, and I look past her, at the closed Dark Place door.

Kat follows my gaze and says, "Don't worry. She hasn't gone anywhere yet. But I think we should talk first. The villain always has to say their piece, after all. That's what happens in the movies, right? I know Haran's a fan."

"Fuck you."

Kat's laugh echoes through the trees, her contempt briefly replaced with a twisted kind of joy, before it snaps back.

"Oh, Sam. You were much more polite last time we met. I bet you're kicking yourself now. You were so close that day to some real answers and you walked away."

"Why are you doing this?"

Kat nods and moves closer. "Yes, of course. The explanation. That's why you're here, isn't it? Sure, you want to keep your sister safe and try to save your girlfriend but that's what's *really* eating you up. *Why.* Why did your silly little secrets get my attention? Why did I screw with you?"

I let the silence sit between us because it's all I can control. She looks down at my hands as I try to loosen the rope and says, "That won't work. Movies have lied to you, Sam. Real people don't escape situations like this."

She stares up at the few patches of sky and lets out a deep breath. Then she crouches next to me and says, "I'll tell you why. Revenge for what your parents did to my father."

"My parents didn't kill anyone."

"Technically, that's right, Sam. Your parents and their friends might not have killed my father, but they sure did a number on him. Do you know how it feels to live out here, to worry every single time you hear a voice in case it's someone coming to torment you? That was our life for years.

"He put those dolls' heads up to keep people away but it did the opposite. It drew them in. He made himself into the bogeyman and I had to live with that.

"When someone knocks on your door, who is it? The

postman? Your neighbor? When someone knocked on *our* door, it was a trick, a dare. I was frightened all the time, Sam. Do you know what that's like? I hope you do now, a little bit.

"I was sixteen when it happened. Old enough to fight back, right? Old enough to come out instead of him and scare those assholes away? Wrong. I was terrified because he'd *made* me that way. I never went to school. I never went *anywhere*. My father taught me everything I knew, and his most important lesson was that the world is a dangerous place. So, I hid.

"You parents might not have killed my father that night, but they broke him all the same. He was different afterward. They tormented him. A man who wasn't hurting anyone. He chased them and he fell and they left him for dead. I watched them do it. I watched my father lying there and I thought I'd lost him forever. That's not a nice feeling, Sam. In fact, it's really fucking horrible.

"When I was sure those kids had left, I went to him. I put my fingers against his neck and I felt the tiniest pulse and heard the faintest breath. Somehow, I dragged him back to the caravan and cared for him. I didn't call a doctor. I didn't ask for help. Because *your* parents and *their* friends proved what he'd always told me. It was us against the world and that world was a nasty place."

A single tear creeps down Kat's cheek. I hold her stare and say, "What my parents did was wrong. I can't imagine how you felt."

"No," Kat whispers, "you can't."

She pulls a box of matches from her pocket and lays it on the ground between us.

"Hope," she says. "That's the name of the girl my dad chased up a tree. But you know that now. You know everything, right?

Well, not quite everything. Did you know that Hope was the one who invented the Dark Place? She felt so guilty about my father that she came into these woods every single week and confessed, over and over again. I followed her. I found out where she lived and I watched from the shadows, even when Dad was 'better' again.

"Although he never was better, you know. Never quite himself. He'd forget things sometimes, and he'd get so angry over nothing at all, because when you fall that far, there are a lot of things that can break."

I picture the man lying in Nightingale House, and as if she can sense it, Kat says, "You saw him, didn't you. How old do you think he is? Eighty? Ninety? He's sixty-one. But time doesn't work the same for all of us."

"I'm sorry," I say. "I know it doesn't mean anything, but I am."

"But would you be if you and your girlfriend weren't tied up?"

I nod and Kat laughs.

"Yes, I think you would. You like feeling guilty, don't you? I *do* know your secrets, after all. You made it a bit too easy for me, coming here every Halloween and whispering all the shitty things you'd done."

I swallow. "You were watching us, all those years?"

"I never stopped watching, Sam. I wanted to hurt Hope and all her friends the way they'd hurt me—by going after their families. I guess you could call it a long-term project. Why do you think I took that job at the slaughterhouse? I needed to stay local. I waited until I knew enough. This year, I decided I had enough to get started—turning all your little secrets into something bigger. I knew your little gang would fall apart once I showed you all how you'd betrayed each other.

"Dom made it so easy—he recorded every word. I could listen, even when I couldn't get close. Haran sold that photo, Dom's spent a third of his life thinking he burned your house down, you hid your secret from them."

I lift my head. "Elisha didn't betray me." I know that much is true.

Kat's smile falters. "Elisha doesn't care about you enough to betray you. All she really cares about is her family."

"That's fine," I say, and Kat says, "Bullshit. Family means a lot to you, too. But you still love Elisha. I've known for a long time that she makes the perfect ending. That's what today is, Sam. The end."

"Where are the others?" I ask. "I know you're not doing this alone."

Kat looks proud and says, "We all have our secrets."

"Are they here?"

She shakes her head. "I'm sure you're desperate to know who they are, but the truth is, it wasn't hard to get people to help me. Dom made a lot of people cry over the years. It was easy finding a few who wanted revenge. But they're gone now, Sam. What I have planned is a bit extreme for their tastes."

What the hell does that mean? I wrestle harder against the ropes around my wrists and my ankles and Kat says, "I'll decide when you're free. When are you going to realize that?"

She picks the matches up and walks over to the Dark Place; then she lights one and watches the flame flare and fade.

"It's funny how something so small can destroy so much," she says. "You let your house burn and your dad suffer . . . all because you wanted a fresh start. You must have felt terrible. That's not something any child should feel. I understand. Like I said, it's a horrible world sometimes."

I fight with everything I have to break free, but the rope is thick and more blood oozes down my wrists. She crouches next to me, stares me out, then whispers, "Have you seen Patrick?" The words smack me hard between the eyes.

Her grin is toxic, because she knows I remember. The girl who spoke to me at the party. She was wearing the mask, and yet it was so close to my face, surrounded by so many other costumes, that I focused on her jet-black contact lenses staring into my soul.

"I said you'd find him," Kat spits. "You got there eventually."

Kat stands and opens the door to the Dark Place and Elisha stares out at me. She's so afraid, and I hate myself for ever bringing her here.

"Here's the thing," Kat says. "I could pull the rag out of her mouth and ask her to tell you her secret but she won't. That's partly because she's ashamed and partly because she hates me. That's fine. I deserve it. But we don't have unlimited time here, so I'll fill in the blanks."

Kat likes to talk. She's been lonely a long time, I think, and now she gets to tell her story. That's my only hope: that, eventually, someone will stumble across us. But that doesn't happen here. We chose this place because it's secluded, far from the walking trails and dog tracks. The perfect place to leave your secrets is also the ideal place for Kat to finally tell her truth.

"Elisha's mom abandoned her. That's sad. But what your girlfriend has never told anyone is that *she* saw it coming.

That's her big secret. The same confession ... every year you forced her to come here."

I focus on Elisha, trying to communicate how sorry I am with my eyes. But hers are full of tears as she stares at the ground.

"Mommy had an affair, didn't she? And you caught her in the act. Thirteen-year-old Elisha watched her mother with another man and she didn't say a word. You could have challenged her. You could have told your father. But you stayed so quiet, you pretended so well, that your mom had no idea that you knew. And then she left."

Tears are streaming down Elisha's face now and I want to wrap her in my arms and tell her everything is okay, but it isn't. Everything's fucked.

"She thought telling her dad would make things worse. She thought *that's* what would break up her family. You were trying to buy him time. It's ironic that you gave your mother the time to fall in love and run away without a word."

Kat shrugs and says, "As far as secrets go, it's not bad. But that's your problem, guys. You don't communicate.

"So, there you have it. My origin story and your girlfriend's dirty laundry. Nice to have things out in the open at last, isn't it? There's only one thing left to do."

Kat pulls the rag from Elisha's mouth, lights another match and tosses it into the Dark Place, then another, and another, until the flames start to stretch and curl. Then she closes the door, kneels next to me, and whispers, "Now she can disappear like her mother."

Everything Burns

Elisha's terror fills the woods, sending birds scattering
from the trees and echoing in its deepest, darkest corners.
Kat stands deathly still, listening, and I want to tear her
apart. There's only one reason she took the rag out of Elisha's
mouth, and that's to hear her screams.

But I'm screaming, too. Yelling as loud as I can for help.
Hoping against hope that someone, anyone, is out there.

Kat grabs my chin and twists my face to hers. "It wasn't
Hope who destroyed my family. It was your father. *He* was the
one who disturbed us that night. *He* knocked on our door.
And now he's going to pay."

"What are you talking about?"

"You've got a thing about fire, haven't you, Sam? That's
what the papers say. They think you burned your own house
down. Now they'll know for certain. Maybe this was a tragic
accident. Or maybe you were finishing the job."

Kat pulls a knife from her jacket and cuts the ropes around my ankles and my wrists. Then, in a flash, the blade is at my throat.

"Here's what's going to happen. You and Elisha are going to die in there and, when your parents find your ashes, they'll be ruined forever. There's more than one way to break a family."

The cold steel pierces my skin, and blood trickles down my neck. My body tenses and Kat snarls, "Don't even think about it. I'll kill you right here if I have to."

Smoke starts to creep out of the Dark Place, and Elisha's screams are replaced by hacking coughs.

Kat's breath is hot on my skin, and she edges closer to the hut, until all I can feel are the flames.

"In you go," she says, reaching for the door with a gloved hand.

Then something smashes into us from the side, the knife falls to the ground, and I see Dom staring into Kat's panicked eyes.

They disappear into the undergrowth and I jolt as someone else's hands touch mine.

"Are you okay?" Lauren says, and I shout, "The hut! Elisha's in there."

Lauren pulls the door open, her body smothered by the smoke before it drifts toward the sky. Then she's dragging Elisha out, pulling her free as the flames drape the walls and swallow the box where Dom hid his phone.

Lauren unties Elisha, who lies faceup in the leaves, panting at the patchwork clouds.

"We saw your car," Lauren says. "What happened here?" But I can't answer yet. There's something we still need to do.

I stand too fast and almost stumble, then try again, slower this time, focusing on each step until my head settles and my legs feel strong. Then I march into the woods, ready to finish this.

Except they aren't here. There's no noise, no disturbance; just the gentle bristle of the woods in the light—calm and welcoming.

I lift my foot and rest it as quietly as possible on the leaves below, but its crunch still fills my ears.

In movies people call out—so I stay silent. In movies they run toward danger—so I slow everything down.

Then I hear something to my right—a grunt and a crash— and I walk toward it. Kat has Dom pinned to the ground, something small and red in her hand. She raises her hand and brings it down and Dom screams in pain.

"Stop!" I shout, but she doesn't. She looks up at me while Dom sobs and holds his side.

"You don't need big knives," she says. "These are the real deal, Sam. It's like slicing through tissue paper."

I start to run, then stop as she holds the knife to Dom's throat.

"You were supposed to burn," Kat says, her eyes full of hate.

She lifts her arm. I launch myself at Kat just as she brings the knife down.

My shoulder strikes her chest, knocking her to the ground. I glance back at Dom but Kat is already up, the knife still in her hand, her face ablaze.

"I'll kill all of you if I have to," she says. "Come on, superstar."

She starts to circle me. I can hear Dom's labored breathing. The woods are spinning and I can't get my bearings.

Kat rolls the knife between her fingers and I imagine her draining all those eggs and refilling them with blood. "You still care about him . . . after what he did to you?"

"It was an accident," I say.

"Your parents would say the same about my father. But they'd be lying. You're a smart kid, aren't you, Sam? You know all about consequences. Cause and effect. They were the cause and this is the effect."

If I keep Kat here long enough, Lauren and Elisha can get help.

"I'm sorry about your dad," I say. "I'm sorry he was the town . . ."

"Crazy person? Is that what you were going to say? He was just a man trying to live his life. You have a house. We had a caravan. You have a street. We had these woods. That was it. Your parents and every other kid around here made him into a monster. They whispered about him around their campfires. They shouted at him in the street until he was too afraid to go shopping. They banged on that door and egged our home and he snapped.

"But he wasn't a bad person. He was gentle and loving and kind. And he would do anything to protect me.

"I couldn't protect *him* because I was scared. Well, I'm not scared now."

Kat marches forward and this is it. She's focused entirely on me and I brace myself as she lunges with the knife. I step back but the leaves are deep here and it feels like we're fighting in shallow water.

"Where are you going to go?" I ask. "You can't stay here after this. You won't see your father again."

Her brow creases as she says, "He knows that. I've said

goodbye," and then she leaps toward me, my back crashing into a tree, and her knife slashes my leg once, twice, as something warm and wet spreads inside my jeans.

This is it. This is how I die. There's no one to rescue me this time. My father isn't here to pull me from the fire, and I imagine me and Dom left in the woods, just like Patrick was.

Will Molly grow up to avenge me? Is Kat just creating another monster, the way our parents did when they went too far?

"Please. Don't hurt my sister," I say, as Kat holds the blade against my cheek. I feel pain, then warmth running down my cheek, and then—

Her whole body is cast in shadow as someone looms over us, the thick branch held high above her head, before it comes crashing down and everything goes black.

Saying Goodbye

There's too much blood. It's smeared over Dom's neck and his arms, and he wobbles as he tries to pull me up.

"It's okay," I say. "I'm okay."

"Liar," Dom says with a smile.

"Is she dead?"

He looks at Kat's limp body, then feels for a pulse. "I think so," he says.

"If Haran was here," I say, "he'd tell you they're never dead until they're dead."

Dom picks up the branch and, for a moment, I think he's going to hit her again. Instead, he staggers.

"We need to get you to a hospital," I say. "You're a mess."

"Have you seen yourself?" Dom replies. "Are you trying to steal my thunder?"

Our laughs hurt but they come anyway. Then I rip a strip

from my sweater and wrap it around Dom's torso as he bites through the pain.

"Do you think you can make it out of the woods?" I ask, and, with his other hand pressed hard against the wound, he says, "I'm not dead yet." But something strange happens to his eyes the moment before they roll back in his head and he slumps to the ground.

"Help!" I scream, over and over until my voice is raw and the word fills every inch of the woods.

White spots dance across my eyes and it feels like I'm drunk but that's not it, because everything's slowing down, stopping, over.

And I see Molly's smile and those amazing eyes. She's talking to me but I can't hear her. Whatever she's saying, she's happy, the joy on her face making the light around her glow.

She is running around the woods, giggling, and I'm chasing her, wrapping her up in a hug that turns into a twirl.

Her legs spin in front of me, and the trees become a hazy green blur. But we don't stop. We keep on spinning until the whole world is a swirl of colors and emotions and I don't think I've ever been happier.

"I love you, Sam," Molly says, the words suddenly clear, and I love her, too, with all my heart.

She only exists because of the fire—one accident forged from another—and I wouldn't have it any other way.

I would tell them now, if there were time. I would tell anyone who'd listen.

". . . Sam."

"It's all right, Molly."

"Sam? It's me."

The picture in front of me splinters and falls away until Elisha's face fills my vision.

"Hey," I say, and she kisses me and says, "Are you okay?"

Am I okay? I don't know. But I think I'm alive, which, to be honest, is more than I expected.

The woods are full of movement and voices, of strangers and friends. Someone's hands are on my body. I feel a mask fitted over my face. Through smeary plastic I see paramedics lifting Dom onto a stretcher and awkwardly carrying him through the trees, while others examine another body that lies still.

"Where does it hurt?" someone asks me, and the answer is "Everywhere." It hurts in my arms and my legs and my head and my heart. It hurts because this didn't need to happen.

So many things could have stopped it, including me, when I sat facing Kat in the slaughterhouse office and she acted like a completely different person. But before that, too. If my dad and his friends hadn't mistaken bullying for bravery that Halloween all those years ago, then none of this would have happened.

Kat wanted revenge for her broken father; a man who wasn't killed, but was forever changed, the day a bunch of loners tried too hard to be cool.

The same as us—sitting in the dark, telling our secrets to nothing and no one, turning an unhealthy obsession into a ceremony with a grandeur it didn't deserve.

The Dark Place is just ashes now. Maybe that's all it should be.

These thoughts spill out of me, falling among the dead leaves as I'm stretchered back to the path, and I want to tell

Elisha everything—I wish I had long ago. About the fire and my guilt about Dad's scars and what it really feels like to be a star with no desire to shine.

And I want to listen, as well, about her mother, and the decisions she sees as mistakes.

But that's not what happens. I'm carried into the ambulance. She watches as the doors close, and for a moment, I wonder if that's goodbye.

Visiting Hours

Mom and Dad sit on either side of my bed, each holding one of my hands.

I don't open my eyes right away. Instead, I listen to their whispers and smile at what I hear.

And then I cry, because I know what happens next.

"Sam," Mom says, "we're here, darling," and Dad whispers, "It's all right, son. It's over now."

Except, it's not. I still have to admit that their bad decisions pushed me into something I can never put right. I still need to tell them my truth.

But nurses hurry in and out and the sound of rickety wheels fills the corridor, so I sit on it for a bit longer.

"How's Dom?" I ask. "And Elisha?"

"They're okay," Dad replies. "It's a miracle that Elisha got out unharmed. And Dom will be fine. He just needs time to recover. You all do."

"Someone else wants to say hi," Mom says, and I see Molly standing in the doorway.

She sways on the spot, uncertainty clouding her face. I think back to when Grandpa passed away and I refused to leave the corner. Then I hold my hand out and wait for her to take it.

Eventually, she steps forward, the tip of one finger brushing mine, and mumbles, "What happened to your face?"

I reach up and touch the bandage, then wonder what state my leg is in, before saying, "I got hurt. The doctors fixed me. They're good at that."

The scar on Dad's right arm reddens as he rubs it, and I think of all the times we've been here.

The best time was when my sister was born—the tiny bundle of perfection that transformed everything.

The worst time was after the fire—Dad's arms hidden under layers of white, Mom's happiness turned to ash, me on crutches by the doorway knowing that, in spite of everything, this was not what I had wanted.

And now there's this—something I can't fully process yet. I hope, eventually, it's something good, or, at the very least, not bad. Because Kat is gone, my family is safe, and all we need is time to heal.

To heal, first you need to hurt. That's why I wait for hours, until the nurses and doctors have been and gone and Molly is dozing on the chair in the corner, and then I take my parents' hands again and say, "I've got something to tell you."

This is a script I know by heart; one I've only ever said in the dark. I close my eyes and reach for the first stubborn sounds, pulling them from the shadows until I look into Mom and Dad's faces and whisper, "I'm sorry."

"What could you possibly be sorry for?" Mom asks. "We're the ones who messed up. We put you and your sister at risk and I'll never forgive myself for that."

I watch them shrinking deeper into themselves—these two broken people who have lived with their guilt for two decades—and I love them.

I love them and I need them because, no matter how hard I stare at their hollowed-out faces, I can't see a reason to blame them anymore.

"I guess," I say, "the only way to free yourself from your darkest secrets is to bring them into the light."

And then I tell them everything.

Revenge

On my first day home from the hospital, Mom knocks on my bedroom door and says, "Look who's here."

Elisha.

My mother stands for a few awkward seconds, has a couple of false starts, then mumbles, "I'll leave you to it."

"Hey," I say. "I wasn't sure if you'd come."

Elisha sits on my desk chair, twisting slowly back and forth. Neither of us speaks for a long time, even though there is so much to say.

Eventually, she stares at me and says, "Did you have nightmares? After your fire?"

I sit up as best as I can and say, "I still do."

I desperately want to help her through this, and the best way to do that is by being honest.

"I knew I was going to die," Elisha says. "I didn't *think* it. I *knew* it. I was so scared, Sam."

"I'm sorry."

"I never wanted to be a part of the Dark Place," she whispers. "I know I put something in there but I didn't . . . get any relief from it. Not like the rest of you. I did it because it was your big deal. But you know what . . . *I* wanted to be your big deal."

"You were," I say, but I see it through her eyes—the importance I put on that tiny hut, the way I lived so much of my life for just one day a year. I know my words sound hollow.

I get it now. Maybe it's because of my parents' love story, or perhaps it's because I'm a fool, but I thought Elisha and I were more than we were, even when all the evidence was proving me wrong.

"I loved being with you, Sam. I loved *you*. But . . ."

"Not anymore."

She stands and pulls something from her pocket. "I've brought you a present."

The cell Elisha places in my hand is old and dirty—like one of those burner phones you see on TV.

"There's only one message," she says, "but I think you should read it."

"Whose is this?"

"It was Kat's. I picked it up that day . . . before the police could."

"This is evidence."

Elisha nods and says, "Exactly."

I flip open the phone and select Messages. She's right, there's only one, sent on the day Kat almost burned Elisha alive in the Dark Place.

I made the call. He's on his way.

"She must have deleted every text that came in," Elisha

says. "Covering her tracks as she went along. But not this one. I guess she was too busy with me. Or maybe she didn't care by then."

I stare at the name above the message. Not a name. Just a letter. *D.*

My stomach turns as I think back to the second call I got that day, from the voice that stirred a memory I couldn't quite touch. Then I dial the number on Kat's phone and wait.

Elisha and I stare at each other while it rings, and then, in a quiet, uncertain voice, someone says, "Hello?"

"Dylan?"

The line goes dead instantly, but I know. The boy I accused of leaking my photo all those years ago, the friend that Haran let take the fall, was one of Kat's helpers. And I don't think I can blame him.

Final Confessions

The five of us stand in the clearing, staring at the space where the Dark Place once stood.

A lone strand of police tape rustles in the breeze, until Haran pulls it free from the bush it's snagged on and tucks it in his pocket.

When he sees my face, he shrugs and says, "A memento."

I guess we have different ways of dealing with this. Some want to forget, while others are happy to remember.

Even now the air is smoky, but maybe that's my imagination. Perhaps I'm destined to never shake the smell of fire.

I look at Elisha and she nods then looks away. It was her idea to come, even after everything. "You need this," she'd said, "all of you."

Sunlight dapples the ground beneath the twisted elms, so I walk over and sit in its patterns. This seems like a good place for what we're about to do—so much better than crouching in the charred remains of a mistake.

"I let my house burn," I say. "I woke up and the fire had already started. But I still had time to run, to raise the alarm. I was so sick of the show ... and my dad's demands ... and feeling like somebody I wasn't ... so I didn't. I didn't raise the alarm. I didn't run. I wanted *Future Force* to end but I almost destroyed everything."

I expected it to come out in a whisper, like it did at the hospital, but this time it bursts free in a shout.

My friends all keep their eyes to the ground as I say, "My dad's scars are my fault. My mom's heartbreak is my fault. The fact that our house has such horrible memories is my fault. If I'd been quicker ... if I hadn't stood there watching my script burn ... maybe the firefighters could have saved everything."

Haran's hand rests on my knee, his silent sign that he's here for me, and a wave of happiness surges over my skin because I need him. I need all of them.

"I betrayed my best friend," he says. "I sold a photo knowing what it would do to him and I did it because I needed the cash. I didn't tell him the truth. And I couldn't hate myself any more if I wanted to."

I put my hand on his and squeeze, and then he turns to me and says, "Are we cool?"

"Of course."

"I did something terrible," Dom says, his voice cracking as his body slumps further toward the ground. "I knew that something was wrong at your house that day and I did nothing about it. I shut the door and I ran away."

"You were a kid," I say. "We all were."

"It doesn't make it better," Dom says.

No, I think, *it doesn't.* But I understand guilt. I know what it can do to you when you carry it on your own. It grows and grows and gets heavier and heavier, but you never drop it. You fight on, your soul cracking under its weight until everything good in your world slips through those cracks.

I rest my other hand on Dom's shoulder, and his body hums like wire. But I don't let go. I stay beside my two best friends because what else is there?

Dom saved my life that day in the woods. He saw my car in his driveway and knew something was wrong. He had no idea he was walking into a showdown with a monster, but without him and Lauren, Elisha would have been lost forever.

"I let my mother get away with an affair," she says. "If I'd called her out . . . if I'd challenged her . . . maybe she would have realized what she was doing was wrong. She might have told the truth. My dad could have done something. Maybe they'd have split up anyway, but . . . at least she'd still be in my life."

"That wasn't your job," Lauren says, and I feel happy that they're friends now . . . and jealous for the exact same reason.

"Malika was the best thing in my world," she says, "and I pushed them away because they reminded me of my failures. *They* succeeded in their internship, I failed. *Their* life was going somewhere whereas mine felt like it was stuck here forever.

"I should have celebrated Malika . . . embraced them. Instead, I made up this girl who took on a life of her own."

I shiver, remembering those taunting messages, those eyes on us. But that was never Sasha Craven. That was Katherine Murphy.

This is what we should have done from the beginning.

It turns out the Dark Place wasn't Dom's idea; he borrowed it from his mother, then twisted it into something bigger. When they were kids, Hope told him and Lauren that there was a place behind their house where they could go to talk and feel lighter. She never explained what she left there, only that it helped. And I guess, for a while, it did, until Dom made his first mistake.

I watch him hold his side and grimace; then I glance at the scar on his neck and wish it hadn't taken so much to get us here.

Then we walk silently back to Dom's garden, where I see Malika staring out of Lauren's bedroom window. They smile and Lauren smiles back and something flashes between me and Elisha; not love, because that's over now, but realization—that some people are meant to be together, and some aren't.

Nightingale House

"Back again?" Mallory asks, and I say, "I don't want him to be lonely."

The receptionist smiles and points down the corridor. "You know where he is."

I stand in Patrick's doorway for a few seconds, watching what he does when he thinks he's alone. But nothing happens. He just stares into the distance until I clear my throat and say, "Good morning."

Even then, his expression doesn't change, only his position, as his head tilts slowly toward me before sinking into the pillow.

For a while, I wondered if Patrick was another of Kat's "helpers"—that's what she called them. But I've been here enough times to know that's impossible.

He is on borrowed time. The least I can do is spend some

of that with him. Every week I ask my parents to come and every week their excuses grow smaller. They're scared. I get that. But this isn't their tragedy.

"I'm sorry she can't come anymore," I whisper. "She'd want to be here if she could."

If he knows what Kat did, no one talks about it. There are no newspapers in his room, and the television never shows the news. But surely that's worse—thinking you've been abandoned. So, I tell him, every time I come. Not everything, just enough to see a moment of understanding in his eyes.

I walk over to Patrick's dressing table and lift the photo of him and Kat when they were younger. A freckled, carefree girl and a father before the taunts got too much. They look happy, and I wonder what would have happened if Dad hadn't knocked on their door.

Maybe I never would have been born, because Mom and Dad got together shortly after. Bonded by fear and guilt. I guess Molly and I both owe our existence to something horrible, and I don't know how I'm supposed to process that. But I do know I can talk about it now. And that's better than burying it in the dark.

"Sam?"

I jolt out of my daydream, convinced Patrick is somehow talking to me. But his eyes are closed now and, when I turn, Hope is in the corridor.

"Two visitors in one day," Mallory says. "This lady says she knows you?"

I study Dom's mother, searching for any sign that she's up to no good. All the arrogance and anger she had that night in the parking lot is gone, replaced by humility.

"Yes," I say. "Hope . . . this is Patrick."

The receptionist smiles and walks away, Hope looking pleadingly after her.

"You should talk to him," I say. "He'd like that."

Hope's lips tremble and tears fill her eyes. "I don't think I can."

I touch Patrick's arm lightly and say, "You have another visitor."

His eyes flutter open and he looks at me, then at Hope, then at the photograph of his daughter.

I've been thinking a lot about the man in that picture—a father who would have done anything for Kat; a man who was taken away from her in increments, with every torturous knock at their door, every shout into woods filled with giggles, every moment he fought to defend something that should have been left in peace.

And then again after the fall, when his health faltered and she coaxed him back. Never the same, but always her father.

What Kat did was wrong but that's not the whole story, because I'd do anything for my family. We all would. I can only imagine the hurt you feel when that family is tormented and damaged beyond repair. I had a taste of it—and it nearly broke me.

"I'll leave you to it," I say, backing out of the room as Hope leans tentatively in and whispers something just for them.

Before I leave, I ask Mallory if Patrick has any other visitors.

"Actually, yes," she says. "You've had quite the impact on his social standing around here."

I don't push any further. I'd like to think that Marcus and Naveen have come. But there's another reason I want to know; I still want to find out who else was helping Kat. There were two more. I can't truly rest until I know if she was the person standing over my sister that night, if it was Dylan, or someone else.

Someone who Dom hurt, perhaps. Kat talked about the people Dom has messed with over the years, and there have been plenty. There were the kids who foolishly knocked on his door asking for candy, and all the ones at school he mocked for kicks.

Those are just the ones I know about.

Dom isn't that guy anymore, but when you've been as big an asshole as he was, it's easy to lose track of your enemies.

Maybe I'll never know.

I walk away from Patrick and the past, the speculation and darkness, and I go home.

The Future

Three months later, my parents sit on either side of me on the sofa, two nervous balls of energy, and Mom says, "I think it's time."

"Really?" Dad asks.

Something strange is happening to their faces, genuine joy trying desperately to break through, pushing the sorrow further and further back until I see the people they used to be.

It's fleeting—their full-on happiness—but its echoes linger and I feel a tentative sense of relief. They've been grim-faced and sorry for so long. It's time the house felt lighter again.

"What's happening?" I ask, and Dad yells, "Molly. Come here, sweetheart."

"You'd better not have set up another Instagram account," I say, and my parents laugh.

Dad deactivated the photography account ages ago, and until now he's shown no sign of chasing more spotlights.

"Relax," he says. "You'll like this."

I'm not sure I will, but I watch my sister drift into the room, then wait for him to fill in the blanks.

"You two haven't had a nice surprise for a while," Dad says. "And we think it's time that changed."

He's nervous, constantly looking at Mom, who nods her encouragement, but Molly is starting to wobble. She looks like a tiny blond volcano about to erupt.

I know what's coming next but it still makes me smile when I hear it.

"We're going on vacation," Mom says, and Molly screeches then runs at my parents, wrapping her arms around their legs.

Dad looks at me and says, "Get in on this, Sam."

"Hall hug," Molly says, as the four of us stand in the middle of our living room, sharing the love.

"Will Lola come, too?" my sister asks, and Dad says, "She'll be happier waiting for us at home, Mol. But it's okay. I'm sure next door will look after her. In fact, Sam, you've been chatting with Chloe a lot lately. Can you pop by and make sure that's okay? I'd rather not put Lola in a cattery."

"Sure," I say. I've been meaning to catch up with Chloe anyway. Considering how good it felt to open up under the twisted elms, I might even tell her what happened.

In the seconds before I knock on her door, I think back to Halloween. I was so desperate to have a decent costume that nothing else mattered. What a sight I must have been, covered in fake blood with Slenderman by my side. But Chloe took it all in her stride.

"Hey," she says. "What's up?"

"My parents want to know if you'd be free to cat-sit.

There's no actual sitting. You just have to pop in twice a day to feed her and change the litter. It's not as gross as it sounds."

Chloe laughs and says, "No problem. I love cats. I'll check with Mom, but it should be fine."

"Cool. I don't know when we're going yet, so we'll drop a key around nearer the time."

"No need," Chloe says. "I think we already have one."

I stop. "You do?"

"From years ago. I think your parents gave us one when you went away for that convention thing . . ." She stops, and I watch as a flush creeps up her neck. "I'm not sure," she goes on, sounding flustered now, "but . . . it rings a bell."

She takes a step back into her hallway.

"Is anything wrong?"

Chloe's voice cracks as she says, "Nothing."

Her hand is on the door and we both stare at it.

"Well," she says. "Keep me posted."

"Right," I reply.

As her front door clicks shut, strange thoughts spark at the back of my brain. Each time one fizzles out, another stirs, because something's not right. After what happened with Kat, I'm learning not to take everything at face value. And yet— what I'm thinking is ridiculous.

I stare at Chloe's house until there's movement at the window—the same one her mother was staring out of that night.

"*You'd think she'd turn the lights back on now,*" Chloe had said when I dropped her home. "*All the trick-or-treaters are in bed, Mother.*"

But that wasn't true. Someone had set in motion a terrible trick. Someone had decided to bring Sasha Craven to life.

In the window, Chloe lifts her hand in a stiff wave, and I copy. Then I quickly walk home, ignoring the excitement downstairs and heading straight to my bedroom.

My thoughts aren't dying out anymore. They are growing— fizzles becoming flames that cause explosions, each one sending moments from the last few weeks splintering off in different directions like fireworks.

On Halloween night Chloe was dressed head to toe in black and I didn't question it, because that's what all the dancers wear. But what if she wasn't dancing? What if she was getting ready for something else and my invite made that easier?

I remember her face when I said Dom's name out loud, and the contempt she didn't even try to hide when they spoke at the party. Was she one of the kids he used to bully? How bad is it that I don't know?

Then I think of the shape flashing past me in Molly's room and outrunning me with ease—just as Chloe used to do when we were kids.

I think of the shards of glass outside our house, as if someone had broken the door from inside then swept up just enough to trick my dad.

That never made sense before—not unless someone else had a key. Our fences *were* too high to climb.

Kat was right—there were so many people she could have called on to help. But only a few could have done everything she needed.

They watched us like we were prey, and we so nearly were. But I know a thing or two about watching. I've learned from the best, after all. So, I stare out of my window until Chloe and her mother silently get in their car and drive away. Then, hours later, I watch when the roar of the engine brings them back.

I watch like everyone used to watch me, and I'll keep watching.

For as long as it takes.

Acknowledgments

Thank you to my wife, Rachel, for always believing in me and encouraging me to pursue my dreams. You are my inspiration.

To our beautiful boys, Charlie and Lucas: You are our greatest achievements and, while it may still be a while before you can read my books, know that you are in every word I write.

Thank you to my agent, Claire Wilson, who has always been my biggest champion. You are always right—even when it takes me a while to realize that—and I am honored to be part of your incredible team of authors.

To my US agent, Pete Knapp: Thank you for working so hard on the other side of the Atlantic. You make it seem like you are considerably closer than that and your insight and support are priceless.

I am so incredibly grateful to my editor, Eileen Rothschild, for bringing me into the Wednesday Books family and for all your work making this novel as good as it can possibly be. I will always remember your enthusiasm for this story at our first meeting and I am delighted to be working with you.

Thank you to Kerri Resnick for designing an amazing cover. I'm so proud of all my US covers, and this fits perfectly alongside my first two books.

I appreciate the hard work of everyone else at Wednesday Books who has been involved with *Secrets Never Die,* with special thanks to Lisa Bonvissuto, Rivka Holler, Michelle McMillian, Melanie Sanders, Eric Meyer, and Gail Friedman.

To Genevieve Herr: Your incredible eye for detail and your wonderful work on this book will never be forgotten. Thank you for encouraging me to write the best possible version of this story.

Thank you to Safae El-Ouahabi and Sam Coates at RCW, Stuti Telidevara at Park & Fine Literary and Media, and Emily Hayward-Whitlock at The Artists Partnership.

I will always treasure the advice and guidance of Tig Wallace, Carmen McCullough, and Wendy Shakespeare, who have all helped me to become a much better writer.

Thank you to all the wonderful booksellers in the US who have helped my first two novels reach unimaginable heights. And, most importantly, thank you to each and every person who has read my books. It is truly a dream come true to have my stories read and enjoyed by others.

Finally, thank you to my mother—for everything.

VINCENT RALPH is the bestselling author of young adult thrillers *14 Ways to Die* and *Lock the Doors*. Both novels are *New York Times* bestsellers, and *Lock the Doors* is also a *USA Today* bestseller and the winner of the Southern Schools Book Award. Vincent owes his love of books to his mother, who encouraged his imagination from an early age and always made sure there were new stories to read. He lives in the United Kingdom with his wife, two sons, and two cats.